Faerie Chronicles

C. L. Kraemer

Published by Rogue Phoenix Press, LLP
Copyright © 2018

ISBN: 978-1-62420-432-6

Cover Artist: Designs by Ms G

Printed in the United States of America

Meadows of Gold

Chapter One

A gentle breeze sighed, undulating the meadow grass lazily and whispering past the forlorn figure slumped on the tree trunk, hands clasped tightly in his lap. Thomas, a forest leprechaun, released a long melancholy breath between his cracked, dry lips. A single plump tear meandered down his stubbled cheek.

The sun sent bright shafts of light through the pine boughs and around the wooden pedestal upon which the morose figure resided. Ignoring the dancing beams, the leprechaun pulled a shuddered breath into his lungs and stared at a spot in front of the stump where a crumpled daisy chain necklace lay withering in the warmth of the afternoon. Another plump tear snaked down his unshaven face.

In the distance, a lone figure scuffed up the lane, which crossed in front of the tree stump. Thomas paid no heed to the approaching form, pulling a thin silver flask from inside his rumpled vest. He blindly opened the lid, placed the opened top to his lips and pulled a deep draught from the container. Refitting the cap to the top, he slipped the silver spirit holder back into his vest. His next shuddered breath was interrupted with a hiccup.

The figure on the road drew closer. Thomas raised his head and squinted his eyes. Was she coming back? He hiccupped and straightened up. Maybe she had been teasing him when she ran away and now, she realized how much he cared for her. His eyes brightened and a smile began to touch his lips.

The figure came around the bend and toward him. The last he'd seen her, she was wearing a diaphanous, thin dress. Had she changed? The form nearing him was clad in leather breeches, a braided leather tunic, and knee-high, soft leather boots. A sword blade strapped to the figure's back flashed in the sunlight. Was Cary so angry she meant to cut him in little pieces? His heart began to pound in his chest and inside his mouth his tongue stuck to the roof.

The figure stopped two lengths from him and raised a hand to shade its eyes from the brightness of the day.

Thomas realized he was shaking. This was it…his life was over. He hung his head.

"Thomas?"

The voice was familiar but it didn't sound like Cary. If it wasn't her…

~ * ~

"Thomas! What are you doing?" Tiamoon, a warrior gnome of the valley clan, stood with her feet planted shoulder width apart in her full leather armor on the roadway to her home. She'd just reconnoitered the meadow area for evidence of the marauding night elves. The local hill clan had been raiding the gnome settlements and wreaking havoc on the inhabitants. The gnome community was rallying together to protect their families against further damage.

Thomas narrowed his eyes and looked through his veil of tears.

"Oh, Tia (hic) moon, itsch you."

Tia rolled her eyes heavenward and leaned toward the wobbling leprechaun, wrinkling her nose in disgust at the sour smell of alcohol surrounding the disheveled lump occupying the tree stump.

"Thomas? How long have you been sitting here?"

"Dunno. What day is it?"

"Tuesday."

"Really?" Thomas lifted rheumy eyes to meet Tiamoon's clear blue ones.

"Yes, really. So how long have you been here, Thomas?"

"Uhm, (hic) since Saturday."

"Saturday!"

Tiamoon stepped to the stump, in the process crushing the daisy chain necklace. She reached out to grab the leprechaun as he dissolved in tears.

"You (hic)… you stepped on (hic) the necklace. (hic) Just like she (hic) stepped on my heart."

"Good heavens, Thomas, pull yourself together. She who?"

She wrestled the drunken leprechaun to his unsteady feet. His weight surprised her. He was sturdy and muscular beneath the rumpled clothing.

"Cary, the love of my life."

"Heavens be cursed. Thomas..."

"Wha-a-a?" He turned red-rimmed, green orbs her direction.

"You fall in love with every female who crosses your path."

"Do *not*!" "Really? Okay let me guess...she flirted with you and teased you until she got you out here at the edge of the meadow where you promised to tell her where your secret stash of gold was hidden if she'd kiss you and be your mate."

His eyes ricocheted in the sockets, making Tiamoon's head hurt.

"You were (hic) sshpying on ussh."

Tia got her shoulder under his armpit and hoisted him up. She wrinkled her nose at the stale body odor emanating from his clothing.

"No, Thomas. It's a pattern everyone in the woods knows. Come on. You need a bath, some food and sleep."

"But what if (hic) she comesh back?"

"Thomas? I can guarantee that won't happen today. Come on."

She dragged him along the road. His head was slumped on his chest and his leather shoes were dragging, toes down, in the soft dirt of the two-lane thoroughfare. After a mile of struggling with the leprechaun, she turned down a single file path winding through the trees. Thomas had hiccupped in Tia's ear through the entire journey, his head lolling from side to side.

She'd reached the end of the path as well as the end of her patience. When the path stopped abruptly at the river's edge, so did Tia. She allowed the momentum of her pace to transfer to the inert leprechaun.

The moment the figure hit the icy water, he screamed.

"You're killing me! Gods in Heaven! You're trying to kill me!"

"For crying out loud, Thomas. Just dunk your head under the water and quit yelling. Maybe if you bathed more often, you wouldn't chase away the ladies."

The figure floundered in the icy stream.

"I can't swim! Tia! I'm drowning!"

"Thomas?"

"Help! I'm drowning!"

"THOMAS!" The roar echoed through the woods.

"Put your feet down!"

Blustering until his face was crimson, the drunken man splashed furiously. His head went beneath the water and he rose up sputtering, unconsciously standing on the stream's bottom. He quit flailing his arms.

3

"Oh."

"Yeah, oh." Tia drew her sword and pointed it his direction. "Now get yourself and your clothing sopping wet. If you even think of getting on the bank without attempting to wash off some of that stench, I'll split you from gullet to gizzard."

He glared at the gnome warrior.

"Fine."

She stood pointing her sharpened blade at him until he and his clothing were sufficiently soaked.

"Now, let's go. My mom will have some stew to put into your stomach."

"But I don't wa..."

Thomas stopped his whine at the glare he was receiving from Tia.

"Lead the way."

Chapter Two

Cary stretched her arms above her head as she yawned. Her moss bed lay in a sunspot inside her temporary oak tree home and she took every opportunity available to steal a nap. Today was no exception. She'd had a run-in with the leprechaun Thomas. He'd gotten sloppy drunk and proposed a union between the two and had the nerve to act surprised when she'd turned him down.

Had he been so drunk as to think his offer of gold could sway her?

"Fool. I have something worth more than his pitiful pot of gold."

She splashed water on her face from the acorn bowl nitched in the cradle of the root of her tree. She wiped her face and hands with an oak leaf. Staring out a gap that served as a window, she noted the rippling heat waves rising to the cloudless sky from the swaying meadow grass. The wind blew hot across her face and she turned from the opening to nibble on some bread. It had been a strange fortnight. Cary still wasn't sure *exactly* what had occurred. She and Conn had been scheming, no, make that planning to undo the wedding of Casey and Kelly and were in right good position to see that happen when, whoosh! they were spirited away along with that pompous human, Florence to—here, wherever here was.

The rustlings across the room set aside Cary's concentration and alerted her to the fact Conn was beginning to move about from his nap.

"Have we food?"

Cary looked at her rumpled roommate. "Always thinking with your stomach, aren't you? If the bread I secured is not enough for your fine palette, then get out and find suitable food."

"Why do I have to be the one to supply the meals?"

Cary fisted her tiny hands to her hips and cast a deadly glare at Conn.

"Because of all the talents in this world, you're gifted at putting food on the table."

He slogged his way to the sink and splashed water on his face. He sucked in a surprised breath.

"That's cold!"

"Might be because the water flows directly from the stream?"

Conn wiped his face and hands and headed for the makeshift door. "I'm out to find food and trace the whereabouts of Florence. As we have lived in this… place for a fortnight, my senses tell me he might be in need of my services. Left alone to his own devices, he fares poorly.

"I'll return then we can sit down and make plans to locate Casey and Kelly. They've been having enough time to learn to dislike each other by now. Our plans will be easy enough to initiate. This time next week, all will be as it should."

"Are you daft?" Cary fluttered to land lightly on her feet in front of Conn.

"Beg pardon?" A scowl covered his face.

"We're not in the green isles, you fool. We're of a different time and different place. I know not exactly and will be out myself to see if I can steal the knowledge from one of the locals. When I have this information, we'll talk about what plans to make. Not before. You go and hunt for Florence, but don't return reeking of wine and foolishness." Cary stamped her foot and turned her back to Conn.

His face reddened and he yanked open the piece of wood they'd been using as a door. He let the bark drop on the ground and flew from the tree.

He buzzed close to the earth, taking in the smells of this new place. There was much greenery here and the trees grew tall and lush. He had to admit to himself Cary was right. This was not the Ireland he knew. What he could smell of the earth was dark, fertile ground. His ears caught the sound of a very angry, very large horde of bees. He shifted his direction and came upon a scene foreign to his eyes. Strangely dressed humans held shiny steel weapons. They seemed to be attacking the forest with a tree-eating monster that buzzed very loudly while eating its way through the wooded area.

Conn was frightened and shot away from the scene. Though certain he could not be seen, he wished not to take any chances. He heard a loud rattling sound and the grinding of metal-to-metal coming very close to him. Darting to hide behind a large evergreen, he peeked at the aberration that nearly crushed him.

It was very large and black. The wheels upon the black wagon had a foreign substance all around them. This padding substance was why the large cart approached him in relative silence. There did not seem to be any horses at the front pulling but the metallic cart moved forward with a deafening high pitched grinding of metal. The wagon stirred up the dust and dirt on the trail. Conn felt a tickle in his nose and, before he could think, he sneezed loudly.

"Ach! I can't be giving away my location. Who knows what monsters lie in wait in this forest? I need to find Florence. I have seen more abominations today than I care to ponder. The explanations must surely be simple." Conn lifted his wings and tentatively flew toward the direction where the sun slid behind the hills. He sensed Florence. With each wing beat, his sensation of his ward grew stronger. He would find his charge and answers would be forthcoming. Until that time, he was charged with being vigilant and wary. Despite Cary's warning, Conn knew he was going to need some mead to settle his nerves.

"She can threaten all she wants, but until she's been as close to the mouth of this monster as I, she can't know the terror. Only mead can soothe this kind of fear."

Having justified his visit to the pub, Conn let a smile touch his lips. Finding Florence was important but not as important as Conn settling his nerves. He couldn't be expected to pump information from his charge and find food without a bit of the mead, could he?

Of course not. He began to whistle a lively reel as he flew toward town. This would turn out to be a positive day after all.

~ * ~

Cary was irritated at Conn. It really was his fault they were in this mess. If he'd been watching Kelly as he was supposed to instead of dashing about the fight egging the boys on, they'd still be back home in familiar surroundings instead of this place. She had no name for this land. All she knew was everything recognizable had disappeared. She needed to find a place where she could get the information without giving away her ignorance. Cary hovered just above the grass line. She sensed other beings close by and headed their direction. As the human voices grew louder, she slowed her flying, finally touching down near a whitewashed building sporting a porch out front. Silently, she climbed up the boxes on the front to look into the window. Her eyes beheld a business selling assorted items. She could hear a bell ring and decided to investigate.

She skittered inside the opened door and sidled up to the wooden counter. Peeking around the side, she noted items in jars on shelves behind the front counter. A human with a white apron stood behind the divider and helped other humans by retrieving merchandise from the containers on the shelves. He would then go to a large metal box, pushed some metal things jutting out from the box and stand back while a portion on the bottom of the box jumped out at him. It was the box which made the bell sound. Cary had flown up to the counter to investigate the box when her skin dimpled in chill bumps. *Someone is watching me!*

She raised her eyes to look directly into the cool, blue orbs of a female night elf. Cary panicked. Night elves! She had not encountered a night elf in years. Now, in this place where she knew nothing, she was going to have to keep her guard up against night elves?

Before Cary could react, Gitty Saun casually leaned over and snatched the faery from her hiding place and placed the tiny being in her leather carryall. "Curses on your father!" the little fae screamed to the darkened leather prison walls.

Well, now she'd done it. She was no smarter for her travel and her current state of freedom was in question. Cary dropped her chin to her hand as she sat on something metallic and uncomfortable. The jouncing of the bag as this creature walked was making her nauseous. If she had been but a moment quicker…

She twittered then chuckled and finally allowed herself the luxury of laughing out loud. She had to give credit to this giant—were she able she would have made the same move. She could only hope the appetizer for tonight's dinner was not being carried in this leather prison.

Chapter Three

Florence sat in his room squinting out the window. He had indeed indulged himself a bit too much last evening. The light in his eyes pierced through his head causing the muscles of his neck to spasm in pain. If he were just to have a bit of the powder the witch woman in his village kept on hand, he might survive this day.

A tap upon his door sent him to moaning.

"What would you ask of me now?" Florence pushed the heels of his palms against his eyes.

"Mr. Florence? It's Dorinda. May I come in?"

His head ached and he tried his best to recall a Dorinda. When the door opened a crack and the smell of fresh soap assailed his nose, his brain kicked into gear.

Ah, yes; the slender serving wench from the tavern.

"Please, my lady. Do enter my chamber."

The door hinges complained with a high-pitched squeal, setting his ears to twitching and his head to pounding.

"Ah, lass. Could you be but a wee bit quieter?"

"So sorry, Mr. Florence. I thought you might be...hungover a bit from last night. I brought some aspirin to help relieve the pain. If you swallow them with this glass of water, it should help take away some of the pain in about twenty minutes."

Dorinda placed two aspirin on the table next to the glass of water she'd brought.

Florence lifted bloodshot eyes to the night table then to his uninvited guest.

"What's this poison you place before me? A draft to kill?"

Dorinda's face drained of color, her eyes widening in horror.

"Oh, no, Mr. Florence! This is medicine to relieve the pain. If you don't want to take it, I'll take the pills away."

Florence looked at the tiny white spots on the table stained with brown rings and burn spots.

"This not be poison?" Dorinda vigorously shook her head.

9

"Medicine to take this evil from my head in less than the peal of one bell?"
She hesitantly nodded.

"Then I shall ingest this...medicine and wait to see if you skirt the truth. But know this, woman, should I expire from your ministrations I shall curse you and all the kinsmen of your clan."

He put the pill into his mouth and started to chew.

"NO!"

Florence squinted his eyes and hunched his shoulders against the reverberation of the shout in his head.

"Swallow the pills whole and wash them down with the water."

Bitterness exploded in his mouth, and he sensed he was close to losing the contents of his stomach. He lifted the glass and washed down the remainder of the pills. A hint of sweetness remained on his tongue as he swallowed to quell the bile rising up his throat.

Dorinda took the glass from his hand.

"When your headache is gone, come to the kitchen and I'll make you breakfast."

A slight nod of his head sent her out of the room. Florence lay back on the soft bed and closed his eyes. His head spun from the events of the last fortnight. The strange clothing on his body had appeared after he had first stumbled into the inn and had been subjected to the jeering of the patrons. The slender serving wench had taken pity on him and steered him to this room he occupied. Somewhere she had secured the local dress of the area so he would not appear out of place. But he *was* out of place and it was up to him to determine his whereabouts so he could return to his life in the emerald land of his birth.

He was respected in his home village. People knew his father was a wealthy man and they catered to his wishes. Somehow the knowledge had not traveled to this village. He would have to right the situation.

Florence's eyes drooped then closed as the aspirin began to work. Within fifteen minutes, he was snoring, the headache temporarily forgotten.

~ * ~

Cary was close to losing the battle with her stomach when the swaying stopped and her leather prison was unceremoniously thumped on to a solid, unmoving surface. As she stood up and tried to get her legs under her, the top of the bag was wrenched open, blasting a glaring light directly on the little fae causing her to throw her hand over her eyes.

"Well, well, well. What do we have here?"

A large, porcelain colored extremity snatched the wee folk by her waist and pulled her into the light of the room.

Cary blinked furiously, trying to adjust her eyes to the surroundings. The abode was as large as any castle she'd seen but not hewn together with any stone she recognized.

A magnificent fireplace stood guard at an end wall but no logs crackled a warm welcome. The furnishings scattered about the room were bulky, imposing and cold, making the little fae shiver.

The large fingers wrapped around the fae exuded warmth. Cary tried to wiggle herself free to no avail.

"I don't think even you have the strength to escape my grip, but you're welcome to try."

Cary turned and cast a wary look in the direction of the speaker.

"How is it you can see me?" She tilted her head to one side considering the tall, pale blonde with fair complexion.

"Because, wee one, I'm not a human."

Cary raised a brow, the hint of a smile touching her mouth. "No?"

Gitty pulled up one side of her lip and snarled. "No! I'd rather have my heart ripped out and fed to me than be part of the human race." She held her chin high. "*I* am a night elf. We are far more clever, smarter, better looking and live considerably longer than those human curs. *And* we are able to see magical creatures of the forest."

Cary pursed her lips together. She crossed her arms and considered this creature that had hold of her.

"So you can see the fae?"

"Yes, and because I can see the fae of the woods, I know you're a newcomer to this area. Who are you and where did you come from?"

Cary stared into the icy blue eyes of this night elf. No warmth radiated from their depths. In fact, she could see nothing resembling compassion in the elf's eyes no matter how hard she looked. She pulled up as straight as she could, unfolding her arms and adjusting her skirt.

"I am Cary of Innisboffin and I have absolutely no idea where *here* is. Maybe you could be so kind as to tell me where I am?"

Gitty chuckled. "Why so you can enchant me and leave? I don't think so. I think, for the time being, you'll be a guest in my home. When I feel I can trust you, I'll let you go, but not until then. So, wee one...back in the bag."

"NO!" Cary squirmed and pushed at the extremity clutching her body so tightly. "I hate the dark and that leather thing makes me sick. Please don't!" She sobbed and struggled, using all her strength. But alas, she was dumped unceremoniously into the pouch and the top was tightened closed.

"Now, what?"

Hiccupping and sobbing, Cary covered her face. Because of that darn Florence and his curiosity, she and Conn were who knows where. The clothing, language and homes she'd seen so far indicated this was not her beautiful Ireland. But if this was not Ireland, then where in all the world could she have landed?

It was a question whose answer would have to wait. Cary's eyelids traveled to her cheeks and before long the gentle snoring of a tiny faerie emanated from the leather pouch.

~ * ~

Florence woke to the sun streaming in his room. He reached up and touched his head, noting there was no pain remaining. Gingerly, he swung his legs to the floor and sat on the edge of the bed. "The little white dots the wench gave me worked. My pain has passed and I'm starved. Think I'll find my way to the kitchen for a meal."

After a brief stop at the facilities, Florence entered the kitchen, his nose taking in the pungent smells.

"Ah, lass. what do you have for me this beautiful morn?"

Dorinda turned and graced him with a shy smile. "Morning, again, Mr. Florence. How does pork, potatoes and scrambled eggs sound to you?"

"Like a bit of heaven." *And home.*

"Looks as though the aspirin worked for you." "Indeed it did, lass. I feel ready to take on the world." Florence noted the sudden sadness in the innkeeper's eyes. "What is it? Has something I said offended you?"

"No, sir. Just your comment about taking on the world leaves me no choice but to let you know of the consequences of your actions last night. You might want to take a seat."

Florence swallowed and pulled out the chair at the kitchen table. He plopped down.

Dorinda fussed around the stove shoveling eggs, bacon and fried potatoes on the platter. She placed the food in front of her boarder who grabbed his fork and dug into the meal. She added a plate of toast on the table within arm's reach.

She poured two cups of coffee, placing one in front of Florence. He grabbed the cup and started to gulp the contents.

"I wouldn't..."

"Owww! That's hot!"

Sitting at the chair opposite, Dorinda cradled her own cup between her hands. "As I was about to tell you, it's very hot. You might want to let it cool for a bit."

Florence touched his fingers to his burnt lip. "Right. Now what were you going to tell me about last night?"

Dorinda gazed into the dark contents inside her mug. She took a small sip then blew out a shuddered breath.

Florence grabbed a piece of toast and mopped up the remaining bits of food from the plate. When he finished the toast, he brushed his hands over the plate, shoved the soiled platter to the center of the table and leaned back to enjoy his coffee.

"Well?"

"Well, Mr. Florence, you insulted one of the new landowners in the valley who you challenged to a duel."

Florence's mouth dropped open. "I what?"

Dorinda squirmed in the chair. "You challenged him to a duel."

Pulling up, he placed the mug of coffee on the table and cleared his throat.

"How...how did that happen?" "Best as I can tell, you called his girlfriend a saucy trollop and he took offense."

Florence lowered his head to his hands. "I take it he feels the need to defend her honor?"

"Yep. And as drunk as you were, you challenged him to a duel with swords."

Florence groaned. "I'm much better with a pistol."

"Too late. The duel is set for this evening at the edge of the meadow. If you don't show, he'll hunt you down and 'dispatch you'."

I've done it now. Not only do I have no idea where I might be but I've riled up the villagers. Florence huffed out a breath. "Tis done now. Have you a blade with which I might practice?"

Dorinda lifted a brow. She rose from the table and reached beside the icebox, retrieving a worn sweeper, its bristles splayed and bent.

"No, Mr. Florence. But I do have a broom. Best I can do on such short notice."

Florence took the proffered weapon, glancing up and down the shaft.

"Will have to do. Thank you, Miss Dorinda. Should anyone seek me, I'll be in the yard… practicing. Please call me in time to clean up before I leave for the inn."

Dorinda hid a smirk. "As you wish, Mr. Florence." *He's gonna get himself killed.*

~ * ~

Conn slipped past a farmer in bib overalls as he opened the door to the inn. The fae winged his way to a corner of the pub and watched the assorted villagers enter and leave. His thirst was increasing with the passing of each human. This place didn't have a designated corner as they did back in his land where the humans understood fae still existed in the land. How was he to slake his thirst if no one offered him mead? His mood darkened until a movement from the corner of his eye caught his attention.

Sitting with his back to the wall, a tall, elegant man ordered himself a glass of mead with a second smaller container set to the side. He carefully moved his long, blonde locks behind his shoulder and looked directly at Conn.

The fae held his breath and froze in his position.

"I can see you, little brother. Come sit with me. Surely, you thirst?" Conn's heart thundered in his chest. He was certain the man had been speaking to another.

"Come. I *can* see you, wee one. I know you must have a great thirst. Join me and quench the fire in your mouth." The hint of a smile touched the blue-eyed man's lips.

Conn was sorely tempted. This stranger had a familiarity about him that made Conn cautious. The long blond hair, blue eyes and ability to see the fae? He shuddered. A night elf; what were night elves doing in this faraway place?

I'm so thirsty but if this elf captures me...oh, what the heck. What more do I have to lose except my thirst? Conn winged his way to the table and landed just out of reach of the elf.

"Greetings, kind sir."

The elf slid the small glass toward the fae.

"And to you, sir."

"Call me Morgan."

"And I'm Conn." The little fae eyed the elf warily. "Can you be trusted, Morgan?"

The corners of Morgan's lips curled in delight.

"I sincerely hope not."

Conn blinked his eyes, furrowing his brow then threw his head back and laughed.

"Ah, good. A man after my own heart. I think we shall get along."

Morgan dipped his head and grabbed his glass.

"You speak the truth, Conn. To a new...partnership."

Conn pushed his glass toward the elf, furiously using his wings to move the large container.

"To a new partnership." He then stuck his head in the glass and pulled a deep draught from the amber liquid.

"Ptah! This is milk for children!"

"You speak the truth but it is the best these villagers can produce. It's better than water." "Well spoken."

The unlikely twosome drank quietly. When the liquid dropped so far down the glass the fae was unable to get to it, Morgan signaled to the barmaid to bring a straw.

"What brings you to this inn, Conn?"

Conn was certain Florence had frequented this place but was still a bit leery of the night elf.

"I felt a need to drown my thirst and observe the humans of this village. Has there been any excitement lately?"

Morgan downed his drink and signaled for another. "Yes, there has. Some blighter showed up a fortnight ago and started horning in on my territory, if you know what I mean?"

Conn took a pull from his straw, eliminating the need to answer.

"Anyway, he comes prancing through the door last night like some nancy-boy and sidles up to my companion for the evening. After several glasses of whiskey, he made a rude comment about her character when she rebuffed his advances."

Good heavens, Florence. Not in town for a moon and you've poisoned the water. Maybe you don't need my help.

"What happened?" Conn balanced himself on the rim of the glass.

"I demanded he apologize to the lady and myself. He laughed, issued more inappropriate suggestions regarding my lady friend then challenged me to a duel."

Conn slipped from the rim and saved himself from falling in the mead by quickly winging his way to the tabletop.

"Does your sheriff *allow* dueling? In my village, the sheriff would lock everyone up should he have knowledge of such a happening."

"I'm above these quaint humans laws. I live by my own rules."

The elfkind's wrinkled nose and down turned lips showed his disgust for the local constabulary.

Conn gulped. He had to ask the question burning in his brain.

"Wha-what weapon did he choose?" Morgan allowed a big smile to lighten his face.

"Fool chose blades."

Conn started coughing.

"Are you alright, friend?"

The fae held up one hand while the other clutched his stomach. He nodded then lowered his head to his knees in an attempt to catch his breath. Once he had his composure back, he pulled upright and continued.

"Can I assume you're talented with the blade?"

Morgan's smile widened. "If I say so myself, I'm very adept with steel."

Oh, you've done it now, Florence.

Conn moved to his perch on the glass' edge.

"So, what would this nancy-boy's name be, Morgan?" He pulled in a mouthful of beer and quickly swallowed.

"I've no idea. What does it matter?"

"The name will be important for placing on the headstone."

"Ah, my little friend, you do have a point. Let me see..." Morgan tapped his finger on his chin. "I believe it was Terrance. No, more along the lines of Lawrence to the best of my recollection. I wasn't really interested in his name; just his apology to my lady friend."

"As well you should have been. If interlopers are allowed to insult your companions, they'll have no compunction about insulting you. You can't have that in your village."

"Thank you, Conn. It's good to see someone who understands my position. I'm afraid my sister isn't as comprehending of a gentleman's duties."

Conn looked at the elf lounging elegantly in the opposite chair. He'd just mentioned a sister so that meant there were at least two of these night elves in the vicinity. He wondered how many were in their clan.

"Tell me, Morgan. When is this duel to occur?"

"This afternoon at the set of the sun." "Shouldn't you be practicing?"

"His defeat can be accomplished with one hand held behind my back."

"Maybe I'll stick around and observe."

Morgan signaled the barmaid. "I'm feeling a mite peckish. Would you care for dinner?"

"Love some."

Conn smiled. His day had morphed from dismal to delightful in the span of one glass of beer. He and Cary may have been stranded here because of Florence but Conn was going to make the very best of it. If Florence had to be sacrificed in the process, well, such were the consequences.

The barmaid brought soup in a bowl for Morgan and, at Morgan's request, a small cupful for *the wee ones* he'd told the barmaid with a wink.

She shook her head and rolled her eyes but complied with his request, as he was known to be a big tipper.

Conn tucked into the soup. *I could get used to this. Wonder where Cary is?*

The thought flitted in and out of his mind. He was too busy eating and drinking to give it any real consideration. Things would turn out as they were destined. They always did.

Chapter Four

Tiamoon had settled Thomas at the family table after coaxing him to change into dry clothing she'd located in her brother's room.

"Don't even think of moving." She narrowed her eyes at the weaving leprechaun.

Thomas picked at the sleeve of the shirt. "This isn't mine. Where's my clothing?"

Tia unbelted her sword and placed it inside a small closet beneath the stairs of the cottage.

"Your clothes are out on the line drying. Maybe some fresh air will help rid them of the stench."

She went in search of her mother. In the back of the small building, divided into equally marked plots, lay the pride and joy of Tiamoon's mother, Skye—her garden. From the cool, damp days of spring through summer's heat, Skye charmed the earth into producing bushels of food. It was in this haven Tiamoon located her.

"Hello, mum."

"Hello, Tia. Can you hand me the trowel near your feet?"

Tia picked up the small spade and carried it to her mother.

"I've brought home Thomas, the leprechaun from the meadow clan. I was hoping you might have some of your potato soup left."

"There's some on the stove. Why did you bring him here?"

"He's a mess. He's been drinking for who knows how long and was visible to any that chose to look. He'd have given us away to the humans."

Skye rose from her knees to face her youngest child. "Daughter, you have to stop bringing home strays." Patting Tia on the shoulder as she passed, she moved in the direction of the cottage. "I'll warm the stew but you have to make the toast."

Tia surveyed the bounty of fresh food growing in the plot. Every year she watched her mom create life from the earth and it still amazed her. She hadn't the patience. Clashing swords was more her style.

Skye had stoked the fire and was stirring the warming soup when Tia strode into the room. On the small table next to the drain board sat the wire toaster and a couple slices of bread. Tia popped a slice into the wire and with a dishtowel opened the heated handle of the cast iron wood stove. Mere minutes provided the needed heat to brown the bread. Smearing the toast with fresh churned butter, she placed it on a small plate and, with a full bowl of heated soup in her other hand, carried the food to the dining table and the sleeping leprechaun.

Tia placed the food far enough away from Thomas as to be safe, then walked to his chair and shook him awake.

"Get up, you fool. My mother has worked hard to provide food for your mangy self. Least you can do is eat it."

Wiping away the drool from his lips, he leaned back and inhaled deeply.

"Smells to be a good potato soup—and toast. I, uh, I think I might actually be hungry." His eyes opened wide and he grabbed for the dishes.

Tia slapped a hand on the table next to his watching him jump in reaction.

"Now that I've got your attention, listen up. You'll eat politely and not make a mess. You'll finish everything on these plates then you'll excuse yourself and wash up. After that, I'm putting you in my brother's room for the night. Tomorrow, you'll go home and stay away from the spirits until next week. Do I make myself clear?"

Thomas nodded, his attention riveted on the steaming bowl of soup.

Tia slid the bowl to him and retrieved a spoon from the sideboard.

She handed him the implement. "Politely."

Watching him devour the contents of the bowl, Tia wondered how he ever managed to take care of himself. Seemed someone in the meadow was always looking after him. *Might be how he planned it.* Tia looked hard at the leprechaun. *Nah, not clever enough.*

She walked to the front of the small cottage and stared out the window to the meadow. The name Thomas had uttered in his drunken stupor was new. She was familiar with most of the meadow, forest and mountain fae in this area and none bore this assignation of Cary. It rang of the old country. She would have to investigate this new visitor.

The loud buzz of snoring interrupted her thought and Tia turned to find Thomas asleep at the table. She bundled him from the chair and dragged him back to her brother's room. Securing him in the bed, she closed the door and went to sit in front of the cottage where she gazed at the scenery.

She couldn't quite put her finger on the uneasiness roiling about her. Her nerves tingled on the top of her skin and she jumped with the slightest provocation. A change was about to happen to her valley, Tia was sure. Just what that change was— she wouldn't even hazard a guess.

~ * ~

Cary moaned and rolled to her back. This was absurd. Why was she tiptoeing around this night elf? The wee folk had taught many of them the magic they used! She had more ability in her tiny finger than the cold hearted, stony-eyed giantess who held her captive had in her entire body. Mustering her courage, Cary stood and began to chant a spell her mother had taught her. Again and again, she chanted the lines, feeling the dormant power surge through her veins. Radiance began to glow around her and the leather container opened. Cary zipped through the mouth of the bag, coming face to face with the night elf.

"I wondered how long it would take before you employed your power." Gitty smirked and reached to grab the tiny fae.

Cary loop-de-looped away, winging herself a safe distance from the elf. "You'll not be holding me prisoner any longer."

Gitty swiped at the floating fae and missed again. A frown marred the porcelain face. "And what makes you think I can't?"

Cary flew straight at the elf and stopped directly in front of her.

"Because the width and breath of my magic surpasses anything you can imagine. I'll have no hesitation to use it to bring you to my size and pummel the life from you!"

Sparks flew from the wee one's fingertips as she pointed at Gitty.

The two stood staring at each other; Cary hovering in front of the elf and the night elf standing feet planted shoulder width apart, hands on hips, glaring.

The air crackled and popped. Wind whipped hair wildly around their heads. The clock on the fire's mantle ticked loudly, echoing in the silence of the room.

Then Cary giggled. Gitty raised her eyebrows and a smile hovered over her lips. The tiny fae clutched her sides as she broke into laughter, her shoulders shaking.

Gitty snickered and soon was laughing as well.

The wee one drifted to the shoulder of the night elf.

"I must say, Madam Night Elf, you seem to be a soul after my own heart. What say we join forces? I can use a partner in this new place who has knowledge and position." Gitty chuckled. "You've proven yourself bold, Cary. I believe you have the flint of a steel blade backed by the powers of a great mage. Your convenient size would help me in my pursuits, too. We have the makings of a perfect partnership.

"Shall we call it done?"

The wee fae flit off Gitty's shoulder and pirouetted in front of her.

"Done!"

Chapter Five

Florence pulled the handkerchief from his back pocket and swiped at his forehead. He couldn't remember the last time he'd sweat this much. Tucking the soaked cloth in his pocket, he picked up his broom and began the parry-lunge-withdraw routine his father had taught him as a boy.

My only hope is the lessons father tried to impart to me will come back automatically.

"Mr. Florence? Mr. Florence?"

Dorinda carried a glass of sparkling water to the red-faced warrior. She handed the cooling liquid to him and watched as he gulped the contents.

"I think you should come inside and have dinner."

"I'm not really hungry."

"It will help to bolster your strength and spirit. You might also consider a shower before you leave. I've washed your clothing and shined your boots. You'll look very dashing in your outfit."

Florence stopped and turned to look at Dorinda. Her blue eyes gave no hint of guile.

"Sounds a good idea to me. I'll shower before dinner, if you don't mind."

"Not at all." *Whew. I'm glad he suggested it first.*

She led the way to the kitchen.

Florence continued to the bathing room and found his clothing carefully laid out. He admired the high gloss of his riding boots and noted his shirt had never been so spotless. It appeared nearly new. He held the trousers to his nose and pulled in the scent of fresh air. His hand lightly caressed the sharp crease, which had been ironed into the fabric. He'd wash himself especially well using some of the sweet smelling soap in the bathing room then smooth his hair with the slicker Dorinda had shown him how to use.

He strolled into the dining room, his nose seduced by the delicious smells coming from the kitchen.

"Have a seat at the table."

Florence set in the chair where a plate and silverware had been placed. Dorinda brought in a plate of crisp, golden fried chicken. She set it on the towel and slapped at Florence's extended hand.

"Not until all the food has been brought out."

He licked his lips. His stomach complained loudly but he knew not to push his luck.

Dorinda finished placing mashed potatoes, homemade gravy, baked biscuits, home grown corn and fresh butter and honey on the table.

"Now we say grace."

The two bowed their heads and Dorinda offered the blessing.

"Lord, please bless this food and those who eat it. Watch over Mr. Florence tonight so he returns safely to our house. Amen."

"Amen."

Florence looked at Dorinda and raised his eyebrows.

She smiled shyly. "Yes, Mr. Florence, you may start." *Eat hearty, man. This may be your last meal.*

~ * ~

The buzz around the meadow increased all through the day.

Tiamoon snagged Cheney, head of the wood clan of gnomes, as he headed toward his forest home and asked about all the excitement.

"Haven't you heard?"

"Would I have asked if I had heard, Cheney?" Tia frowned and crossed her arms.

"Uh, right. We've had visitors arrive in the last two weeks who seem discontent with the peace of our valley."

"What are you talking about?"

"A human arrived and was accompanied by a couple of fae I've not seen before." Cheney nodded his head at the fact.

"You wouldn't happen to have the name of the fae, would you?" Tia dropped her arms to her sides. He furrowed his brow and narrowed his eyes. "To the best of my recollection, the she-fae is called Mary. No, that's not it. Derry, no, humph." His eyes rolled to the sky as he thought. "Cary! That's it. She's Cary and he's Conn. The human they accompanied has some fancy girly name like Flossie, or Francis. Something like that."

So this was the name of the fae Thomas the Leprechaun muttered in his drunken stupor.

"What has all the valley folk wagging their tongues so furiously?"

"The human male challenged Morgan to a duel...with swords." Cheney's grin covered his face.

"Is the man out of his mind?!" Tia began to pace. "He'll be skewered. We can't have these humans and night elves dueling in our valley. If the human is killed, the human authorities will come out here and trample our homes in their zeal to find the culprit."

"Hmm. Hadn't thought of that."

"Apparently nobody has. When and where is this to happen?"

"Tonight at the meadow's edge. All the valley-kind will be there. Listen, I want to go home and eat before the duel. I'll see you there, Tia."

With a quick wave of his hand, Cheney disappeared into the greenery of the forest.

It was bad enough the night elves were raiding the homes of the faerie and gnome clans. With teamwork and dedication, the gnomes, faeries, wood nymphs and other small folk of the valley might be able to protect their homes and hold back the scourge of the elves. If humans got involved in the mix, the valley folk would surely lose.

Tia shuddered at the thought. With someone else responsible for patrolling the meadows and forests tonight, she'd planned a quiet evening at home. Taking care of Thomas had drained her energy. However, her quiet evening would have to wait.

Anytime the night elves were involved in a fracas, nothing good happened from outcome. Tiamoon needed to witness this event and plan accordingly.

~ * ~

Morgan pulled the brush through his white hair one last time, settling the locks behind his shoulders.

"Looking magnificent." He smiled at the reflection in the mirror. "My lord, brother. You're worse than any human woman I've met. I take it you have a heated rendezvous tonight?"

Morgan slowly turned to face his sister. "I have a meeting but not with one of the local women." A smile touched one corner of his mouth accenting the dimple in his cheek.

"I've been challenged to a duel."

Gitty had sprawled across the white divan. Her eyes grew in astonishment. "You? Dueling? Please. Whatever brought this on?"

"There's a cretin of a human being who showed up a couple weeks ago and tried to sweet talk his way into my territory. Last evening was the final straw. He insulted my lady friend and I demanded an apology.

"He's the one who challenged me to a duel. He just made the mistake of choosing swords."

Gitty sat up and considered her brother. "Well, if nothing else, I can give you the edge on swords. Next to me, you're the best swordsman in the clan."

Morgan rolled his eyes. "I can outfight you any day, sister. Once I've finished this interloper, we can set a time and date to meet and prove who's best."

Gitty propped her feet on the table in front of the divan.

"No thanks, little brother. I've better things to do with my time than beat you soundly at a sword fight."

Morgan huffed out an impatient breath. "I haven't time for this. I'll be at the meadow's edge at twilight should you wish to witness my victory."

He flipped his cape over one shoulder and pulled open the heavy wooden door, allowing it to close behind him.

Gitty turned to the small figure seated quietly on the back of the divan. "Well, Cary, fancy a night on the town?"

The little fae's eyes lit up. "Yes!" She flew up and turned a somersault before landing on the night elf's shoulder.

"Lead the way, partner."

Chapter Six

Rays of rose-colored light extended warm fingers from the setting sun to the golden meadow in the valley. Surrounding mountain sentinels glowed a deep burgundy and purple, hiding their forests in indigo shadows.

Standing head and shoulders above the gathering crowd, a lone white-haired figure towered, replete with flowing cape and polished black boots. Securely tucked at the figure's side in a hand-tooled leather scabbard shone a finely honed sword engraved with the bearer's name and family crest. At his feet, a plain practice weapon reclined.

Morgan unconsciously brushed his hair behind his shoulders as he unbuttoned his cloak. With a flourish worthy of a film star, he whipped the cape from his shoulders and folded the plush material in one smooth motion. Sunlight flashed off the hardened steel blade and he placed his bundle on the cleanest log he could find.

Conn winged to the cape and took a seat. He winked at Morgan and wiggled his brows. There was nothing quite as exciting as a good fight. Rubbing his hands together, he giggled. If Morgan quickly dispatched his opponent, maybe they could go to the pub and have more mead before he went back to face Cary.

With carefully staged movements, Morgan drew his weapon from the scabbard, the quiet hissing of the blade against the leather lost in the growing murmur of the multitude.

Morgan was a patient man, but the cowardice of his opponent was becoming evident by the lack of his presence. Should the interloper fail to appear, he would win by default and not have to break a sweat. He felt confident this stranger was more bluff than action. More to his advantage. He would appear as the wounded party and fall back in the good graces of the ladies.

Just as Morgan decided to resheath his weapon, a ruckus at the back of the growing mob caught his attention. People parted and a lone figure in riding breeches, white billowing shirt and shining boots marched toward him.

Pulling a monogrammed handkerchief from his sleeve, the outsider whipped it across Morgan's cheek.

"I formally challenge you to a duel."

The corners of the night elf's lips curled in amusement. He pulled himself tall, staring directly at the man and replied.

"I accept your challenge." Turning to the crowd, he searched but was unable to see his sister. *Where is she?* "Is there someone here who will act as the referee?"

"Didn't you pick one before now?" A raspy male voice from the gathered mob hollered.

Morgan drew himself to his full height. "There was no time."

"I'll referee." From the midst of people, a parting of the crowd showed a small being swathed in leather from head to toe and carrying a blade upon her back.

Morgan raised a brow and looked down his aquiline nose. "And who might you be?"

Tiamoon looked around at the gathering. She would need to be... cautious with her response.

"I'm Tia from the far side of the meadow. I have knowledge of dueling and can be an impartial referee."

Morgan let his eyes rove over the small creature standing before him. Should it decide against him, two swift swings of his blade could end this creature's existence and no one would be the wiser. *Why not?*

"I've no objection." He turned to his opponent. "And you?"

Florence blinked his eyes to be sure he was seeing the sight standing before him. His knowledge of the wee ones imparted to him in bedtime tales covered gnomes and as sure as he was standing here getting ready for a sword duel, this being was a gnome.

"I've no problem."

Morgan swung his blade with his wrist, twirling the shining metal past his shoulders.

"Shall we begin? I've provided you a weapon over there." He indicated with a jerk of his head toward the practice sword on the grass.

Tia strolled to the weapon and lifted the metal spear. She drew her thumb down the blade and turned to glare at the night elf.

"The blade is dull. You will give him a stone and allow him ten minutes to sharpen this weapon."

Morgan rummaged in his pocket and tossed a whetstone to his opponent.

"There. Ten minutes, no more."

Tia looked toward the crowd. "Is there someone with a watch?" A hand went up.

"Please let us know when ten minutes has passed."

Shirring sounds of stone against metal and shuffling feet filled the air. The spectators soon began to mumble and fidget.

"Time!"

Florence looked up, a shadow of fear passing over his face. He regained his composure and walked to the blonde giant. He handed the stone to its owner.

"Thank you."

Morgan smirked. "You're welcome."

"Please make a large circle so the challengers have plenty of room to spare."

The crowd shuffled back, raising a dust cloud silhouetted in the twilight. When sufficient space had been acquired, Tia turned and looked at both men.

"Stand with your backs to each other."

When the two competitors were back to back, it was clear Morgan had the advantage of height and arm length.

In the crowd, Dorinda watched in horror and wrung her hands.

Leaning against a tree behind the majority of the gawkers, Gitty propped one leg up against the trunk. Her line of vision was unimpaired by the shorter townsfolk.

Cary settled on her shoulder, her eyes popping at the sight of the opponent. What the devil had Florence done now?

"Are they really going to fight with swords?"

"Looks like it."

Good heavens! Fool was going to get himself killed! He was better with a firearm than a blade. Unfortunately, all she could do was sit back and observe.

"Who do you think will win this?"

"Oh, Morgan will make quick work of this. You watch." Cary fretted for a moment then settled to study the duel. Florence had been given his chances. After all, wasn't the fault his they were stuck here?

The referee continued.

"Please take five paces. One...two...three...four...five. Now turn and face each other."

Morgan whisked around and looked into concerned brown eyes. He could sense fear from the intruder. *As well he should be.* He pulled his weapon to the front and grasped the hilt with both hands. Quickly he covered the ground between himself and his opponent just as the man had put up the blade in front of himself.

Morgan swung down with crushing force pushing the blade to the ground, the clanging of steel on steel echoing between the darkening mountains.

Florence sucked air into his lungs. The fierce attack of this blonde giant had taken him by surprise. He shoved upward, catching the steel of the other man's sword and flinging it up toward the giant's shoulder.

The blonde warrior turned into the surprise move and jammed Florence's weapon up and over, catching the blade and flipping it from his hands. Morgan then pirouetted and ran the interloper through from front to back.

Shrieks and cries were all the gathered observers could do. On the ground, red staining the white shirt, lay the stranger.

Morgan walked to the edge of the meadow and wiped the blood from his steel. He'd do a careful cleaning when he returned home.

Dorinda burst through the throng and ran to her houseguest. She fell to her knees, gently cradling Florence's head in her lap.

He looked into her eyes and smiled weakly. Mouthing the words, thank you, he expelled his final breath.

She hovered her hand over his forehead and sensed the spirit had left his body. Lowering her head, she allowed tears to course down her cheeks.

Cary watched curiously from Gitty's shoulder then flew closer to observe the reaction of this other human. The female human was crying real tears over Florence. *How strange.* She, Cary, was supposed to be his guardian and, yet, she couldn't bring herself to feel sadness.

Winging her way back to the night elf, she realized she'd changed her alliances. This was the fate of her new life. Nothing ever stayed the same. Gitty stood and straightened her leather jacket.

"I might as well congratulate Morgan. He'll be impossible if I don't."

The pair wended their way through the meandering crowd. As they neared the edge of the meadow, Cary's narrowed her eyes. *If I didn't know better…*

"Well, brother, you did well. Congratulations."

Morgan turned to face his sibling. "Where were you? I couldn't see you in the crowd. Did you catch the whole thing?"

"Yes, I saw the whole thing. I thought duels were supposed to be between equally matched opponents."

Morgan shrugged his shoulders as he leaned to pick up his blade.

"I can't help it if he chose the weapons. Point is I won. Thought I might head to the pub and have a beer or two. Care to buy me one?"

Cary dropped from Gitty's shoulder to the log holding the cape.

"Conn! You devil! Where have you been? Why weren't you searching for Florence? Explain yourself!"

The male fae jumped from his perch at the bark of his name. He twisted around and winged backward.

"Cary! I, uh, I was looking for Florence." He pointed to the form lying recumbent on the ground. "See? I found him."

Cary punched him in the chest. "You idiot! How are we supposed to get home now?"

Conn winged his way above Morgan's shoulder. "I'm not sure I want to go home. What's there for us? More work? No thanks. I like where we are right now."

Gitty and Morgan looked at the two fae arguing.

"New friend, sister?"

Gitty bristled at Morgan's tone. "Yes. Just like yours. Useful and very devious. I see a way to get what we want without putting ourselves in danger."

Morgan slipped his blade into the scabbard and grabbed the cloak from the log. "Tell me over a brew. I've worked up a thirst and I believe my small friend is in need also."

The siblings moved in the direction of the tavern while the wee folk continued their argument as they winged behind the night elves.

From behind a tree a small figure emerged.

I need to find out what they are up to before everything I know is destroyed.

Tiamoon pushed out a breath between her lips. She was going to have to go into the lion's den. If it meant saving her people, then so be it. The lion's den it was.

She set off toward town. This time tomorrow she would have the knowledge she needed to formulate a defense plan or die trying

Chapter Seven

Darkening shadows stretched long across the valley. Tiamoon, lounging against her favorite oak casually swinging her blade, surveyed the meadow. Chills inched down her back, setting her nerves to tingling. Seeking solitude from the crush of the humans in the pub, she'd returned to observe the mortician's ministrations to the outsider. His body would reside in a pauper's grave. Tia could only hope his soul would find better accommodations.

Rocks crunching beneath boots alerted her to the approach of unwanted visitors. Two night elves deep in conversation strode her direction. She squinted her eyes and caught the flickering of wings from tiny fae surrounding the elves.

Tia felt her chest tighten. Faeries and night elves didn't normally mingle. *This doesn't bode well for the rest of us.* She leaned over and pulled her blade toward her as she slowly rose and slipped around the tree in sync with the night elves movement.

"What are you rambling on about, Morgan?" Gitty slowed her pace. "You're going to collect your practice sword, aren't you?"

Strolling to the red-stained metal shaft, he bent down to retrieve the implement. "Of course. We'll need every blade in the coming days. Weren't you listening at the last clan gathering?"

Cary and Conn, sensing a squabble brewing, flew themselves out of danger's range and hovered above the siblings.

Cary leaned toward Conn. "You smell of mead and tobacco. I thought you'd gone to search for Florence?"

Conn snapped his head her direction. "I was tracking him down. I can't help it if the journey took me to the pub, can I?"

Staring at the blood soaked ground; Cary wrinkled her forehead in consternation.

"Well, you did a slap-up poor job of finding him, now didn't ya?"

Conn noted her brogue deepening. If he didn't defend himself now, she'd start a railing that wouldn't stop until his ears bled.

"I located Morgan who let me know where Florence was to be. It's not my fault the fool went and issued a challenge he couldn't win. Besides, I was hungry and thirsty. What was I to do? Morgan was kind enough to offer me food and drink. Saying no would've been impolite."

Cary flew to inches in front of Conn's face. Gritting her teeth, she lowered her voice to just above a whisper. "You're his faerie godfather, Conn. Your responsibility was to guide him and watch over him. What about that?"

The fae straightened his back and reverse winged until he could look Cary in the eyes. "I guided him through his childhood. His decision to disregard my advice as a man had nothing to do with my efforts. I couldn't force him to use his common sense. Don't place the blame on me for his boastful nature. Florence developed that without my help and against my guidance."

Cary's wings slumped and she heaved a sigh. "Tis the truth. We can but lead them. We can't force them to use their knowledge. I'll give you that, Conn, but if I find you're only purpose in going to the pub was to quench your own thirst..."

He held up a hand. "On my honor as a fae godfather."

She eyed him suspiciously. *I've naught but to believe him.*

Their attention was drawn back to the night elf siblings sniping at each other. Gitty pulled her sword from the scabbard and twirled the blade, switching the fine steel claymore from hand to hand.

"Why should I listen? Most of the talk is you boys blowing your own horns about your conquests. I can live without knowing how many notches each of you has on your belts."

Tiamoon hunkered at the foot of the oak, her dark brown leather blending with the tree's bark coat. She keened her ears, held her breath and concentrated with all her being.

Morgan whipped around, covering the distance between himself and his sister with purposeful strides. His arm shot out and grabbed the twirling blade, yanking the weighty steel from her grasp. Standing toe to toe with his older sibling, he narrowed ice blue eyes at her.

"You arrogant ass. The council voted to interrupt the raids on the valley folk. Someone has gotten to them. They're talking about setting down a peace treaty with the locals. Do you really want to live on your little piece of land?

"We started this because we're far more intelligent than the local villagers and ruling is in our blood. Wasn't it your plan to own your own mountain and valley? Have you discarded that idea?"

Gitty placed her hand in the middle of his chest and shoved him.

"Don't ever get in my face like that again. I'll cut out your heart and feed it to you." She snatched the saber dangling in Morgan's hand. Flipping it up and sheathing the metal, she walked toward the road then turned.

"I'll have my kingdom and you won't be allowed inside the borders." She tromped toward home, rising dust with each stamped footstep.

Morgan watched her ramrod straight back march away from him.

Cary sped up to catch Gitty.

Conn winged lazily to Morgan's side. "Is she going to be mad forever?"

Morgan jumped. "You startled me. No, she won't be mad forever, but being on Gitty's bad side is not good. I'd never tell her to her face but my sister is a formidable opponent. It's best when she's *got* my back, not trying to attack it. By the time she gets home, she'll come around to see things my way."

Morgan wiped the bloodied cutlass on the dew-laden grass until the blade appeared clean.

"What *are* you planning to do, if I may ask?" Conn cocked his head ever so slightly, frown wrinkles creasing his brow.

Morgan looked about the area.

Tiamoon held her breath and concentrated on trying to hear the night elf's plan.

Morgan meandered to the edge of the clearing and gazed at the meadow surrounded by forested mountains.

"This land is the richest I've ever seen. The local villagers are ignorant farmers and laborers with no knowledge of the wealth beneath their feet. So far, our clan has been able to flash a few gold coins in their eyes and buy up the property. The humans aren't the problem. This Depression they complain about has made them easy targets.

"No, it's the forest folk; the fae, gnomes, leprechauns, nymphs and sprites that are causing us the biggest concern. We need to run them out of the area. If they can't pay taxes, they can't live on the land. But the little blighters have dug in and won't be chased away."

Morgan turned to Conn. "Your people are very tenacious, little partner. Maybe you can offer me insight into a way to get them to leave?"

"Uh, I, uh, will have to put my mind to the task. Let me think it over and I'll get back to you." Morgan leaned over and picked up his practice cutlass. "Don't take too long. We're planning a raid in the next few days and I want to be certain I'll have success. Before the next moon, I will own all my eyes can see."

He set a fast stride down the same path Gitty had taken, the little fae winging frenetically to keep pace.

Tiamoon counted to twenty then emerged from her hiding spot. Things were far worse than she'd imagined. She needed to rally her clans and pull in as many of the fae and others as she could.

She slid her blade in its casing on her back and trotted down the road toward her home. As she neared the cottage, she smelled the sweet wood her mother burned in the fireplace. Tia vaulted over the gate and burst through the front door.

"Mum, mum!"

Stirring a vessel on the potbellied wood stove, Skye started at the noisy intrusion.

"Why in the world are you yelling? Slow down, Labhoise, and take off your boots. You're tracking in mud all over my clean floor."

Sitting at the table looking a sight better than Tia had seen him in two days was Thomas who quirked an eyebrow and one corner of his mouth her direction.

"Labhoise?"

Before the last syllable had left his lips, a blade with razor-honed steel was at his throat. He gulped, feeling the cold steel prick his skin.

"Yes. It is my name but will never be uttered by the likes of you. If I find you have spoken this to anyone in this forest, you won't be able to tell anyone of your stash of gold.

"Are we clear?"

Thomas slowly moved his head up and down.

Tia removed the blade from his throat and propped it in the corner. She sat on a three- legged wooden stool by the fire's side and removed her boots, wiggling her toes to bring warmth to them. She gazed at the crackling flames, sagging on the small settee. Her simple life was getting too complicated and all of the problems pointed to the interlopers in the valley: the night elves. Skye, her warring leathers traded for the comfort of a house smock, stirred the vegetable stew. Glancing at her daughter, she sensed unease in the young woman.

"What bothers you, daughter? What creates such deep longing and confusion?"

Tia stood and turned her back to the fire's warmth. She clasped her hands behind her and rocked lightly on the balls of her feet.

Nodding in Thomas' direction, she questioned. "Has he had any of the spirit today?"

Skye narrowed her eyes at the leprechaun.

"Not as far as I can tell. I upturned his flask in the sink and have kept a close eye on him while he was here."

Thomas shot a thunderous glare at Tiamoon. "I'm as bloody sober as I ever want to be, thanks to you. Can't say much for the condition."

"Good." She walked to the table and sat opposite Thomas, indicating her mother should sit.

"What I have is news...not good at best, disastrous at worst."

The frown melted from Thomas' face and Skye leaned toward her daughter.

"Wha-what news?" Thomas' voice shook and his lip began to quiver.

"Quit thinking of yourself, Leprechaun. This news will affect all the inhabitants of the valley."

Skye held up a hand. "If this is serious, I need to have my pipe to think. Thomas, would you care to indulge?"

"Yes, ma'am."

Tia huffed out an impatient breath. She tolerated her mother's smoking but wasn't an indulger herself, never having developed the taste for it.

After Skye and Thomas had packed and lit the long ebony carved pipes, Tia began to relate the information she'd gleaned from the night's reconnaissance as the other two settled in to listen.

Wispy tendrils of fragrant smoke curled above their heads. Skye and Thomas kept the pipes clenched tightly between their teeth and refrained from commenting. "What I'm about to tell you came directly from a night elf known as Morgan. He and his sister reside in the abode on the top of the hill that overlooks the valley. To this point, they've caused little problems...or so we thought.

"I've just learned they are buying up as much of the land from the humans as they can. Somehow, they have gold when others do not. They aren't worried about the humans. They are worried about the valley folk.

"Morgan mentioned the other clans have become tired of warring and are happy to settle with what they've received from the humans. He, on the other hand, wants as much land as he can get and domination over the entire valley: magic *and* nonmagic folk.

"He's making plans to raid in the next few days. He wants us gone before the set of the next moon."

Skye pulled deeply on her pipe. She appeared to be concentrating on a spot across the room. Slowly, smoke trickled from her mouth, lazily clinging to her burnished red hair.

"I've been part of the talks with the night elves."

Tia raised her eyebrows.

Skye pulled the pipe from her mouth and pointed it at her daughter.

"It's not necessary for me to tell you everywhere I go. You were busy patrolling the valley."

"At the last meeting, we'd come to an agreement to sign a treaty. If the young bucks have taken it in their minds to start raiding, I think it's time to call in the head of their clan. The elder night elves are tired of the warring and wish to settle on the lands they have now. There's enough for all of us to live without encroaching on the other's territory.

"I must think on this, daughter. It's time for dinner."

"Food?" Thomas put his pipe on the table and rubbed his hands together. "Sounds good to me!"

"Bah! All you think about is your stomach." Tia got up and grabbed the bowls and spoons. Maybe her brain would work better if her stomach were full.

It couldn't work any worse.

Chapter Eight

Shuffling sounds filled the room as participants from the clans settled at the table. One side of the long wooden slab seated heads from the night elves; facing them were the gnome, faerie, leprechaun and wood nymph clan leaders.

Skye stood and cleared her throat.

"I want to thank everyone for attending tonight. We have much to discuss. I'll get directly to the point. Are all the clans represented?"

She watched a familiar figure rise across the table from her, his white hair flowing around his muscular shoulders.

"All the representatives of the night elf clans are here." The smooth baritone of the speaker reverberated in the room.

Skye swallowed hard. *I have to keep my mind on the proceedings.* She pulled in a calming breath.

"Thank you, Aethel. I think we can achieve our goals quickly so we can all go to our homes before the sun rises this time." A shy smile covered her face.

Ahhh! That man makes my knees go wobbly.

Aethel stepped around his chair, moving to the head of the table.

"What is so urgent we need to meet three days prior to our scheduled time?"

Skye moved so she was opposite the clan leader. Her palms had begun to sweat and she knew if he got too close he'd be able to see her heart pounding wildly in her chest.

Pulling to her full four foot eleven inch height, Skye plunged ahead.

"Are you aware within the last rising and setting of the sun a human was killed by a night elf?"

Stunned expressions and crushing silence was her answer.

Skye avoided looking directly at Aethel. Her eyes connected with the other clan leaders as she continued. "A young night elf known to frequent the meeting places of the humans engaged in an altercation with a newcomer to the valley. Their verbal sparring peaked in a duel challenge."

Whispers morphed to murmurs and the participants at the table sent furtive glances toward Aethel, whose flushed face belied the straight line of his lips and determined set of his jaw.

"The humans gathered last evening in the meadow next to their drinking place. When the challenge had been dealt and accepted, two figures stood in a circle of witnesses.

"It's my understanding the actual duel was brief; the night elf dispatching his opponent painlessly and quickly."

Aethel pulled out the chair at the head of the table and dropped onto the wooden seat. A vein on the side of his neck visibly throbbed.

"When the duel ended, the humans went to their pub and continued as though nothing had occurred. Their keeper of the dead came out and took away the remains. What happened next is of concern to each and every council member here."

Skye paced the floor, biting the side of her lip and contemplating how to cautiously phrase her next thought.

"A conversation was heard between the victor of the duel and a female night elf."

Aethel's shoulders flinched.

"The young night elf boasted of a raid to be staged in the next few days. The tone of his comments indicated we have young ones not willing to listen to the judgment of their elders. He spoke of power, possession and domination of all creatures of the valley.

"If this is indeed the climate of feeling among the young warriors, we could be facing dire consequences."

Skye looked around the room and noted each clan member deep in thought. It wasn't a comforting sight.

"I'm asking for your solutions to stop this bloodshed before it happens."

"You're wrong."

She looked up to face the voice of dissention.

"What makes you say that, Glade?"

The night elf of the woods clan stood and peered down his straight nose at the gnome leader.

"I have spoken to my clansmen, young and old, and they tire of the constant threat of war. Many of the young men are seeking to settle and raise families. Who is your source for this outrageous story?"

Skye gritted her teeth. Glade was known to be argumentative. Sometimes, she thought, just for the sake of arguing.

"I don't wish to speak the name."

"There you have it." Glade slapped his hand on the wooden tabletop. "If you won't reveal your source, how are we to know what has been spoken is the truth? Maybe you're making this up to catch us off guard and attack us." He shrugged his shoulders. "Who knows? Unless you can provide a witness to this conversation, we only have the word of a...gnome."

The curl of Glade's lip left no doubt about his feelings.

The door to the meeting hall slammed shut.

All heads turned toward the sound.

"You dare to call the head of my clan a liar?" A young male gnome planted his feet shoulder width apart, sword drawn and at the ready.

Skye turned to the figure. "Terran, please. The man is entitled to his opinion."

The gnome Terran strode to Skye's side. "Aye, he is, but not when he fouls the clan's honor."

The night elf Glade yanked his sword from the casing and, in two swift steps, stood next to the gnomes, weapon in hand, towering dangerously over the two.

Aethel rose, his chair scraping across the floor. He threw out his arm, toppling the cutlass from Glade's hand.

Whipping quickly around, right hand fisted and swinging, Glade's dark green eyes sparked as Aethel caught the thrown punch mid-air.

"Glade." Aethel's low warning held menacing undertones.

The night elf of the woods clan wrenched his hand to his side.

"This is not over, Aethel. You may head this council, but I don't recognize your authority and won't be bound by the decisions made here."

He leaned in and dropped his voice. "Prepare yourself and your little friends. I believe Morgan has the right idea and I may consider joining his campaign." Stepping away, he gave a quick jerk of his head. Chairs dropped to the floor of the meeting hall as several clan leaders jumped up, clomping their boots and banging the doors on their way out.

Skye pivoted on her heel and headed for the door. Hesitating at the exit, she twisted to face the rest of the clan members shuffling to leave the table.

"I think we'll need to regroup and meet at another time. I'll send messages via the mouse network. Everyone take care when traveling homeward. Tonight has shown we've come no further than we were a year ago. Terran, we head for our home. Aethel...good to see you again."

Skye acknowledged the night elf with a quick head bob. She left the meeting hall and slipped the dagger from her belt, hiding it up the sleeve of her shirt. Terran trotted behind, his hand on the hilt of his blade, surveying the landscape in all directions. In a complete reversal of previous congresses, tonight's meeting put the council back to where each clan had stood at the very first get together, and Skye no longer felt safe in her land.

She feared a bloodbath was about to ensue, regardless of the careful negotiations accomplished to this point. There really was nothing as headstrong as a young man trying to prove himself to the world.

Skye tread lightly, scanning the surrounding meadow and woods as she moved toward home on soft leather boots.

Terran, straining to hear beyond the hushed footfalls of Skye, brought up the rear; walking in the same spots.

Skye was deep in contemplation. She'd fallen for persistent attention lavished on her when she'd been but a young warrior. A tall, elegant white-haired night elf had stolen her heart and sweet-talked her into ignoring the common sense whispering in her ears. Furtive meetings in dense forest locations had produced many memorable nights...and a daughter. The night elf had disappeared out of Skye's life as quickly as he'd appeared.

It wasn't until many years later she'd learned of his arranged marriage to the daughter of a chieftain, putting an end to generations of warring between the clans. The woman quickly gave birth to two children: a daughter and a son, expiring while giving the son life.

She felt blessed her daughter resembled her and not the father, making explanations unnecessary. Skye and Terran reached the cottage. Smoke spiraled from the chimney and a candle glowed in the window.

"We're welcomed," Skye whispered.

"Good, I'd hate to have to fight my way back in my own home."

Skye could tell her son was smiling. Joy bubbled through his voice.

A quick entrance and the two warriors stood inside the living room. Thomas, the leprechaun, was snoring in the armchair facing the fire, his feet stretched in front of him, pipe smoldering in the abalone shell on the side table. Tiamoon sat on the three-legged stool, gazing into the fire.

"Hello, daughter."

She swiveled on her seat to acknowledge her mother when she caught sight of another figure skulking in the shadows of the room.

"Who's there?" She sprung from the stool clamping her hand on the fireplace poker and wielding the implement as a weapon.

The figure chuckled then burst into laughter.

"Do you know how silly you look, sister?"

Tia glared at the figure until his words connected with her brain.

"Terran?" Tia set the poker against the flagstone hearth. "Is it really you?"

The young gnome stepped into the glowing ring of light cast by the fire.

"Yes, sister. It's me."

Tia quickly covered the floor space and smothered her brother in a hug.

"When did you arrive? What have you found out? How many bought swords are we facing?"

Terran wiggled free from her grasp and held up his hand. "Whoa, big sis. Let me unstrap my weapon and sit in front of the fire. My body is tired from the journey. I wish a warm cup of mother's broth and to remove my boots."

"I'll get you the broth and some bread but you're on your own for taking off your boots." Tia wrinkled her nose, much to Terran's delight. "It's good to see little has changed since my leaving." Setting in the other armchair facing the fire, he ripped the bread into pieces and dipped a piece in the broth, bringing both to his mouth. Eyes closed in delight; he swallowed and released a long sigh.

"I have missed this."

Skye slipped to her room. The children could update her with the latest news in the morning. The council meeting had tried her patience and worn her out. There was also the matter of seeing Aethel again. It had been many a year, but her heart still skipped a beat and her stomach hurt every time she spotted the night elf. A good night's rest would put things back into perspective.

~ * ~

Tia watched as her brother gorged himself on the broth. When he had finished and removed his boots, she drew the stool next to his chair.

"What have you found, brother?"

Terran stared at the flames dancing in the hearth.

"The threat we've suspected is real-very real. There is a faction of night elves determined to rule this valley. They have enlisted the help of mercenaries from afar and make plans in the dark of the night. The elder clansmen have no knowledge of the plans or the mercenaries. I think we're on our own."

Tia used the poker to shove the logs in the grate around then added a new one on the dying stack. Flames flared up, expelling heat and light.

"What are we to do, Terran?"

Brother and sister stared into the fire.

"Nothing tonight. I'm exhausted and can't think clearly. After a good night's sleep, I'll tackle this problem again."

Tia rose and strolled to her room. Terran was right. The evening had dragged and Thomas' constant whining about not having any liquor to drink had worn on her. She was no good to anyone at this moment. Sleep, indeed, appeared to be the best idea.

Chapter Nine

Wan flaxen rays of sunlight reached across diaphanous pillows of fog covering the dew- laden meadow. Gitty stood holding her coffee cup, staring at the light playing off the mist. Steam curled around her nose, wafting the pungent smell of freshly ground coffee beans to her olfactory senses.

Before her lay the fertile meadow gently sloping up to the velvet green mountains covered in usable forests. A smile touched her lips. *My meadow, my forests.*

Oh, yeah. Morgan might have illusions of power, but Gitty would guarantee the reality of ruling. From what she had ascertained about the meeting last night in the few mumbled words her father had spoken as he had stomped past her to his bedroom, the peace committee had been disrupted and temporarily put on hold. It was her duty to make sure the treaty was never signed.

Morgan stumbled into the living room and through to the kitchen. Several minutes later, Gitty heard him plop himself on the settee.

"Tough night, little brother?" Gitty turned to face him.

Squinting up at her, he grunted.

"Aren't you just the picture of polite conversation today?"

Morgan gulped a large mouthful of coffee. "Better things to do than make small talk with you. I've an important meeting to attend. I'll be out all day."

Gitty raised a brow. "Really. Since when do you leave the house before 4 pm?"

Morgan rose from the couch, grabbed his cup and tromped toward the hallway.

"I haven't time the time to argue, Gitty. My future is something I plan to mold myself, and I have an appointment with destiny."

Gitty blew out an exasperated breath and rolled her eyes. "Dragons and trolls, Morgan. I've barely had time to down my coffee and you're spouting rhetoric worthy of Shakespeare. You must've been drinking tainted mead, for it's surely gone to your head."

She looked around the room, noting she'd not seen Cary since storming from the meadow last evening. Had the tiff between the siblings frightened the little fae?

Gitty shrugged her shoulders. While the little fae was a welcome diversion and having her as a spy in the faerie camp would give Gitty a huge advantage, she'd done fine before the wee one appeared on the scene. Morgan appeared and moved toward the back door. He was attired in the clan's red-brown colors; a dark brown cloak about his shoulders, black polished riding boots on his feet. His hair was tied back with a dark brown leather strip and he carried his fighting steel.

"I'm taking a horse from the stables. And Gitty," Morgan turned to face his sister, "I wouldn't go out after dark."

He departed before she could reply. Moving back to the window, she watched him gallop down the driveway on his brown steed. Out of the corner of her eye, she spied the tiniest distortion in the air. Peering to the valley, she scrutinized each inch of the scene below her. As she was about to give up and get more coffee, the air directly in front of her wavered.

Gitty sucked air to her lungs. *There's old magic here. If the Ancient Ones have been brought in, Morgan and his friends could be in trouble. Heck, we'll all be in deep trouble.*

Aethel ambled through the living room and toward the kitchen, dark circles under his blue eyes. He grabbed a cup from the cupboard and poured coffee for himself. Sitting at the kitchen dinette, he spooned two teaspoons of sugar into the black concoction and stirred.

Gitty slipped in behind him and watched as he dropped his head to his hands. "Are things alright, Father?"

Aethel groaned. "No. Did you know your brother was involved in a duel last night?"

His question echoed through the room. He lifted his head and looked into the guilty eyes of his daughter. "As I suspected...you knew and you were there. Before you try to deny it, there were witnesses."

"Who says I was going to deny it?"

"Your brother and his renegade friends will be the death of us all. I've spent the night tossing and turning with the knowledge we are one step from war with the humans. We can't afford war with the humans. And if that isn't enough, my senses tell me there is Old Magic being used close by.

"My skin is crawling from the spell casting."

Gitty went to the stove and pulled out a frying pan. She collected eggs from the icebox and sliced bread from the breadbox. Muttering under her breath, she proceeded to magic the eggs to cook and bread to toast. Fixing the food on the plate, she handed it to her father. "Thank you. This should help."

"Why are you so determined *not* to war with the humans? We're superior to them in every way and should control this entire valley, not the other way around. They should be trying to get along with us." Gitty dropped her long frame into a chair opposite her father.

"The world doesn't always work the way you think it should, daughter. You must remember we're visitors here."

"Not if we own all the land."

Aethel looked up from his food. "If the humans don't wish to sell to us, how do you propose we get ownership of the land?"

She leaned back in the chair and looked at the ceiling, her mind churning, as she formulated a non-confrontational answer.

"Magic."

The clattering of the fork on the china plate rang through the kitchen.

"You would magic the inhabitants to turn over their land to you? What about when they awoke from the spell? What then?" Aethel's eyes had turned a steely gray as he fixed an angry glare on his daughter.

Gitty stared at her father. *What's happened to the fearless warrior of yesteryear who'd peered into the jaws of death and charged ahead anyway?*

"By the time these witless wonders came around, we'd own their property and they'd have to pay taxes to live on it. We'd be the rightful rulers of this land. What else matters?" She furrowed her brow in disbelief.

Aethel stood, set his plate in the kitchen sink and magicked it clean then turned to his offspring.

"Take yourself elsewhere for the day. I'm not sure I can control my anger enough *not* to destroy you. Don't show your face to me until the rise of the sun tomorrow." Fists clenched against his side, Aethel stomped from the kitchen.

Gitty smirked. *Just as well.* She retired to her room and rummaged in her clothing chest. Many months had passed since she'd ridden her horse. Today would be a perfect time to remedy the situation. She pulled the white chaps from the chest and lashed them on, grabbing her long duster and a white hat in case the skies opted to dump rain on her. She tromped to the back porch and sat on a wooden chair, slipping into her riding boots. The night elf craftsman who'd created her gear had spent many months bleaching the leather to a sparkling white. Gitty had demanded the leathers be created the old way, by hand, not by magicking the material to the desired color.

She slammed the door and strode to the stables, covering the quarter acre quickly in her fury. Her father had grown weak in his time in this inconsequential valley, but she had not. She'd watched him succumb to the taming imposed by the council. No night raids for him, no. He'd sat by the fire reading the old texts, trying to apply their wisdom to the new situation.

She could have told him it wouldn't work but he didn't want to hear it.

Gitty swung up on the finely crafted saddle and yanked the reins to the bit of her mare, directing the animal to the driveway running by the castle. The sooner she was away from here the better. She touched her pouch to ensure there were coins for necessities. A quick kick to the mare's flanks and she galloped away from the mountain's top. By the time she returned, her plan would be set in motion, father or no father.

~ * ~

Conn rubbed his hands together and flew loop-de-loops in delight.

Cary pumped her wings, feeling the lack of use in her shoulder blades.

"Why are you so happy? I'm tired, hungry and I want to sleep in my own bed. I can sense we're close to the place we settled in but I'm not completely sure I can find it. Will you stop acting foolish and get us home?" She scowled Conn's direction.

"There's going to be a wa-a-a-r-r-r. There's going to be a wa-a-a-a-r-r-r."

Cary stopped mid-air, hovering. She grabbed Conn's arm and jerked him around to face her.

"You're an idiot. Don't you remember the last time these humans fought? There was bloodshed all around us. We nearly lost everyone we cared about!"

"Pshaw! This time the magical folks will win and these humans will be gone. We'll have control of the meadows and forests again." Conn danced a jig.

"CONN!!"

He stopped and turned to stare at Cary.

"What is your problem? This is good news for us all." "You've been listening to that Morgan elf. *We* aren't from here. *We* know nothing about these humans, this land, the night elves...need I go on?"

Conn floated, winging lazy circles around Cary. "I have been listening to Morgan and I agree with him. The Others here are very backward. They're nearly the same as the Others we left back home. How could we not succeed here? Once the night elf clans conquer the valley, we'll have free reign to do what we want. Isn't it great?"

He zipped up and turned somersaults in the air.

Cary moved in the direction she thought the oak where they were staying grew. "All I want is to go home to Ireland. This place is different. They talk funny and no one really believes in us here. I'm homesick and I want to go home. I don't want to see these Others kill each other over pieces of land."

Conn shrugged his shoulders. He'd never really understood Cary's love of the land. Oh, sure, he loved his Ireland, but this land was green and there was much to be gained by starting new. Maybe he could conjure that big red travel thing which had brought them here. If he could just remember the conjuring spell...

~ * ~

Aethel sat on the ledge of his bedroom window peering in the direction of the meadow. He couldn't shake the image of Skye from his mind. She'd aged, but then so had he and she'd apparently married, as had he. The young warrior Terran, with firm jutting jaw, straight back and tenacity reminded Aethel so much of Skye, he'd bet his best stallion the young gnome was her son.

He found his heart aching with the need to touch her again and flinching a bit in jealousy. What would have happened had the two of them mated? Ah, but these were the meanderings of a lifelong past. It could never happen. Night elves married and mated with night elves and gnomes married and mated with gnomes. Some lines weren't crossed. It didn't matter if he'd loved Skye. There, the truth had been revealed.

Sure, his wife had been tall, lean and elegant, just like Gitty. Unlike Gitty, his Ella had possessed a kind heart and they'd grown to appreciate each other, but Aethel had not loved Ella. It saddened him to lose her when Morgan was born.

Seeing Skye again brought a rush of feelings he'd thought dead. Oh well, not much he could do now. Because of his two renegade children, the valley and its inhabitants, including Skye and her family, were in great danger.

Aethel stood and looked over the meadow. They might think him old...but it was up to him to prove them wrong and save the valley from their arrogance. He might have propagated them but he didn't have to like them. It was a sad fact, but Aethel's children had become his enemy, and he was determined to win this war. More than the night elves and gnome lives depended on his success.

Chapter Ten

Everything about the scene before her was wrong. Scorched spots blackened the earth and marred nearby trees. Splintered branches littered the ground and the scuffmarks crisscrossing the forest floor hinted at recent activity. Reaching over her shoulder, she guided the tempered blade from its leather encasement and held the weapon in front of her.

The air wavered and Tiamoon froze in place, holding her breath. The flesh on her arms rose and hair on the back of her neck prickled. Magic had been used here recently. She moved leather-clad feet slowly, silently around the edge of the scuffed area. Her lungs ached for air and the side of her lip pulsed where she clamped down with her teeth.

Tia poked the shrubbery with her blade. Under a mulberry leaf, wings crumpled beneath a tiny body, lay an inert fae of the wood clan. Tia let go the breath she was holding. The sight was worse than she could possibly have imagined. Moving quickly, she reconnoitered the area and discovered eleven dead fae and one barely clinging to life.

She placed her blade on the ground and knelt at the male fae's side.

"Who did this to you?" She placed a leaf over the tiny one's body.

Very faintly, the male whispered. "Morgan."

She leaned her ear close to his mouth. "Who?"

"Morgan."

Buzzing about her head alerted her she was not alone. Again the annoying buzz sounds, and now, pinpricks of pain. Tiamoon tried tracking the sound with her eyes. Just when she thought she'd determined the source, a stab of pain would distract her.

"Stop! I'm not sure why you've targeted me but stop. I'm not the enemy."

She stood still as the oaks growing nearby, listening as the buzzing slowed to the swishing sounds of many tiny wings.

Two male fae flew to the front of her face and pointed lances her direction.

"Do not move, gnome. We've seen the damage you've inflicted here." The speaker swept an arm at the lifeless bodies scattered on the ground. "You may have had the upper hand with my kinfolk but I bring reinforcements and we won't be so blindly trusting."

Tia watched as a multitude of faeries appeared before her eyes. She sheathed her sword. Slow, measured steps took her to a stump where she opted to sit and allowed the emotion of the sight she'd stumbled upon to overtake her. A tear meandered down her cheek.

"Such waste; such destruction. Your poor kinfolk had no chance. This is the work of the night elves. I can only guess they stunned your warriors and dispatched them with no conscience."

The male faes darted looks at each other and continued to hold their lances on the seated gnome.

"You lie. You're trying to divert attention from yourself from the heinous act of murder!"

Multitudes of wings fluttered with the murmured agreement of the crowd.

Tia stood. "No. I was searching to find the elves before something like this occurred. I'm trying to stop them. Everyone in the valley will be in danger if they gain the upper hand and take over.

"I've no quarrel with you. I think we need to join forces against the night elves. If all the forest and meadow folk get together in a united front, we can make sure the valley stays ours. If we don't, we'll be subject to the whims of the night elves."

The two male fae lowered their lances and winged backward.

Tia watched as they drew several others from the throng and conferred among themselves. She could only hope her argument was strong. It was difficult to gauge the fae community. For the most part, they were very unreliable, concerned only with life's enjoyments. But many were deceived by this attitude and knew not what fearsome warriors they could be when their homes were endangered. Most magic had been gifted to others by the fae. The extent of their magical understanding had never been tested.

Tiamoon was not about to be the first to test the depths.

The two male fae winged to her, their lances, once again, pointed her direction.

"We can't trust your word. All we know is we came to help our kinsmen but found most of them dead and you hovering over the last one breathing. Your prowess with a sword is legend, gnome. It's not beyond reason to think you inflicted all this destruction.

"We will handle our own affairs and take care of our own families. It might be in your best interest to leave this valley. Word will spread and you won't be welcomed in any community."

Tia clenched her fists at her side. "Do you threaten me, fae?"

The throng of faeries buzzed forward pointing weapons her direction. "Fine. I offered my sword to you and you refused. Don't call on me when you find yourselves under the grinding boots of the night elves. I take my leave."

She turned her back on the warriors, leaving and keeping to the edge of the woods. Her heart pounded and she ran a tongue over her dry lips. She was in a precarious position. The night elves would run roughshod over the inhabitants of the valley if something wasn't done, but her offer of services had met with rejection.

The fae community was suspicious of all outsiders, a fact Tiamoon knew. But she'd relied on her being part of the magical folk of the area to help her win their trust, an obvious mistake. This valley was in for a war like no other and everyone, except the night elves, stood to lose.

I'm not sure I can stand by and watch my people get slaughtered.

A solution was needed and soon. At the moment, Tiamoon wanted to get home without becoming the next victim in the fray.

~ * ~

Gitty galloped her stallion across the meadow to the edge of the verdant forest opposite her home. An old ally had been rumored to be in the area. Slowing her steed to a walk, she kept herself vigilant. The old growth woods could shield many an opponent. Her horse tugged at the reins and snorted impatiently. Halfway up the first hill, the stallion stopped and could not be coaxed to move one step further.

Gitty kicked his flanks but the beast would not budge. In an angry huff, she flung her right leg over the saddle and dismounted, turning to stare down the shaft of a highly sharpened sword. Startled ice-blue eyes rose to gaze into deep green orbs.

"Glade." The whispered name floated through the air.

"You'd best be careful, Gitty. Next time, your opponent might not be as taken with a blonde, blue-eyed amazon." His lips curled into a smile that reached his eyes.

He lowered his weapon and stepped forward, gathering her in his arms and crushing her lips beneath his.

Gitty sucked in a deep draught of air when he released her.

"What makes you think I wanted that?" She furrowed her brows at him.

A deep bubbling sound echoed beneath the forest's green canopy.

"Because, my love, you didn't fight me in the least and I still hold you in my arms." She tried to wiggle free but the arms holding her gently tightened as her captor pulled her close.

"I won't lose this opportunity to make up for lost time, love."

Glade lowered his lips and stopped just above hers.

Gitty waited but he moved no further. When she could stand it no longer she reached up and closed the space between them, slipping her arms around his neck.

He groaned deep in his throat as she pulled from him.

"It has been too long Gitty Saun, too long. I've missed your sharp tongue and quick wit. But most of all I've missed holding you in my arms. How have you been?"

"After all these years you ask now, Glade? Where did you go? Why didn't you contact me? You could have magicked a message to me. What happened?"

The dark-haired night elf pulled back, grabbed the reins of the horse and slipped his arm around the blonde amazon's waist.

"This is not a safe haven. I'll explain once we've arrived at camp."

He led her through a maze of trees and bushes, paths twisting, turning and doubling back on themselves. Just about the time Gitty felt truly lost, the thick forest opened to reveal a camp with many traveling caravans.

Curious eyes watched the striking couple enter the campsite.

Glade led the stallion and Gitty to a wooden caravan. Brightly painted designs covered the outside. Stairs descended from the door to the forest's floor and Gitty noted the wooden wheels were covered in rubber. Glade tied the steed to the side of the vehicle near a filled water bucket. He slid his hand beneath Gitty's arm and directed her to the caravan's door.

"Go inside. I'll bring hay for your stallion and give him a quick brushing."

Gitty turned to protest but Glade had disappeared.

She climbed the steps and entered the box on wheels. Surprised at the space within, she sat at a table and looked out a portal to the outside. The floor of the caravan was covered in hand woven rugs. Colorful pillows dotted the table benches and hurricane lamps hung from metal hooks protruding from the walls.

Glade came through the opening and slid next to her. "What do you think of my home?"

"This is your home?"

"Has been for the last twenty years."

"I thought your family had a castle in the old country."

Glade heaved a sigh, his shoulders drooping. "We did. For millennia we had a castle with lands, rivers and towns. But the last one-hundred-fifty years have taken their toll on our land and clan. With more than a dozen wars happening, the last World War causing the most damage, my people have had to flee our homeland."

"Couldn't you just fight back?"

"We have magic like you but these humans, these Others, have weapons so destructive we were outmatched. Before we could organize and protect our lands, they had bombed the earth from beneath us. We fled over the North Pole and through Canada to come back here. Some of our southern cousins recalled these caravans from the early wandering night elves and created them for us here. They're mobile and contain all we need to survive. They'll do."

Gitty looked around. A shy smile touched her lips. "Yes, they will."

Glade gazed at her porcelain face. "Gitty, my love?"

"Hhmm?"

"What is it you want from me?"

She turned wide eyes on him. "What makes you think I want something?"

Glade burst into laughter. "Because I know you. We had a great love—once—but I've never known you to pine for a man, and *need* is not in your vocabulary."

Gitty felt heat rush to her cheeks. She hated it when Glade foresaw her every move. It was one of the reasons she'd walked away from him. He knew her too well.

"Okay, fine. My brother Morgan is gathering troops around him for a takeover of the valley."

"I was aware he was purchasing land from the Others at a rapid pace but I didn't know he was serious about a war."

Gitty nudged him to move and scooted from the table to pace the small room. "I'm not really sure he wants to go to war but he wants to appear powerful so others will respect him."

"That's a dangerous undertaking, isn't it?" Glade frowned.

"Yes and he has no experience commanding anybody, let alone a bunch of young night elves out for blood."

Glade leaned back and crossed his arms. "So why are you so concerned? You have no love for the humans of your valley?"

Gitty turned a lopsided grin his direction. "Because *I* want to control the valley and I *do* have experience commanding a group of blood-thirsty night elves."

He chuckled. "Aye, you do. Well, Gitty, my love, would it be worth my skin?"

She tilted her head and looked at him from beneath her eyelashes.

"Aye, Glade, aye."

Chapter Eleven

Smoke curled lazily from the chimney as Tiamoon padded toward home. She could only hope Thomas had decided to leave and quit living off the kindness of her mother.

The gate creaked as she opened it, reminding her yet again of the need to oil the hinges. She pushed open the cottage door and was met with the spicy aroma of mulled cider. Her stomach growled and Tia made for the stool by the fire.

She shed herself of the blade and scabbard, standing them next to the hearth before sitting to peel off her boots and stick her feet near the fire. *What am I to do?*

A hand reached around and placed a mug of the warmed cider in her grasp.

Tia turned and looked up at her mother. "Thanks."

"What troubles you, daughter?"

She sipped from the cup and contemplated.

"I came across a scene so horrific today, I can barely think on it."

Skye felt a shiver course down her back. "What would that be?"

"I set out to find the night elves. I'd heard from some of the river faeries Morgan and his cronies were traipsing through the woods destroying all in their path. I was wary, at first, but was forced to re-examine what I know about Morgan. He's no stomach for bloodshed, only for wooing the ladies.

"I started at the south woods and crept my way through the wood nymphs' glen. As I neared the woodland faeries home, I realized I couldn't hear any of the birds singing. No insects were buzzing and the air around me pressed heavy on my skin.

"I slowed my pace and silenced my footsteps. The ground in front of me was scorched and several trees had blackened spots on the bark. Branches lay broken on the ground. I let my eyes sweep the landscape and they fell on the most horrible of scenes. Scattered about the ground were dead faeries, their wings and clothes burnt, weapons scattered. I noted one male fae in front of me struggling to breath. I leaned down to see if I could help and he whispered one name...Morgan."

Tia looked up at her mother, eyes spilling tears. "Mum. They had no chance.

Morgan killed them all! How could this happen in our valley?"

Skye dropped into the seat by the fire. *How, indeed.* She would have to find a way to contact Aethel and incorporate his help. The humans could be expected to fight and kill each other. It seemed to be what they did best, but the valley folk were better than that. They were supposed to get along and help each other. This... slaughter was unthinkable.

Skye placed her hand on her daughter's shoulder, feeling the young woman's body shake with emotion.

"Is there more to this, Labhoise?"

A deep sigh escaped the young gnome warrior. "Yes. They accused me of causing the deaths of the wee ones."

Blue eyes filled to the brim with tears looked pleadingly at Skye.

"How could they possibly think I would harm any of them? I offered to help them find Morgan, but they told me they didn't want my help and to stay away from them.

"Mum, what am I to do? I can't just stand by and let them be massacred."

Skye pulled Tia into her arms and held the young woman, stroking her red locks and allowing her to cry herself out.

"Whatever we attempt, child, we must do under cover of night. We'll protect our forest and meadow from those who would destroy the lands and us. This is not done. We won't lie down and let them annihilate us."

~ * ~

Dorinda gave the table one more swipe with the wet cloth and stepped around the back of the bar. Her keen eye noted the strange foreigners who'd started hanging out didn't come in as often as they once had.

The dandy Morgan was in almost every night, but all the others like him had quit appearing in her pub. She wasn't too disappointed. Oh, yeah, she liked the income, but the tall fair-haired men made the local boys nervous and caused more fights than she wanted to referee.

The women loved the attention but soon realized most of the foreigners had little or no money and were looking for a sugar mama.

It was while she'd been waiting to use the one restroom she'd heard the local females talking.

"Did you hear that braggart Morgan tonight?"

"No, what's he done now?" "He was talking about buying the Thompson's farm. I didn't even know Bill and Joyce were selling. Did you?"

"No. Wait a minute. Didn't he say he'd bought the Williams' land last week?"

"Yeah. He did. What's he up to? He has enough money to buy a bunch of farms in the valley but can't buy his own drinks? I've had it with him. Beside, that new guy he brought in, the one called Glade? Well, he's really much cuter, anyway."

Dorinda stepped behind the door when the two women left the bathroom. She watched as they walked back to the restaurant. The news she'd just heard was very disturbing. She'd investigate first thing in the morning when the bank opened.

Morning arrived in a blaze of sunshine. Dorinda gazed out her kitchen window at glowing golden rays. She stood at the sink finishing the morning's dishes. With Mr. Florence gone, there were only two residents at her inn and and they were leaving this morning for Eugene. When she'd made mention she needed to do some banking in town, Mr. Jones offered to give her a lift to the city. She'd take the afternoon bus home and arrive in time to get the bar ready for the evening crowd, if there was one.

She donned her going-to-town dress and grabbed her spring hat. You could never be sure in the early months of the season if it would rain or not so Dorinda brought an umbrella and a slicker. She stopped by her desk and opened the business drawer, retrieving a slip of paper which she stuffed in her bag. Quick stepping to the front door, she locked the handle and crawled in the passenger seat of Mr. Jones' business coupe.

Conversation was polite and brief on the way in, each rider enjoying the passing scenery.

Dorinda thanked the gentleman when he dropped her at the bank, wishing him luck on his business trip and inviting him to stay at the inn should he pass that way again.

She straightened up and marched boldly through the front door and up to the receptionist.

"I'd like to see the president of the bank, please."

The older woman peered over her glasses at Dorinda and raised an eyebrow. "May I ask what this is about?"

"No. I wish to discuss personal business with the president."

The woman rose from her seat and pointed at a straight-backed wooden chair positioned at right angles to the desk. "Take a seat. I'll see if he's available."

Dorinda fretted with her umbrella, turning the handle in her fingers and chewing her bottom lip as she listened to the clicking sounds of the receptionist's heels on the bank's marble flooring. She noted the smell of Murphy's oil and let a smile slip to her lips. She used the same oil on the pub's bar top. She started at the brusque voice interrupting her thoughts.

"Mr. Clive will see you now."

The receptionist frowned as she pointed to the partially opened door titled 'President'.

Dorinda nodded at the receptionist. "Thank you."

One hour later, Dorinda emerged from the President's office, agitated at the news she'd discovered. She felt pushed by the urgency of the situation to contact all the farmers and businessmen in her town. A meeting had to be held as soon as she could possibly get people together. The face of the valley was changing and not in a positive way.

~ * ~

Glade sat up and stretched his arms. He'd have to remember to purchase material for the women to create more rugs for his floor. There wasn't much difference from the earth's ground and his caravan's rug covered wooden floor; both were hard and cold.

Rising up and quietly slipping out the door, he made his way to the stream to splash cold water on his face. His heart pounded wildly as he thought of the silken haired she- elf sleeping in his bed. Were he to settle into monogamy, Gitty would be his first choice. She, on the other hand, was only interested in power and had made that abundantly clear when they spoke last evening.

He'd watched her eyes glitter with the thought of owning the valley below this mountain, controlling all the inhabitants. He sucked in a breath when the ice-cold snow runoff hit his face. His whole body shivered as he splashed more water against his skin. He needed his wits about him this morning as he gathered his clan to share the decision he'd come to last night.

What he had said in the council meeting was true; his clan was tired of moving from place to place and desired nothing more than twenty or so acres away from the humans to create their own town and settle. What he was about to do was throw them into the heat of battle; the reward was the entire mountain. Once Gitty conquered all the other clans with his help and bought all the property the humans had, she would sit on her hill and rule as the queen she fancied herself.

"Morning, love." Glade twisted to face the silver-haired night elf. Sunlight backlit her hair, casting a glow about her face.

"Morning. Did you sleep well?"

"Yes, but as I told you last night, you could have lain with me."

Glade smiled as he ran his hand down her cheek. "No. I will only lay with you if we are mated."

Gitty humphed. "That's not going to happen."

Glade grabbed the bottom of his tunic and blotted the excess water from his face.

"You made that brutally apparent last night. Where are you headed today?"

The pair moved in the direction of the base camp.

"I think I'll head to the village and start asking around. I'm sure there are some of the Others who haven't been approached by Morgan yet. If I can buy their land before he makes an offer, I'll be on my way to owning all I see."

Gitty leaned over and placed a kiss on Glade's cheek. "Good luck with your meeting today. I'll send a messenger bird with our next move. Thanks for the great night's sleep."

With the flash of a smile and wave of a hand, she swung up in the saddle of her stallion and reined him to leave the camp. Glade had magicked the directions back to the valley into the steed's ear the night before.

Glade watched her leave, a strange sensation settling over him. The sight of her back felt very final. He shivered and moved to the caravan. A good breakfast then a gathering of his clansmen. Today, they would begin their future.

Chapter Twelve

Dorinda got off the bus and scurried home. She had just enough time to start her letters to the local farmers. She knew ten days was almost too short to ask folks to come to a meeting, but the information she'd received at the bank put an urgency to her task. She gathered her writing tools. If business were slow tonight, she'd be able to get all the letters done and posted by tomorrow's mail.

The quiet life everyone once knew was about to go up in flames.

~ * ~

Skye sat at the head of the table; Aethel faced her from the opposite end. The last two weeks in the valley folk lives had taken a decided turn for the worse. Reports were trickling in from survivors of raids on outlying communities. Forest gnome clans, wood nymph clans and even the laconic leprechauns were taking up arms. The survivors straggled in to the meadow and collapsed in the homes of cousins.

After Skye's third cousin, a forest gnome, had stumbled to her cottage with news of total annihilation of two communities by night elves in forest green leathers, she called this emergency meet.

Tension filled the room and weapons rattled in nervous apprehension.

Skye stood. "Thank you all for taking the time from the protection of your homes to be here. I know most of you are not in the mood to talk peace but how about we talk cooperation?"

Protests passed among the seated participants and glares were directed Aethel's direction.

Skye called for silence. "We, too, have heard the stories from survivors, my own cousin, Etain from the forest clan, watched the invaders tear down her village and burn the trees. She heard them laugh about leveling the northern clan's homes. Had she not been hunting mushrooms, she would have perished."

The company of magical creatures rose from their chairs and moved

C. L. Kraemer

Aethel's direction.

"Stop!" Skye held her blade with both hands in front of her, chair on the ground where she'd jumped up. "The next soul who moves will be cut in two."

"Why shouldn't we slice him in pieces and hang the bits from all the trees? It's *his* people who are doing this."

Skye inched forward. "Do any of you doubt my word?" The room was filled with mumbles and grumbling.

"Then set yourselves down and listen. If you can't or won't listen, I'll confiscate your weapons or, better yet, let you try to handle this alone. How long do you think you'll last against several clans of rogue night elves? A day? A week? How long?"

She slammed her sword on the table and planted her feet shoulder width apart, fisting her hands on her hips.

The clan members put away their weapons and scowling, sat in the assorted chairs, grudgingly giving Skye their attention.

"Thank you. I will vouch for Aethel."

He snapped his head up and stared at the warrior gnome.

"I have known this particular night elf longer than most of you have been on this planet. His heart is pure and his intentions honorable. He can no more choose his heritage than your or I but this man...this night elf guarded this valley from outside sources long before your families settled here.

"When my cousin described the invaders of her village, I knew immediately what we were facing. Glade has been true to his word. He and his clansmen are terrorizing the mountains and valley.

"Singularly, we stand no chance of saving our community. However if we unite, pool our resources and plan wisely, I believe we can defeat these marauders and run them out of our lives forever.

"Who's with me?"

Silence permeated the room. Each clan leader glanced at the other.

"Fine. Then you can kiss your loved ones and dig holes in the ground to be buried because alone we won't make it."

Skye grabbed her blade and headed to the door.

"What about him?"

She spun around to face the speaker. "Who?"

"The traitor night elf." Skye walked to Aethel and placed her hand on his shoulder, ignoring the spark she felt flame in her heart.

"You call him a traitor; I call him a hero. He could have easily decided to throw his sword in with the mercenaries burning their way through our homes, but chose instead to stand up and be counted with us. His life is in danger every moment of the day because of his choice.

"Can you say the same?"

Low conversations buzzed in the air until Fergus of the river gnomes stood.

"I'll throw my sword in with you. But only if you lead, Skye."

Heads around the room nodded.

Skye stood straight and lifted her chin. "Fine. I'll take the lead on this but there is one hard and fast rule."

"What?"

"Do *not* question my orders or my authority. The first time either is put in doubt, I'll walk away and leave you to your own devices. Are we clear?"

"Aye."

"Form the circle."

The clan heads circled, facing the center, and placed their blade tip on top of the next.

Skye was the last to place her blade on the wheel of steel.

"These blades will fight for heart and home, until this land is again our own."

"To the death!"

Skye put up her free hand. "No. To life!"

"TO LIFE!"

The cry echoed through the building. When the swords had been sheathed and clan leaders filed out, Aethel stood from his seat.

"You took a huge chance today, Skye. Why?" She gazed into the blue eyes which set her pulse racing. "Because I truly believe you are a man of honor, Aethel. You could have decided to throw your lot with the mercenaries. The one thing I didn't mention in the meeting was my cousin described a she elf with flowing silver hair in white leathers. You and I know there is only one person who fits that description."

"Gitty."

"Yes. But I didn't want these chieftains to have that bit of information. They wouldn't have united. They don't understand children who don't obey their parents. In our culture, it isn't tolerated or understood.

"Will you be able to help us even if it means working against your own kin?"

Aethel moved close to Skye. "Yes. I have love for my children but I don't have to like them. I do, however, wish to protect those I love and like. Will you allow me that honor?"

Skye felt the heat rush to her cheeks. It'd been a long time since any man had brought such personal feelings to the top of her heart. As much as she tried, denying her feelings for Aethel was going to be near impossible. She still loved him as much as ever.

She cleared her throat. "Thank you for helping our community."

Aethel leaned over and picked up her hand, placing a gentle kiss on the top. "My pleasure."

Skye slipped her hand from his, knowing her cheeks were blazing red.

"Won't you be in danger if you go home?"

"Probably. I'll bunk at the inn until we've secured our valley. What about you? You surely can't go home with Glade and his clan roaming the woods."

"Hhmm. I hadn't thought of that. Well…"

"Allow me to pay for a room for you at the inn, too."

"Aethel…"

He smiled at her dangerous tone. She was always independent and determined to make her own way. It was a trait he admired.

"As you just pointed out to me, the danger out there is real." Skye huffed out a deep breath. "Fine. But know I'll have the innkeeper marking down the costs so I can repay you."

Aethel smiled. "Of course."

Skye grabbed her sword and sheathed it. "Let's go. I find myself sporting a great hunger. You?"

"Aye. The innkeeper is quite a good cook. The food will fill the belly and please the soul."

Marching out the door and down the dusty road, the unlikely duo headed to the small community of humans. The war had begun.

Chapter Thirteen

Gitty sat in the caravan reveling in the tales Glade was spinning of his conquests of the small towns and villages.

"We galloped in and, blades whirling, took down all the menfolk. As you would expect, some of the women were in gear and fighting back so my kinsmen felt no remorse in taking them down too.

"Ahhh, Gitty, it was a sight. The first hut was set ablaze and the others went up in the blink of an eye. What a vision! I believe we'll be in control of this land in less than six moons. Taking their land is as easy as swirling a finger through water.

"Our deal is still in place, right?"

Gitty stretched her legs under the table and pushed her arms over her head.

"Of course. I just set the paperwork in motion to buy this mountain for you. When the bank manager approves the sale and issues the money to the human, we'll own everything you see.

"Will that keep your kinsmen happy?"

"Yes. Some of them are beginning to grumble a bit. They want a challenge in battle. So far none of these outposts have provided them a contest worthy of their talents."

"Tell them to have a little patience. By the fall of the first leaves, they can start wooing their sweethearts and planning little warriors."

Smiling, she rose from the table. "I've enjoyed the tales of valor, love, but I must go home. Can't have your kinfolk talking, can we?"

Glade blocked her path and snatched her into his arms. He leaned down and pulled her earlobe gently into his mouth. Releasing the soft tissue, he whispered.

"No, can't have the neighbors telling stories out of school."

Gitty moaned and turned her face to his accepting his lips. Fire raged through her body, tingling her skin and taking away her breath. She pushed him away.

"I-I have to go."

She rushed out the door and leapt on her stallion, galloping away from the camp to the sound of laughter chasing her out of the woods.

~ * ~

Dorinda stood in front of the assorted group, feeling her knees threatening to give way. She cleared her throat.

"Thank you all for showing up on such short notice. We don't often get together like this, but what I learned recently made me feel this was something of an emergency."

"What is it, Dorinda? You finally getting hitched?"

A ripple of laughter circled the room. Dorinda couldn't help but smile.

"No, Ollie. There's still no man in my life. You volunteering?"

More laughter.

"Okay, okay. I'm sure some of you have noticed we have had quite a few new folk in our community."

Heads bobbed up and down in agreement.

"Now, normally, as a business woman I wouldn't say that is bad, but what I've noticed is these folks seem to be flashing quite a bit of cash around."

"And that's bad?"

The group snickered.

"No, Dave, it's not unless you start thinking about how many of your neighbors are no longer in this room. Anybody seen the Thompsons lately? How about the Williams or the McCoys? Tell me, who else is missing?"

The gathered group started looking around and murmuring. Realization started to dawn on the members present.

"Dorinda, what's happening?"

"I made a trip to town to make my final payment on the inn and restaurant and got the bank president to talking. In the last three months, ten folk have sold their places to the family up on the hill—the Sauns. Most of the sales went to the young man, Morgan, but it seems the girl, Gitty, is now starting to purchase land.

"Have any of you been approached?"

Several hands rose in the air.

"Do you see what's happening here? If we don't watch out, they'll own every bit of land around here and all our hard work will be for nothing. To be honest with you, I don't think I want to live here if they become the main landowners.

"I've watched that young man when he comes in the pub. It makes my skin crawl just to think about it. If that doesn't scare you, think about this...Morgan Saun had no problem running a sword through a stranger who insulted his lady. What would he do to someone who hunted on his land or tried to plant wheat in his valley?

""We need to hang on to our property. If they're bound and determined to buy it, make them wait. What's the big hurry?

"Okay. I've said my piece. Who wants lunch?"

Dorinda watched as the members of her community bunched in small groups. She might not be able to completely stop the sale of her valley, but the Sauns weren't going to walk in and take over. Not if she had anything to say about it.

~ * ~

Tiamoon moved her feet slowly and watched every movement she made. Whispers had the night elves planning a raid on this settlement tonight. She, Terran and a dozen of her family clan had volunteered to patrol the perimeter of the village.

The shadows at the edge of the meadow stretched long into the forest backdrop. Every movement set Tia's teeth on edge. Her muscles ached from the intense control and her hands itched to be fighting.

"Tia." The whisper reverberated off the pines.

"What?" She couldn't stop the irritation in her voice. Of all people, Terran should know better than to try and communicate when they were on silent watch.

"I need to answer the call of nature."

"Now?"

"Yes."

"Then be as quiet as you can."

Muffled steps crushed against the needle strewn forest floor. Tia's ears keened to hear any unusual movements.

"AAAAHHHHHH!!!!"

"TERRAN!" The sound of her brother's cry set Tia racing in the direction she recalled him going.

"TERRAN!"

Thundering hoof beats came toward her. In her quick estimate, she guessed a dozen horses were heading her direction.

"INTRUDERS! INTRUDERS!"

She clutched her sword to her chest and nitched against a large pine. As the hoof beats rumbled closer, she muttered. "Please forgive me."

Turning the blade side away from the animal's shin, she grabbed the blade and swung the handle side at the animal with all her might.

The horse stumbled, sending the rider to the ground. Behind him two others went down. Tia rushed out and finished the night elf with a swift blow. She quickly glanced at the figure on the ground and caught her breath. She'd just put a sword through Glade. The ashen color of his skin indicated her prowess had not lessened since the last war.

Not having the time to think further on the situation, Tiamoon soon dispatched two other elven warriors. She ran between the trees to the village. Slowing her pace to a trot, she noted smoke rising from the chimneys and lights in the windows. She spun to face the remaining warriors headed this direction but heard no hoof beats echoing through the pines.

Tiamoon slowed her breathing and narrowed her eyes. A movement in the trees set her teeth to grinding as she tensed to fight. Three forms headed her direction. Two upright figures dragged a limp form between them. Tia's muscles went into overdrive.

She moved silently toward the trio.

"Tia?" A whisper pierced her concentration.

"Frey?"

"Yes. We've Terran and he's hurt bad. We need to get him to the healer."

She ran to the cottage known to house the healer and knocked on the door.

A sliver of light cut the darkness of the night as the gnome witch peeked out the door.

"What is it you need?"

"My brother is badly wounded. We need your healing powers." "Bring him to me."

Tia ran to relieve one of the warriors. Moving with urgency, the gnomes made their way to the healer's cottage. Directed to a cot by the fire, Terran was laid on the straw mattress.

The healer turned to the warriors, centering her gaze on Tiamoon.

"Go. I will send for you when I have ministered to him."

"But..."

"Go. Your bond to him is too strong. It will interfere with my healing efforts."

Tia glared at the healer but left the cottage. She was a warrior, not a healer, and could respect the witch's need to perform her magic in private.

When the sun rose above the eastern mountains, a small child came and tugged on the tail of Tia's cloak.

"You must come to the healer's."

She hurried to follow the child and knocked before entering the cottage of the witch.

The woman looked up. "I'm truly sorry but they damaged his life source. I could do nothing to save him."

Tia looked at the broken form of her brother. She clenched her jaw, spun on her heel and left the healer's cottage. Barging past the gathered warriors, she barked orders.

"Give Terran a warrior's burial then head to your homes. The night has been long and we need rest before the next attack."

The men glanced warily at each other. Many had fought with her in the last war and knew this look did not bode well for the enemy. Many night elves would lose their lives to pay for the death of Tiamoon's brother.

Chapter Fourteen

Morgan paced the living room end to end. His deal on the Huff land had fallen through and for no reason he could fathom. He'd offered them more money than they could hope to get in a lifetime, yet just as they were about to agree to his terms, they changed their mind. The same situation occurred with the Millers down by the stream. If he didn't know better, he'd swear someone was undermining him. *Gitty?*

Scuffing across the floor in house boots on her feet, she meandered through to the kitchen, an enigmatic smile on her face. She hummed a Celtic tune she recalled her mother singing years earlier.

"What are you so happy about?" Morgan scowled at her.

"Why not? From what I hear, the forest elves are ridding the surrounding mountains of all the worthless creatures usurping our land."

Morgan stared at his sister. "What did you just say?"

Gitty rolled her eyes. "The forest elves are ridding the mountains of all the scum. Dragons, Morgan, don't you ever read?"

"Why? Won't make me rich."

"Seems you're not getting that way by your own means. Maybe reading will help you become the noble landowner you think you should be." She smirked his direction.

"I knew it! *You're* the one who's undermining my deals." He shot toward her, fury overcoming common sense.

Before Morgan could reach Gitty, she'd pulled a knife and held it at his throat, the blade inches from his Adam's apple.

"Don't tempt me, little brother. I've always wanted to be an only child. If your deals aren't working out, it's not because I'm undermining them. It's because you're a poor negotiator. I'm not experiencing problems."

He backed away and shot her a dirty look.

"If father were here, he'd tell you to back off. As the heir apparent, it's your duty to support me and my efforts."

Gitty's brows furrowed as she stared at her brother. She broke into laughter and walked away. "But he isn't here, is he? In fact, I haven't seen him in several weeks, Morgan. Have you?" Morgan gazed out the window and mulled over Gitty's statement. She was right. He hadn't seen his father in several weeks. He walked back to the master bedroom and entered. The bed was properly made and a light layer of dust covered the furniture tops. Opening the wardrobe, Morgan noted Aethel's riding boots were missing and his leathers appeared to be gone. He quick-stepped his way to the stables. Several fighting blades used by Aethel were missing, as was the thoroughbred mare he always rode.

If Aethel was gone then...he liked the idea of being the head of the house.

Gitty passed him on her way to the barns.

"Don't get any wild ideas about being the boss."

He whipped around. "What?"

"You had that dreamy look on your face like when you think you're going to get your way. Father is still in the area, just not here right now. I've seen him come in, change his clothing and leave. He usually checks to see if either of us is here.

"I believe, little brother, he fears us. If your buying deals are falling apart, our own father maybe responsible. What will you do if he's the one spoiling your plans? Kill him?"

Morgan growled. "I wouldn't be the first or the last to commit patricide, I suspect. I need to regroup. Where are you going?"

Gitty flipped her hair over her shoulder. "None of your business. Don't wait up. I'll be home late." She trotted through the stable opening, reappearing on her steed, and galloped down the driveway.

Morgan fumed as he stomped into the house, slamming the door in his wake. He could sense Gitty was scheming against him and now he had to contend with his father conspiring against him, too? *What to do? What to do?*

"Well, pacing the floor here won't get things done. Maybe there's a young maiden new to the valley who'll appreciate my attentions. A bit of mead will help clear the brain and set the mind to working. That's what I'll do...go to the pub."

Grasping his night cloak, Morgan swung the cape about his shoulders and headed to the barn. He'd find a solution to his situation at the pub and things would go his way in the morning...just like always.

~ * ~

Gnomes, leprechauns and clans of fair night elves tromped in and out of the inn. Dorinda hadn't seen this much business in her family's restaurant, well, ever. During the evening hours, magical folk she'd grown up hearing the tales of came in for food and meetings. Her back rooms were beginning to resemble war rooms. Maps were constantly being unfolded and lines followed by fingers. Murmured conversations soon overtook the music from the radio. When she entered the room with beverages, the dialogues would cease until she left. No matter. Dorinda was thrilled to know the valley where she resided was guarded by the magic folk.

She started leaving plates out on the hearth at night and at the back door. Let the people talk. She knew she was ensuring her safety.

During the day, the farmers and villagers began to stop by and keep her posted on the offers being made by the tall blonde female and male newcomers. Offers met with negative answers.

But of all the wonders in her world, Dorinda was most fascinated by the unusual couple residing in her inn. She tried not to stare, but they brought looks to themselves from everyone.

It had been a month since she'd held the meeting with the village folk and the tall gent and tiny lady in leather clothing sat at a table in her restaurant speaking in low tones. Dorinda watched them, a spike of envy touching her heart. The pair were obviously in love, but something about their conversation suggested they held the worries of the world on their shoulders.

She came over to fill their water glasses.

"Excuse me, miss?" The gentleman's blue eyes held her attention.

"Dorinda, sir. How can I help you?"

He glanced at his companion and she nodded her head.

"You believe in the wee folk, don't you?"

"Yes. My mum was from the old country."

His smile sparkled lighting up his face. "Good. Could you spare my companion and me some time after you close tonight?"

"Sure. I can meet you in the sitting room around 10:00 pm if you wish."

"Perfect."

Dorinda watched as the two held hands. Her curiosity was wildly peaked. If she could only make it until ten without exploding...

~ * ~

Gitty tore through the forest. She hadn't heard from Glade in several days. He always sent a messenger bird after a successful battle and she hadn't heard a thing. Her stomach ached with worry. Slowing her steed, she pulled him to a stop and dismounted. She tied him to the nearest tree opting to walk the rest of the way to the caravan camp.

She followed the trail she'd memorized, breathing easier as the forest opened to the clearing. But the scene unfolding before her struck fear in her heart. The fire pit was black and dark. There were no caravans to be seen anywhere and by the disturbed dirt on the forest floor; the inhabitants had left in a hurry. Gitty ran to the spot where Glade's caravan had stood. Jammed into the ground through his green jerkin was his bloodied sword. Next to the sword stood his riding boots covered in blood.

Gitty sucked air into her lungs. Dropping to her knees, her fingers trembled as she reached out to the boots.

"No." The word whooshed from her mouth.

Snapping twigs alerted her to the presence of another. She looked up to see a haggard- faced, young forest night elf.

"Twelve went out, one came back. Keep your mountain and your wretched valley. It's not worth the price. He loved you more than any other woman and would have presented you many healthy sons. You wasted his life."

The young warrior spit on the ground next to her, turned on his heel and disappeared into the towering pines.

Gitty sat on her heels, determined to be strong, but the moment her hand touched the soft, green leather jerkin, she broke down and wept, the sighing wind through the pine boughs harmonizing with her keening wails.

It was at that moment any compassion felt by the she night elf disappeared.

Chapter Fifteen

Cary and Conn hid beneath the oak their wings shaking in fear.

"So you want to stay? For what? To spend the rest of your life hiding in a tree?"

Dozens of footfalls trampled past the oak and down the road.

Conn buzzed to the center of the room. "I'm not afraid. I just didn't want them to find you."

Cary narrowed her eyes at him. "You're a fool and a liar. What I wouldn't give to find that big red thing that dropped us here and fly away home."

Conn crossed his arms and lifted his head. "I'm not a liar. I'm not afraid."

The ground next to their tree rumbled and rocked the roots of the tree.

Cary screamed and flew to Conn's arms. "What is it? Are we going to die?"

Conn shook her from him and winged his way to the tree's opening. He peeked out the door. Turning, he flashed Cary a huge smile.

"Your magic seems to work just as well here as it did back home."

She furrowed her brows. "What are you talking about? I haven't cast a spell in many moons."

He wiggled his brows. "That big red thing is outside the door and the mangy mutt is running around sniffing. You ready to leave?"

Before he could blink his eyes, Cary had zipped past him and found the opening in the red thing. Recalling the thunderous, rowdy crowd of warriors who'd just passed by, Conn was a wing beat behind her.

He'd had enough adventure for one lifetime.

~ * ~

Morgan swaggered into the pub and reconnoitered the room. There were no night elves, no gnomes, no magic folk at all in the inn. The only woman at the bar was a grandmotherly type drinking cola.

He sauntered to the bar, removed his cloak and sat on a stool. Dorinda appeared and walked toward him. "He's not welcome here, innkeeper."

The deep voice boomed through the empty room.

Morgan swiveled his chair to look upon a familiar face.

"Father. Since when do you give orders in this place?" A sneer marred the young night elf's chiseled features.

"Since the council gave me the power over all things in the valley and mountains. We've watched you try and steal what these humans have worked so hard to earn by playing to their sense of security. No longer, Morgan. You are not welcome on these premises. Your presence is offensive to all creatures magical and nonmagical.

"When you took the life of an Other without regard..."

"But *he* offended my companion and *he* is the one who issued the challenge." Morgan smirked, his knowledge of the rules of dueling well honed.

"Truth that may well be, but you could also tell from his ways and clothing he was not of this time."

Morgan shrugged. "I can't help it if he didn't know where he was."

"And that attitude is what has gotten you banned. Until this generation has grandchildren or has passed on, you will confine yourself to the castle grounds starting now."

Standing with his hand on his blade, the young night elf glared at his father. "Are you going to enforce this decision?"

Aethel stood tall. "If you force me, I'll do whatever it takes to obey the council's decree. Don't push me, Morgan. I *will* cross swords with you and I'll win."

The air crackled with electricity and the two night elves faced each other. Morgan dropped his hand from his sword.

"This is a poor excuse for a proper pub anyway. I'll find my entertainment elsewhere." He snatched his cloak and stormed from the room.

Dorinda watched the older night elf melt away from the room. She looked up to see if Betty needed another cola only to find the seat empty. As the time was nearing ten, she locked the front door and started to clean up. At the appointed time, Dorinda joined Skye and Aethel in the dining room. The three sat at a table staring at each other.

"What is it you wish to talk to me about?" Dorinda's voice wavered.

Skye smiled and gently touched her hand. "Don't be afraid. We're not here to harm anyone. We've watched you with the Others. You sense things they don't and

I suspect you have the magic about you."

Dorinda felt the heat rush to her cheeks. How could this small woman see so well?

"Uhm, yes. It's strong in my family. My grandmother was a healer back in Ireland before we came here. I've been taught the old ways since I was a child."

"Aha! I knew I'd been feeling old magic in the air." Aethel rose from the chair and began to pace. "Are there many other humans with this power?"

Dorinda shook her head. "No. I'm afraid once I'm gone the old magic will die. No one in this country believes as I do and I don't believe they want to. They're too busy trying to survive in the here and now."

Aethel stopped pacing and stood behind Skye. "We asked you here to be an ambassador for the Others until the uprising has been quelled."

Dorinda sat back in her chair. *Me? An ambassador?*

Skye reached a hand out and touched the innkeeper's lightly. "You know that Aethel and his kin are night elves, right?"

"I guessed."

"I'm a gnome. While originally of the forest clan, I moved to the meadow and joined them when I wed. There are also wood nymphs, leprechauns and wee folk in the surrounding areas. We need an advocate who can make the Others, the humans, understand our plight. I know most humans in this country don't believe in us but they seem to listen to you.

"Will you speak for us?"

Sucking air into her lungs, Dorinda's only answer was a large smile.

Aethel patted Skye gently on the back. "I told you she would."

Skye rolled her eyes and huffed. "Men." Aethel turned his attention to Dorinda. "The worst of the uprising has passed but there might be pockets of resistance to the peace plan we've set in place. We need you and your kind to be wary and let us know when unusual happenings occur. We'll send out our warriors to keep control of the few. I promise no human will be harmed."

Dorinda looked to the earnest faces of her guests. "How can I say no?"

"Then it is done." Aethel patted Skye's shoulder.

"It's done." Skye nodded her agreement.

"It's done." Dorinda agreed.

~ * ~

Tiamoon stood at the cottage's door gazing on the carefully manicured yard. When Skye had learned of Terran's death, she'd come back and worked furiously in the yard for three days, digging until her fingers bled. Tia knew her mother had watered the plants with her tears.

But Tia had been surprised when Skye had gone back to the inn, especially when Skye sent word via the mouse network she'd be staying with Aethel, the night elf.

Skye had instructed Tiamoon to retrieve a diary she kept in her wardrobe. The contents would explain her actions.

As instructed by her mother, Tia had read the early pages and received the shock of her life. She was half night elf. She wasn't sure whether to scorn herself or deny the connection. What she did was send a message to her mother to find her happiness.

Maybe among all the death there would be a spark of love and a promise of life. Only time would tell.

The Lending Library

Prologue

Follow the highway that hugs the shoreline of the river about fifteen miles into the dense forest. A covered bridge spanning the water appears on the right side. Turn your vehicle slowly onto the creaky, wooden single lane passage and after holding your breath and praying the bridge holds your vehicle, follow the narrow lane for three miles. The transport through a rainbow of greenery is unlike any other spot on this planet. Towering pines reach their evergreen arms to the sky creating a canopy that provides a cool shelter for the creatures of the forest. As the fading blue of the overhead sky begins to morph into inky darkness, the road wends itself past a slatted building tucked into a crook within the wooded landscape. The clapboard siding could do with a coat of paint and visitors must wonder if the shaky building will stand another year in this coveted haven. Much of the outside bears the weathered scars left by years of rain and a slight green sheen to the sides indicate the moss which cushions the foot on the forest floor has decided to overtake the structure thus returning the elements back to their beginning. The one inconsistent in this picture is the sturdy, new porch hosting miniscule tables and chairs.

A sign out front bears white, chipped letters of explanation:

The Lending Library—open 24 hours. Welcome.

Linda Brown moved to these woods so long ago she'd forgotten the actual date. She hated the isolation at first, but after spending ten years being miserable, she realized she had a choice to make—move or learn to adjust. She adjusted.

It was after she'd adjusted to her situation she discovered mail order catalogs and book clubs. When her husband Donald passed away, she gave away all the earthly things he had felt so important and built shelves in every room except the kitchen to store her books and create her library. She moved her small bed into the old pantry adding a small window so she might see the "little people" when they came to visit her before she fell asleep.

Friends from her socializing days stopped visiting. People in town began calling her the Witch of the Woods and quit passing by the house. Linda didn't care. She had her library and the wee ones.

Chapter One

Ailidh wobbled precariously on her high heels.

Kayne smirked. "Having problems, dear?"

"Shut up!" she snapped. "I need to practice this until I get it right. We don't really have many options left open to us, Kayne. You had better practice, too."

He stopped and steadied himself on the railing of the porch. He wriggled his feet out of the closed leather shoes that encased them.

"I don't know why you insist we wear these ridiculous articles of clothing. This long- sleeved shirt cuts off the circulation to my hands not to mention the lack of space for my wings and these long pants chap my legs.

"Worst of all, are these horrendous leather shoes. They pinch and make my feet swell. Why do we have to go through all of this? I don't understand." Kayne grumbled.

Ailidh sighed and slowly, *patiently* explained to him, once again, why they were practicing.

"Remember last Wednesday when Keegan and Connal lost their dwelling? The sound of their tree crashing to the ground was deafening. The Others are moving out more and more. We will lose our home if we don't act first. Now, put your shoes back on and walk for just five more minutes."

Kayne wrestled his shirt off and threw it to the porch's deck. He pulled the long pants off his body and left them in a heap next to the shirt. Bending forward, he touched his toes gingerly as he gradually unfurled his lacey wings. Slowly, he pulled himself to an upright position. Shoulders back, wings completely expanded, he lifted his 18-inch form to its full height and looked at Ailidh defiantly.

"I don't need to fit into the Others' world. They need to adjust themselves to my world and leave us alone."

Ailidh, teetering, grabbed the lower railing of the porch and shook her head.

"Kayne, most of the Others don't even know we exist. How can they adjust to something they don't even believe?"

"They adjust to animals, don't they?"

"The animals chose to be seen. We did not. Remember? Our great, great grandfathers took a vote and decided we would endanger ourselves more if we continued to be visible to the Others. At that time, they didn't have all the machinery they have now. They moved into our lands at a slower pace. Now, put on the clothes and try to adjust."

"No." Kayne kicked at the clothing on the porch. "I'm going to get a magazine and a cup of coffee. You can stand here and practice day and night for all I care."

He turned on his heels and lifted himself off the ground with his delicate appendages. He lazily winged his way into the open window of the building marked *Lending Library*.

Hovering until he landed on the balls of his feet, he folded the wings tight to his torso and walked to the corner of the building signed Coffee Shop. He sat in a small chair snugged close to the matching table. Sliding the Newsweek someone had tossed on the table toward him, he flipped through the pages. Minimized for easier handling, the magazine was still large enough to require both of his hands to turn the pages. A diminutive nymph in a waitress uniform with a "Chrissy" nametag took his order for a latte. Ten minutes later, she returned with the steaming liquid in a cup.

"Thanks, Chrissy." Kayne picked up the cup carefully and took a sip.

"No problem, Kayne," she had a surprisingly deep voice for a nymph. "Where's Ailidh?"

Kayne jerked a thumb over his shoulder toward the front porch.

"Practicing," he grunted.

"Oh," Chrissy mopped the table next to Kayne's with a wet rag then flew daintily to the kitchen with the dirty cups and saucers she'd picked up. One of the resident dryads of the valley, Chrissy was living in the tree behind the Lending Library. Her home across the meadow had been one of the first destroyed.

Ailidh is right. Kayne frowned at the silent admission. The Others were invading his world with frightening, swift, uncaring swaths into the forestlands. Soon there wouldn't be an Ancient tree left. While, at a glance, their movements seemed random, even careless, Kayne had noted a pattern, albeit haphazard, to their actions. Months earlier he'd watched from a safe distance as the huge screeching yellow machines ripped up his ancient wood friends and squashed their bodies beneath armored tracks. He could never be sure whether the squealing had been the old trees or the vicious yellow machines. After the first occasion of watching as they destroyed a sea of Ancients, Kayne had left on shaky wings and flown home. Ailidh was furious at him, thinking he'd been with his friends drinking honeysuckle wine. He couldn't stop throwing up long enough to tell her what he'd seen.

When the thunder and growl of the angry yellow tree destroyers rumbled over their living room ceiling several months later, Kayne sat Ailidh down and explained what had happened that fateful night. He took her soft, dainty hand in his and looked into her sparkling moss green eyes.

"We must be prepared to move from our home."

Ailidh's exquisite wings trembled. "Why?"

The earth near the entrance to their home groaned and bits of dirt drizzled from around the doorway.

Kayne pointed up. "That—that—monster will reach into our home and pluck us up with no regard whatsoever. I've seen it rip out the Ancient trees in the glen over by Drystan's home.

"The night you thought me so drunk I could not speak, I was ill from watching The Others kill the Ancient trees and destroy homes of our friends. I couldn't stop being sick long enough to explain to you. When I finally got the horror of that picture out of my mind and stopped throwing up, you'd gone to bed—angry. I didn't want to disturb you."

Ailidh's face blanched and she slumped to the cloth-covered chair Kayne had so carefully carved from a branch the Ancient tree had gifted them.

"Wh-wh-why? We've not harmed them. Why do they want to rip out our homes and make us move?"

"I don't know my love, but we've got to find a way to fight back or we'll be next."

Kayne had soothed Ailidh's fears that night, but she began a campaign to move to Faetown and get out of the meadow and woods they called home.

Kayne sighed. She'd get her way and they'd move, but he wasn't going without a fight.

He felt a soft rush of air caress his cheek and looked up to find Ailidh alighting gently on her bare feet, her toes inflamed and angry looking.

He nodded to her. "Better get the Librarian to wrap those before they swell too much. Wouldn't want to put your *shoes* in the rubbish bin." Licking several fingers, he turned the page, the crinkle of the slick paper echoing off the wall of books.

When his smarmy comment met with silence, Kayne looked up to see a large tear meandering down Ailidh's cheek. He dropped the magazine to the table and hung his head, pushing out air between his lips. He'd done it again. He'd hurt the one woman who put up with his attitude and still loved him. Most women of the Fae would have kicked out his boastful self long ago not tolerating his pride and pomposity. Not Ailidh. She'd just look at him with those enormous sparkling moss green eyes, pat his hand and kiss his cheek. Kayne, unlike most Fae men, preferred one mate and one mate only. He never had understood the need to wing from inviting mossy bed to inviting mossy bed.

He reached out and grabbed the wayward drop heading toward the fine line of Ailidh's jaw.

"I'm sorry, my love. Let's see if the Librarian has something to ease the pain." Kayne lifted himself from the chair and fluttered to the back of the building.

On the door was a sign. It read: "Rap loudly. Human hearing."

Kayne pounded on the door, settled himself on the floor, and waited.

Slowly the big door opened; before him stood a giant of a person. He sucked in a deep breath and felt his wings tremble.

Pulling up a stool, the giant Librarian sat. She was nearly at his eye level. A gentle smile touched her lips and crinkled her gray eyes. The essence of wild roses swirled lightly on the air.

"Kayne. How can I help you?"

Her soft voice purred quietly to his keen hearing.

Kayne opened his mouth but nothing came out. He coughed, stepped back then winged himself up a foot. At this level, he was looking in to the kind eyes.

"Ailidh… Ailidh has been practicing with those high heel shoes, and now her feet are swollen and hurting. Do you have something that would help?"

Linda thought for a moment. "I do believe I have something to ease her pain. I also have some Epson salts you can take with you so she can use them tonight. Wait here."

Rising from the step stool slowly, she walked to the back of the small room and opened a cupboard on the wall. Taking out a box and a bottle, the Librarian returned to the doorway.

"May I come out and administer to her?" Gray eyes questioned as she stood with the medicine in her hands.

Kayne hesitated. Ailidh liked the Librarian, but he still didn't trust her. After all, she was one of the Others. He turned his head and saw his mate trying to stifle the large tears meandering down her cheeks by swiping at them with the back of her hand.

"Yes. Please. She's in such pain." Linda was surprised. Very few of the wee folk had become comfortable with her presence. Ailidh was the exception, so getting their permission to move about her own home was necessary if she was to keep them coming into her library.

"Lead the way, Kayne." She wasn't above playing to his male vanity.

As they got closer to the tiny faerie, Ailidh straightened in her chair and sipped from her coffee drink. She was a bit startled to see the Librarian out in the building. She didn't come out in the daytime for fear of scaring away the wee folk that gathered. Something must really be wrong for her to take such measures.

"Librarian." The sweet sound of Ailidh's voice carried to the odd pair approaching her.

"Ailidh. How are you today?"

"I'm well, thank you. What brings you out of your room?"

"Kayne asked me to see to your feet. He mentioned you were suffering and asked if I could help."

Ailidh shot Kayne a glare. "My toes are swollen and hurt a bit, but they will heal without help, thank you."

Linda could sense a fight brewing and opted to take the diplomatic way out.

"Well, let me give you some of my healing helpers. Use them if you like and if not, hang on to them. At some point in the future, they might come in handy. These little orange pills here relieve pain from the inside out, small dose aspirin. I believe you have this remedy in a leaf you brew; this is just easier to take and not quite so bitter. Just swallow them, don't chew, and in about 20 minutes you should feel some relief from the aching."

Linda gently shook the box of Epsom salts.

"These salts work if you place them in hot water and soak your feet. They're called Epsom salts and can be quite handy for those days when you've trekked too far. I'd be more than happy to get a tub so you could start the healing now."

Ailidh looked at Kayne's worried face and the concern on the Librarian's face. She pushed out a sigh.

"All right. If it will make both of you happy..." She watched relief flood the faces of the two people she cared about the most. If this would stop her feet from throbbing... she'd try anything.

"I'll get Chrissy to give you a hand." Linda took a step and hesitated. Turning, she asked, "Is that all right with you?" Ailidh nodded.

Linda trod lightly on the old oaken floor. As she came close to the kitchen, she stopped, waiting until all her clothing had stopped rustling. She cleared her throat and closed her eyes. She'd made an agreement with the small ones to ask permission before peering directly at them—it was considered polite in their realm.

"Chrissy?" Linda whispered.

"Yes, Librarian?"

"May I speak with you?"

"Of, course, Librarian. Let me dry my hands and I'll join you."

Linda sighed quietly. These wee ones had taught her to slow her world down. It was a lesson she greatly valued.

The whirl of wings wisped past her face and she scrunched her eyes tight.

"Please, Librarian. I thought we had agreed we would not stand on the formalities. Open your eyes. I wish to see your storm-cloud colored eyes."

Chrissy maneuvered herself to sit on the hand railing that separated the kitchen from the main floor.

Linda relaxed her features and allowed her eyes to open; before her sat the tiny nymph. She had clad herself in a fifties-style, carhop uniform, ingeniously made from the petals of daisies and roses.

Linda allowed a smile to touch her lips. "You're looking very... official today. Any particular reason?"

Chrissy shifted her position. "Yes, I was reading on the Internet that servers used to get something called tips. Every server I saw had a uniform so I decided I like this style best and put it together. Maybe I'll get some tips."

Linda was finding it very hard not to laugh aloud. "Well, Chrissy, I don't really think you have a need for tips."

Chrissy pushed her lower lip out and furrowed her brow into a thunderous frown. "Why?"

Linda caught herself before a grin covered her face. "Because tips are paper money customers leave if they think the server has done a good job. Since you live here in the forest and most of your housing, food, and needs are met without having to buy anything, paper money doesn't really have any value, does it?"

Chrissy's lip pulled in and she smoothed her brow. Her face took on a quizzical look and she tilted her head. "I think you're right. Well, this uniform would be wilted by the end of the day, anyway. I'll just wear my regular clothes tomorrow.

Was there something you needed, Librarian?"

Linda allowed herself a small chuckle. "Yes. Ailidh has injured her feet, and I wish to get a pan large enough for her to fit in both her feet. I'll need to have water warm enough to melt these salt crystals and then a towel available for her to dry her feet."

The little nymph narrowed her eyes and puzzled the situation. "I know there are some large pans in the very back of the cupboard. Will you come in and pull them out?"

Linda hid her surprise. She never entered the kitchen when Chrissy was working. Her size terrified the little nymph and it was, again, one of the agreements they had made. Moving very slowly, Linda entered the tiny room. She crouched on her knees and opened a very tiny door. In the back was a small, quart size, sauté pan which she was sure was the pot the little nymph meant. Using two fingers to slide out the pan, she pulled it from cupboard and placed it on the top.

"Is this the one you meant?"

Chrissy buzzed into the room and looked at the pan. "Yes. I'll warm some water in it in the microwave..."

"Uh, don't do that. The one thing that won't work in the microwave is metal. If you'll allow me, I'll find something plastic..."

Chrissy smacked her forehead. "Librarian, don't worry. I'll just have to use my magic. How silly of me to forget heating water is one of the first things we're taught. So, if you'll leave?"

Linda rose slowly from the floor and feeling somewhat like a pretzel, backed out of the small space. She rolled up to her full 4 ft. 8 in. height. It felt good to stretch her cramped muscles.

"I'll leave this to you, Chrissy."

Turning she noted Ailidh and Kayne deep in conversation. Something about the body language of the two wee ones was very wrong. It made Linda think. These two were not the only faeries to come into the library and whisper in frightened, muted tones. Linda was determined to find out what was causing such consternation among the Fae community. From the trembling of their wings, she needed to move fast or her tiny folk would be gone, and Linda would be alone with her library full of books.

Chapter Two

Linda crept toward the huddled bodies of Kayne and Ailidh. She stopped, her eyes cast down, and cleared her throat. Her ears picked up the rustle of wings.

"Yes, Librarian?" It was the melodic voice of Ailidh.

"I was wondering if I might speak with Kayne privately for a moment."

Frantic whispering ensued. Linda was hoping the two would decide soon as her neck was beginning to pain her.

"Please look up, Librarian."

Linda brought her eyes up to face the piercing forest green orbs of the tiny faerie.

"What do you want with my mate?" A tiny eyebrow slowly arched upward.

"There has been some unrest within the…" she hesitated.

Calling the faeries by that name could bring a world of problems on herself and the library. She frantically searched for the proper terminology.

"…the Hidden Ones' community."

Ailidh and Kayne smirked at each other.

"It's okay to call us faeries, Librarian. You have our permission." They saw her shoulders relax and she breathed a sigh of relief.

"I've noticed many of my patrons whispering in hushed tones and frowns have replaced the happy smiles once exhibited. I'm very worried and hoped Kayne might enlighten me as to how I might assist."

Chrissy arrived, carrying a towel-wrapped, steaming pan of water. She placed the pan on top of the towel on the floor in front of Ailidh.

"There. I've brought some of the salts to sprinkle in the water once you've slipped your feet in the pan, Ailidh."

Kayne turned toward his mate. "I'm going to talk with the Librarian outside. I'll be back shortly." He kissed Ailidh lightly on her forehead and winged his way out through the open window.

Linda moved carefully toward the door listening to Chrissy fuss over Ailidh and her sore feet. "What were you doing to get your feet so swollen? Oh, Ailidh, they must really hurt. Here, slip them into the water. See, isn't that better? Now, I'm supposed to sprinkle these crystals in… Ooohhh, look! They fizz!"

Linda allowed a smile to touch her lips. Chrissy had been a godsend in the small community. Unlike most forest nymphs, she was determined to be successful in a businesslike way and had welcomed the opportunity to work and be around an Other. Linda couldn't understand the little nymph's need to be human. She would've given her right arm to be a fae of the forest. Oh, well, seemed no one was happy with their lot right now.

Linda slipped out the door and quietly sat on the second step. Kayne had drawn up one of the chairs to the edge of the top step and was tipping the legs back.

"What is it you want to know, Librarian?"

"Kayne?"

"Yes?"

"Can you read?"

"Yes, Librarian. Quite well. As the first son, my parents made sure I was well educated. They felt having the ability to read the Others' language would help me to keep the community safe. I've tried to keep up with the news by reading the daily papers when I can find them."

Linda nodded. An old mystery had now been solved. When she and Donald had first moved here, their paper was tossed on the front porch. Out of seven days of a week, four of those days the paper would go missing. They never could figure out why. So Donald constructed a paper holder and set it at the end of the driveway. Toward the end of his life, the only exercise he got was to walk to the newspaper box and get the daily paper. They never lost a paper again.

"Good. It will make my request a little easier then. I've noted my patrons are very upset. They gather in clusters in the coffee shop and start discussing—something. I'm not sure what it is because if I venture out to get a book, all conversation ceases. I'm beginning to get hostile looks. From what few snatches of conversation I gather, there is construction machinery damaging your homes?"

Kayne turned his head and looked at this Other. Should he let her know what was happening? Would he be betraying his kind? What if she could help?

He weighed the options and decided. "The machines, you call them bulldozers, are moving swiftly through our forest and homes. They seem to strike without a pattern. We're terrified and unable to do anything. We don't know how to make them stop." Kayne sighed. "I'm afraid we're all going to have to move to Faetown."

Linda blanched. Her faeries were going to leave the forest. She couldn't have it.

"Has anyone come close enough to read the name of the company on the side of the machine?"

Kayne flinched and pulled back. His eyes were wide, his jaw had dropped open and his wings began to beat furiously against the chair.

"Get close! Are you mad? Those machines would crunch us in a minute, and no one would know!" He shook his head. "No, no one has been close and I wouldn't ask anyone to try."

Linda waited for his wings to stop churning. When Kayne folded them against his back, she knew he'd settled down enough to broach him with her idea.

"I asked because if we could get the name of the company off the door of the bulldozer , then we might be able to check on the computer to see who owns the construction company. I'd be able to check official records to see what the project is requiring them to work so haphazardly. From that point, we might be able to formulate a plan to stop the destruction of the Ancient Ones."

Kayne's eyes popped open. "You know of the Ancient Ones?"

Linda nodded. "I had many years to study before you wee ones showed yourselves to me. I know of the Ancients. It angers me to see them systematically destroyed for no reason."

Kayne shook his head. The librarian was amazing him with her revelations. She seemed so in touch with his kind, and he knew... well, nothing about her. He turned his deep brown eyes her direction.

"Why would you aid us? You're one of... them?"

He watched anger flash across the face of this Other. As quickly as it had surfaced, he saw it replaced by a kindly smile.

"I always knew of you wee ones. Before I married the Mr. and took his name as my own, my family name was O'Rourke. The little folk have long been welcomed in my family's homes. "The cups and saucers, plates and silverware you use in the coffee shop were all forged and molded by my great, great, grandfather. Our hearth always featured food for the fae. I grew up with faerie…" she glanced quickly to Kayne at her slip of the tongue.

He smiled and nodded forgiveness.

Linda cleared her throat and continued "...friends. They didn't change—I did. As I got older, they seemed to disappear, and I began to believe seeing them had all happened in my head.

"Then we moved here. Chrissy was the first to show herself."

Linda smiled. The day she arrived had been a particularly tough one. Donald, her husband, had been so sick; Linda knew he wasn't long for this world. She'd had to make a decision to like living in the woods or sell everything and move back to San Francisco.

She had sat on the front porch—Donald having finally fallen asleep—and stared into the woods surrounding their home.

Suddenly, there she was standing on the top step, her wings poised elegantly.

Linda remembered holding her breath not sure the sight before her was real.

~ * ~

The two stared at each other.

The Librarian not daring to move.

The nymph not sure if she should speak, and when she did ,where to start.

Chrissy spoke first.

"Might I have a cup of coffee?"

Linda blinked and released the breath she'd been holding.

"Black?"

"Sugar and milk if you have it."

Linda nodded. "I'll bring it out. Have a seat."

She backed slowly toward her front door. Ever so gently, she opened the door and sprinted to the kitchen. She put a cup of coffee in the microwave warming the brown liquid. As she waited, she looked around for a container small enough to fit the nymph's hands. As she was beginning to panic, she remembered the tea set, forged by an O'Rourke hundreds of years earlier and passed from one generation to the next.

Moving quietly through the house, she went into the second bedroom and grabbed the set. She washed everything in the kitchen sink then filled the small coffee pot, sugar bowl, and creamer. Adding a cup next to her own porcelain teacup, she balanced the tray as she measured her steps to the outside.

She wasn't certain she would find the tiny wood nymph on her porch. She *had* been up for the previous 24 hours taking care of Donald. She could have hallucinated the tiny mite.

Upon opening the door, she spotted the miniscule visitor still seated on the porch. Noiselessly, she placed the tray on the top step, sat, and poured a cup of coffee for her guest, nodding her head to the sugar and creamer containers.

"Please… help yourself."

She poised her cup while the nymph doctored her drink. It wasn't until the little creature had taken a sip of her coffee that Linda spoke.

"I don't want to seem ungrateful but… what brings you to my home?"

She brought the cup to her lips and pulled a sipful of the warm liquid into her mouth.

"Because I need your help."

The liquid seemed lodged in her throat. Linda swallowed hard and looked at the tiny beauty. She cleared her throat.

"You need *my* help?"

Golden brown eyes reminding Linda of the bark of the oak trees surrounding her small home stared up at her.

The wood nymph nodded her head.

"One of the machines that the Oth… your kind uses came and tore my oak tree, my home, from the ground. I was down by the stream enjoying the day and dipping my feet in the coolness when I heard the screams of the yellow machinery. I hid myself behind a boulder near the edge of the trail running past my tree. If I would have been inside…"

The tiny nymph shuddered, her wings rustling to the very tips.

"…anyway—I was wondering if I might stay in the old oak behind your dwelling. I've checked and it appears vacant." The tiny visitor looked so lost, Linda felt her heart melt.

"Of course."

The little visitor's shoulders dropped. "Thank you. And thank you for the coffee."

"I'll try not to disturb you. Do you need help moving in?"

"No. I'm carrying everything I now own."

The two sat drinking their coffee. When they had finished the pot, the nymph rose, her wings working lazily, and turned to Linda.

"You're different than most of the Others…"

"Linda."

"How is it you can see me?"

Linda watched the effort the nymph was exerting to keep herself aloft.

"Well…"

"Chrissy."

"Chrissy, as you appear to be very tired…"

The visitor bobbed her head in agreement.

"…why don't we save that discussion for another time?"

A slow nod of the tiny head, bobbing of the body, and the nymph winged to the end of the porch disappearing around the side of the house.

Several years and many cups of coffee later, the two had formed an unusual friendship.

Chrissy's home destruction was the first Linda had heard of the decimation of the Ancient forest and the homes of the fae folk. It was not, unfortunately, the last.

As the fae started to trust Linda, thanks to Chrissy's concerted efforts, and had begun to use the Lending Library, she picked up on the whisperings and saw the trembling wings more often.

~ * ~

Now she sat with Kayne hearing yet again another tale of unprovoked, wanton destruction of the ancient forest and fae folk homes.

Linda looked at Kayne. "If you can remember the name on the side of the dozers, we could use the Internet to track the owners. There has got to be a way to stop the devastation."

Kayne shifted on the step.

"I was trying to stay away from the machines."

Linda watched the color rise to his cheeks.

"I understand and I would have done the same thing. However, anything you can recall will help us to halt this killing."

Kayne thought for a moment. He closed his eyes and scrunched them tightly.

"I think I recall a triangular shield with a long sword crossing from the top left through the bottom right. There was also a name… black… black catco. That's it. It was black catco."

Linda rose. "Great. Let's see if we can find some information about the company on the Internet."

"Excellent idea. A chill has begun to descend on my wings."

Kayne winged his way inside.

The librarian waited until the faerie had disappeared into the building.

Maybe, just maybe they'd get somewhere now. She hoped so. The daily razing of the forest was moving dangerously close to her home.

Like the wee folk, Linda feared the bulldozers… and like the fae folk, she had nowhere else to go.

Chapter Three

The setting sun spiked light off the gray circular tower of the multi-storied, river rock building covering two acres of the mountaintop. Wrought iron gates set in stone walls protected the summit fortress known as Citadel Saun from the rest of the world. The castle had overlooked the valley for as long as the residents could recall. Very few recognized the design as a direct copy of the Bothwell Castle in Strathclyde, Scotland.

Gitty stood in her dining hall at the long oak table. Chandeliers hanging on cast-iron chains from the 25-foot ceilings shed light around the long narrow dining hall. A crackling blaze in the man-sized fireplace emitted enough heat to warm the cavernous room. Strewn across the 16-foot tabletop covering the slab's magnificent wood swirls bordered in gold leaf, lay a topographical map of the eastern 25 miles of the valley closest to FaeTown. The tall, muscular night elf leaned over and drew large red x's on areas noted to be home to groves of oak trees.

"There's one less bunch of trees to search."

A sneer marred the fair face. Ice blue eyes pored over wavy lines showing mountains, rivers, valleys, and acres upon acres of wooded lands.

"That wretched little raisin of a leprechaun better not have lied to me, or I'll let Lancelot have him for dinner."

A 40-pound cat with glowing yellow eyes prowled its way around the leather clad legs of the elf. She reached down and pulled her pointed nails along the thick black fur of the animal's back.

"Soon, my love, soon."

Leaning closer to the paper, Gitty noted she was nearing the edge of the Ancient One's land and had yet to find what she sought.

"If we don't come across something soon…" She let the thought die.

The cat growled deep in its throat; the hair down the center of its back standing on end.

Gitty tried to ignore the cat's warning, but the sound of soft leather on flagstone disrupted her concentration and she looked up to see who dared to interrupt her.

"Oh, it's you." Gitty shrugged and turned back to view the map.

"Wow. Don't let your sisterly love overwhelm you at my return." Morgan strode his way to his sister's side and the map that seemed to have ensnared her constant attention.

"I just can't figure out the little raisin's rhyme. 'A stand of oaks That all can see, Hides the fortune You seek from me.'

"I've bulldozed nearly all the oak groves in this valley and have yet to find the miserable little beggar's fortune. If I don't come up with it soon, I'll put him on the rack and torture the information out of his leathery hide. Then Lancelot can have him for dinner."

The cat yeowed at the mention of its name.

"That's right, my sweet, leprechaun for dinner."

Gitty traced a road with her fingernail. In her own writing, she'd drawn a house and noted, *Lending Library*. Directly behind the structure, per notes she'd written herself, was an enormous oak tree shading the building. The towering perennial housed several forest creatures and covered the building with shade in the summer. Gitty had dismissed it as inconsequential. She was beginning to reconsider.

"Maybe the leprechaun was playing with his words."

Morgan leaned over her shoulder and peered at the squiggly lines and circles on the paper.

"I think, sister, you need to get a hobby. This looks to be a child's attempt at art."

Gitty huffed her impatience. "It's a topography map, you idiot. If you weren't so busy trying to enchant every female that passes by you, you'd realize our time will be coming to an end very quickly if we don't find some sort of gold to purchase the land."

Morgan straightened and looked at the hunched back of his sister. "What in the world for? We're elves; we have no need for the things humans consider so important."

Gitty dropped her head to her chest and pushed out a sigh. "You fool. Of course, we don't *need* money. If we want to continue to live in this castle and keep the grounds human-free, we need to be able to purchase the land around it to stave them from our fortress."

Morgan's brow furrowed. "Why? No one *owns* the land. The land belongs to all who live in the forest."

Gitty whipped around, fisted her hands on her hips, and glared at her younger brother.

"You, mushroom brain, have been thinking with your sexual organ and not your head. If you'd taken the time within the last 100 years to notice, man has begun *buying* all the forest. Somehow they have found a way to own what was not ownable. If we don't use their paper money to purchase what was ours by rights, we will be thrown off our family's land.

"Are you going to go and get one of their jobs to bring in some of their paper money?"

Morgan pulled himself to his full 6' 5" of height. "I don't need a job. I'm elfkind."

"Well, elfkind, help me locate the leprechaun's fortune or you'll be elfkind living in a cave and bathing in the river."

Gitty resumed her position at the table studying the map.

Morgan looked at his older sister. She was not one to mince words. He thought about his latest ventures into the nightclubs of the humans. The females were drawn to him as bees congregated around the hive, but the moment they learned his looks were not attached to money, they disappeared. He'd spent more than one night in the company of some troll of a woman due to the lack of this paper money of which Gitty spoke.

Morgan moved next to his sister and looked at the map.

"The only thing I see is this place here."

Morgan's finger rested under the simple drawing Gitty had made of the Lending Library.

Chapter Four

Linda dragged her hand through her hair, scrunched her eyes shut, and tilted her head back. She'd been sitting in front of the computer for hours trying to track the business name Kayne had said he spotted on the side of the excavation machinery. What she located was a maze of business organizations bleeding into other organizations all circling back to Black Catco. No one seemed to own the company, and there was no paper trail on the county site indicating a permit issued to bulldoze the woods surrounding her home.

She sighed deeply and brought her head forward squinting at the stream of light spiking her eyes. Glancing at the clock on the computer, she moaned.

"God, I didn't realize how late… make that early… it was. I need sleep, or I'll be as grouchy as Simon Stockington on a good day."

Linda emitted a tired giggle. No one could be as grouchy as the ancient mailman. Feeling woozy and lightheaded, she left a note for Chrissy asking her to watch the library while she got some sleep. The destruction of the Ancient Woods and faeries homes would have to wait. Otherwise, her thinking capacity would be worthless.

~ * ~

Chrissy opened the door to a dark interior.

"This isn't good."

The bluish hue of the computer screen caught her attention and, after flicking the switch to lighten the room, she allowed her curiosity to guide her. Taped above the computer display was a note from the Librarian.

Please watch the library today. Up all night researching. Need to sleep.

Chrissy moved the cordless mouse and watched the screen flicker to life.

"Oh no."

She sharply sucked in a breath at the image on the screen. Centered on the computer monitor was a triangular-shaped shield. From one upper corner across the face of the shield to the lower corner, a long blade was pictured. Above the sword and shield was the heavily printed word, *Black*, and under the image was one other word, *Catco*.

"Not again. I thought she'd left the area. Damn!" Chrissy muttered. "Tiamoon, you'd better be close by. We really need you now." Turning off the computer, the little nymph trudged to the kitchen to start her day. She was going to have to call on the mice to get a message to the warrior gnome, Tiamoon. If Black Catco was in the area, the Lending Library was in trouble... as was everyone who lived in the surrounding woods.

Chapter Five

Ailidh tittered nervously as Kayne placed their luggage in the wagon. The dog pulling the vehicle shuffled in place, his actions bobbling the bed.

"Silas! Hold still!" Bram huffed.

"I'm anxious to get going. I'm only doing this as a favor to Ailidh, you know." The terrier mix turned to look at his business partner.

"I know, I know," Bram arranged the suitcases in the bed of the wagon. He fluffed the pillow on the seat and pulled out a blanket to cover the slender shoulders of his dainty passenger and her mate.

Ailidh winged to the front of the wagon and settled herself in front of the dog, Silas. She looked into his dark brown eyes and smiled. Resting her hands on his furry muzzle, she placed a tender kiss between his eyes.

"Thank you, so much, Silas. This is a tough move for us but knowing you care enough to take us there helps. Really, it does."

Kayne watched his mate work her wonder on the dog. If dogs could blush, he was sure Silas would be red to the roots of his fur. He figured to get things moving before it got too late.

"I think we should be moving before it gets dark. We have a long way to go my love."

Ailidh nodded but didn't move until she'd wrapped her arms around the dog's neck and squeezed gently. "Thank you."

She winged to the wagon and hovered over the seat next to Kayne.

He laid the blanket on the wooden bench and when she had set herself down, he wrapped the woolen spread around her body.

She shivered and leaned into him. "Let's get started. We have one stop to make before we leave the woods."

Bram clucked his tongue and Silas took off at a trot.

Ailidh and Kayne turned to catch one last look at their home.

"I sure hope this works out," she whispered to him.

"Me too."

~ * ~

Chrissy sat cradling the hot cup of liquid in her hands. It had been a long time since the *Black Cat* name had appeared. The last time the name had been uttered, the fae community was nearly wiped out. She couldn't—wouldn't—let that happen again. Tiamoon needed to be contacted; but how?

No one had heard from the warrior gnome in several years. After the last debacle, she'd left the glen swearing never to return.

Chrissy rolled her eyes. Kayne's brother, Keegan, had rejected every command the warrior had issued. His insubordination came close to undermining the defense of the woods and the inhabitants. Only after Kayne had thrashed him soundly had Keegan agreed to pitch in with the others and fight for their homes.

She felt the rise of panic. How was she going to find the warrior? Her reverie and questions were interrupted by the squeaking of the front door.

"Going to have to get that hinge oiled." She put her cup on the table. Standing, she blinked in surprise at the visitors.

"Ailidh, Kayne. You're here awfully early today. What brings you in?"

Kayne stepped toward Chrissy and extended a hand. "We're leaving the forest and wanted to stop by to thank you for helping Ailidh the other day. Will you let the Librarian know we've gone?"

Chrissy's mouth hung open. "Leaving, why?"

Ailidh looked at her feet, a shy smile touching the corners of her mouth.

"My sister invited us to live in Faetown with her. I've always told her no, but the other day when the huge yellow machine the Others drive nearly destroyed our home, well... " Ailidh lifted her chin, crossed her arms, and stood straight. "...I just made up my mind I'd had enough. I'm tired of living in fear. At least in Faetown my home won't be torn down."

She gave a nod of her head. "That's what my sister says."

Kayne shrugged his shoulders. "Where Ailidh goes, so go I. Thanks again, Chrissy, and please let the Librarian know how much we appreciate her help."

Chrissy pushed out a sigh. "Best of luck to you both. Send me news when you settle. I'll keep watch on your home—just in case things don't work out and you decide to come back to us." Ailidh straightened her shoulders. "They will work out. I'm determined."

Chrissy cast a glance at Kayne. He was shaking his head slightly. She knew he would support Ailidh no matter the cause but recalled many an argument where he had been vocal about not wanting to live in the city. This change of heart meant Ailidh was very, very frightened.

The two faeries walked to the porch and down the steps to the wagon bearing their belongings.

Chrissy watched with a feeling of hopelessness as the pair departed.

I have to contact Tiamoon. Somehow, someway. The forest is in grave danger and we need a champion… the sooner, the better.

Chapter Six

Tiamoon paced the floor of her hut, the sound of her pliable leather boots whispering over the river stones. She couldn't sit still. She wasn't sure what the problem was, but she *just* couldn't sit still. This feeling of... restless dread permeated every pore in her body. She found herself whipping around at every creaking branch outside her window, jumping with every snap of wood in the fireplace, and in general, trying to escape her own skin.

Something was wrong in the forest; something was terribly wrong in *her* forest. She could sense it. A high keening carried on the drift of clouds pushed by the winds of the south filtered through the evergreens. The last time the woods spoke to each other in such worried tones, Mt. St. Helens exploded and killed many old friends. The feeling in the forest was taking on the same trepidation as it had in May 1980.

She stepped out her hut door and stood in front of her home listening. Restless trees swished their branches through the air, groaning in fear and expectation. The bushes rustled nervously and the only other sound was the throaty hooting of an owl searching for dinner. All else was silent—too silent.

Inside, she reclaimed her chair facing the fire. She bent forward and stirred the stew simmering in the pot hanging over the fire. The fragrant smell of cooked vegetables curled around her nose and her stomach grumbled at her.

"Yeah, yeah. Soon."

A quick dip of the wooden spoon in the pot and she brought the steaming liquid to her mouth receiving more complaints from her stomach. The hot tangy liquid burned the edges of her lips, and she blew across the top of the spoon to cool it. A second test proved the cooling to be a success, and she gulped the food down.

"It's cooked long enough. I'm hungry."

Tiamoon dipped her bowl into the mixture pulling the dripping wooden container toward her. As she was about to tuck into the stew, a scratching at her hut's door halted her progress. She dropped the spoon into the filled bowl, precious liquid splashing over the side. Rising from her stool, Tiamoon set her dinner down and stomped to the door.

"This had better be damned good."

She flung open the door and stared out at the dark night. As she was about to roar her anger at the wind, a tapping on her boot directed her attention downward. Standing before her was a mouse with a note clutched between its teeth.

Tia snatched the document from the creature's mouth. "Thank you. My jaws were beginning to ache."

Tia nodded.

"I'm to wait for a reply."

Tiamoon stepped out of her warm home and glanced around the nearby woods. There was no unusual movement, nothing out of the ordinary; just an early spring wind blustering through the tree branches.

Stepping inside she motioned the mouse to enter.

"Sit next to the fire. I'll bring water and some food."

"That would be lovely. It's very chilly this evening."

Tia humphed an answer as she fetched a container in which to dip water from the pail. She pulled a small bowl from her cupboard and filled it with the soup which still bubbled in the cooking cauldron on the fire.

Her hostess duties fulfilled, Tiamoon sat in her chair and opened the message.

Forest facing destruction from unknown assailant. Need your help, again. Please come as soon as possible.

C.

Tiamoon crumpled the note in her hands.

"Why should I? The last time I helped they ignored my advice and exiled me off the land. I don't care if they all get pushed into Faetown and never have a home again."

"Beg pardon?" The mouse pushed aside its empty bowl.

"Nothing. It may take me some time to come up with an answer."

Settling itself next to the warmth of the hearth, the mouse replied. "Take your time. My bones need warming, and this fire is very inviting."

Tia finished her soup and dipped out another bowl as she tried to formulate an answer to the message that wasn't as bitter as she felt. She realized much time had slipped away as the mouse began to snore gently.

She threw several large logs on the fire, washed out the bowls, and crawled under the covers on her bed. The goose down comforter gifted her by the Valley geese held her body warmth, causing her eyelids to flutter and close. She still had no response for the mouse to take back but maybe a good night's sleep would bring the right words to her mind. Tiamoon sighed deeply and drifted into a restless slumber.

~ * ~

She rose from her bed and rubbed her eyes. There was something dark gray in front of her fireplace.

"What the…" she furrowed her brow as she tried to place the strange apparition on her hearth. Grabbing her boots, she pulled the supple leather over one foot then the other. She leaned to grab her sword from it resting place next to her bed and stalked silently on leathered feet toward the intruder. Her journey to the hearth halted at the piece of crumpled paper on the floor.

The sword slid quietly into its sheath on her belt, the events of the previous evening replaying in her mind.

"Oh, yeah… an answer."

Tiamoon grabbed her fur cloak from the hook by the front entry and braced herself for the chill and probable rain of the morning. She pulled open the door and found herself squinting at the brightness assaulting her.

"Wonders never cease."

She trod around the side of the hut and gathered wood to start the morning fire. Above her a formation of geese headed north squawking noisily as they left the approaching summer.

Hoisting the wood in her arms, she muttered, "Looks to be a hot summer."

She bobbled the load to the front of the hut and pushed the door open with her foot shoving it closed behind her. Padding to the hearth, Tia dropped the cut logs on the flagstones.

The gray lump stirred. From the mountain of fur a furiously moving nose and twitching whiskers appeared. Tiny, bloodshot eyes blinked rapidly and peered at Tiamoon.

"Ah, yes. I really can't thank you enough for allowing me to share the warmth of your fire and dryness of your hearth. Have you an answer to send back?"

Tia sighed. She'd like to tell them to handle their own problems; they were so certain they didn't need her the last time, but Fae Forest was her home. She was as tied to it as if the land had born her. Last night's message had put understanding to her restlessness of the last few weeks. She watched Mouse stretch. Tia moved forward arranging the logs in the fire pit and set flame to the wood. The night's chill began to subside from the hut's interior.

"I have fresh bread baked by one of the local lasses in payment for a favor I did for her. Let's have some bread and water. After that, I'll give you a reply."

Mouse's ears perked up and his pink tongue slipped out around his lips.

"You know, you're not obliged…"

Tiamoon held up a hand. "I know. I also know it's better to work with a full stomach."

"That's true." Mouse wiggled himself as close to the fire as he could without singeing his fur. "Ah, but this feels good."

Tia had gone to her pantry to retrieve the bread and returned with a full bowl of water and thick slice of bread. "You'll be pleased to know the sun shines today. No rain to soak your fur."

Mouse's eyes brightened. "How wonderful! My senses tell me we are to have a long, hot summer."

Tia nodded. "The geese fly north as we speak."

As the two ate in silence, Tiamoon intently watched Mouse. He shifted and cleaned his whiskers.

"Have I dropped crumbs on my coat?"

Tiamoon stood. "No, no, that's not it. I think I may have a solution to you having to carry the message back in your mouth."

Mouse smiled. "That would be welcomed. I get so tired I have to stop more often than I should. Any help would be appreciated."

He watched her rummaging under her sleeping spot. All sorts of curious items emerged from beneath her bed until he heard her exclaim, "Aha! This is just what I wanted."

She turned and held up some kind of log-shaped item with a long string attached.

Mouse's eyebrows came together. "What is it?"

Tiamoon explained as she walked toward him. "This is an old quiver I haven't used for a very long time."

Mouse's frown deepened. "A what?" "Quiver. It's used to store arrows when you are hunting and need to carry more than one with you. That's why it has a securing strap."

"Oh."

"I think if I extend the strap as far as it will go we'll be able to strap it to your back. Once that's done, we can put a message inside, create a cover for the end and you'll be able to travel without holding the message in your mouth."

Mouse sat on his haunches and smiled. "When do we start?"

"Let me reply to the note you brought me and we'll get things set."

Tiamoon padded to the cupboard where she stored her dishes and pulled open a drawer. Lifting out a pad of paper and a pen, she stood at the counter and formulated a reply to the note. She rolled the answer into a cylinder and placed it inside the quiver. Opening the second drawer of the stand-up cupboard, she located a knife. Kneeling down on the floor, she pulled the quiver to her and punched a hole in the very end of the leather holding strap. Next she got up and started toeing through the items on the floor she'd pulled from under her bed.

"There."

She bent down and pulled two items from the floor using her foot to shove the rest of the stuff back under the bed.

Mouse watched as she placed a piece of tanned leather over the opening of the quiver and secured it with a leather thong.

"That should hold everything inside. Now, mouse," Tiamoon turned to the messenger, "I need you to allow me to put this around you."

Mouse looked at the contraption, thought of his aching jaws the previous night, and nodded.

Tia slid the cylinder up his arm, over his head, and settled it between his shoulder blades. Noting it slipped easily, she moved back to her bed and got on her hands and knees.

"I know it's here somewhere." She reached beneath and pulled a long strand of leather to her as she sat on her knees. She looked at the strand then at the mouse with the quiver hanging off its side.

"I must make an adjustment." The mouse sat back on its haunches.

Tia took the leather strand in hand and walked around the mouse. She stopped behind him and a smile began to slowly emerge on her lips. "Bingo."

"What?"

"I'll be just a moment. Don't worry if you feel tugging. I'm not doing anything that will harm you."

"I guess I just have to trust you." Mouse felt a tugging and heard a soft zipping sound.

Tiamoon stood in front of him with a leather end in hand. "Hold this please."

He grabbed the end and waited.

She had the other piece of the leather strand and standing in front of Mouse, grabbed the end she'd handed him and tied the two together. She adjusted the quiver until the cylinder was positioned squarely in the middle then she cinched the strand to a comfortable tightness.

Mouse patted the leather at his waist. "The missus says I need to lose some weight. Guess she's right."

Tia smiled. "Well, I'll never tell. If I had more time, I'd fashion this to fit more comfortably. For now… this will do."

Mouse wiggled back and forth, the cylinder on his back staying in place.

"I think this is great. I'll be able to move faster, keep up my pace, and get home sooner. I've no complaints."

Tia threw her cape over her shoulders, opened the door, and walked outside with Mouse.

"How long will it take you to get back to Fae Forest?"

Mouse considered for a moment, sniffed the air, and narrowed his eyes against the light.

"If I can find Grizelda's Flight Service, two days. If I'm on foot, a fortnight."

She nodded. "Well, be careful. All sorts of creatures are waking from winter's sleep right now."

Mouse hopped into the field, his gray fur disappearing within the tall grass. Tiamoon strode to the back of her hut. She untied the cape and slung it over the top rail of the fence. Drawing her sword, she crept toward the first outcropping in the field behind her hut. Tia's senses tingled. The skin on her arms prickled and her ears tuned to the sounds of the land.

"It's been a long time, my friend, but your sleep time is over. Ha!"

She jumped up and jabbed a well-used straw dummy. The arms swung around wildly, a flail at each end with the ability to deliver painful, bleeding wounds. Tiamoon dropped to the ground under the swinging arms her sword clutched tightly in her hand. She crawled on her stomach until she was beyond the dummy then ran the obstacle course twice until her undershirt lay soaked against her skin. Pushing aside wet strands of her hair, she plodded back to her hut. She divested herself of her sword and heavy cloak. The wall at the back of the hut sported a heavy velvet curtain which Tia pulled back, to reveal a modern bathroom: shower, toilet, sink, and storage for towels and linen. She turned on the faucet in the shower until steam roiled to the ceiling. Dropping the last of her sweat and dirt-covered clothing to the tiled floor, Tia slipped under the scalding liquid allowing the water to soothe her aching muscles.

"I will not be run from my forest again. I may ache and pain now, but in a fortnight my body will be the weapon it once was. I can only hope you are the cause of this, Gitty..."

The mention of the name caused Tiamoon to shudder, even within the scalding cascade of her shower.

"...this time, you'll face eviction. I'll see to it."

Chapter Seven

Ailidh's head swiveled from side to side and up and down. She'd never seen such wonders as there were at this city at the edge of the forest where her sister resided.

"Kayne, will you look at how tall those buildings are. They must be the size of the old oak in the middle of the forest. I thought the Lending Library was big but compared to these… " Her green eyes resembled the saucers the librarian placed under her teacups.

Kayne narrowed his eyes. All he could see was the dirty concrete streets filled with trash floating in the light breeze which seemed to push them into town. There were strange vehicles parked near the concrete pathways and people seemed to be rushing around, their heads staring down as they quickly walked to and fro. The gray colored buildings *were* the height of the old oak, probably 50 to 100 feet tall in Others measurements. Unlike the oak, these monstrosities were dead, lifeless, and gritty.

"Yes, Ailidh, it's very different from the forest."

"I know. I think I'm going to love it here. There's so much happening and the town feels… alive!"

Kayne snapped his head to look at his mate. Her face glowed and she smiled as she hadn't in many a month. He couldn't remember her smiling like this since the Other's machines started tearing up the forest.

A pain touched his chest. He'd been gone less than a week, and he missed the smell of the meadow near their dwelling, the damp of the moss-covered streambed nearby, and the rustle of leaves in the branches of the tree above their home. He was here in Faetown because he loved Ailidh. That was the only reason. Plucking up courage he didn't feel, he answered.

"I think this is going to be… an experience." He slipped her hand into his and gritted his teeth in to a smile. *For Ailidh.*

The dog and cart drew up to a curb in front of a tall brick building. Kayne counted ten sets of glass above extra large windows at ground level. The façade of the building was plain red brick with light gray accents. He noted the panes looked like eyes peering out at the world. In the center of the building at the top of the ten-step staircase was a set of double doors featuring etched glass casements. Kayne looked up in time to see one of the doors swing open and a faerie with blue-tinted dark hair fly down the steps.

"Ailidh!"

"Cadhla!" Ailidh jumped from the cart tearing her hand from Kayne's and ran to hug her sister. They were a contrast in color. Cadhla was dressed in a black long-sleeve shirt, black jeans, and black high heels on her feet; her blue-tinted, short-cropped, dark spiky hair shimmering in the light streaming between the buildings. Ailidh was attired in her forest clothing of grass green diaphanous skirt, buttercup yellow blouse, and bare feet, her blonde hair billowing in the breeze.

Kayne shook his head. How could two such opposite people have the same parents? The answer was beyond him.

The two girls jumped up and down hugging as they danced in the street.

"Come inside and see my place. We have about three hours before I have to go to work so we can catch up." Cadhla linked her arm through her sister's and led her up the apartment steps.

Kayne looked at Bram and Silas and shrugged his shoulders.

"I guess we get to unload the cart."

"Better you two than me," Silas said. "Soon as you're done taking stuff out of the back, I'm taking a nap. My pads are sore."

Bram started to grumble about good-for-nothing, lazy help as he moved suitcases from the cart to the sidewalk. He frowned deeply as Silas lay down when he and Kayne were finished.

"Useless mutt. If he didn't own sixty percent of the business, I'd fire him."

Kayne smirked, knowing Bram wouldn't know what to do without his business partner and best friend.

"I know what you mean."

The two men hurried up the steps dragging suitcases hoping to find the giggling faerie sisters. They barged through the doors and stood inside a lobby with ceilings as tall as an oak tree. Both men gawked at the ornate paintings on the walls and ceiling, gold accents glistening in the light of the day.

"Wow!"

"You can say that again," Kayne said.

"Hello?" Cadhla called to them from a square hole in the wall. She motioned them over and pushed her hand against the side of the opening until they'd dragged all the suitcases inside. Once she removed her hand, the wall slammed shut on them. Kayne, Bram, and Ailidh started pounding on the wall.

"Open up!"

They stopped and gulped air as the floor started shaking and the walls groaned. Each one clutched their stomach.

"I feel like I'm going to be ill," Ailidh turned to Cadhla.

She smiled. "It's an elevator. Sort of a moving room. This is a faster way to get to my apartment than walking up ten flights of stairs."

She could see the confusion in their eyes. "I'll show you when we get to the top. I live in the pent... in the top of the building; similar to the top of the tree—the highest branch on the tallest tree in the forest. You'll see when we get there."

The floor shuttered and bounced and the feeling of movement stopped. The wall opened into a hallway with rugs all across the floor. The three forest faeries stepped tentatively on the carpet. When the floor proved stable, they pulled the suitcases out of the moving room and turned to watch the wall shut again.

Cadhla motioned them to follow her. She walked to the end of the hallway and opened a large door. The trio followed her inside, Kayne and Bram bumping into Ailidh who'd stopped in the entry. Before her was floor to ceiling glass showcasing the top of the city and the woods beyond.

"It's, it's so beautiful!" Ailidh dropped her suitcase and darted to the window. Her eyes swept the rooftops of Faetown and caught sight of the forest leading to the mountain. She could just make out the castle of the night elves. The sight made her quiver.

Cadhla had eased up next to her sister. "I know. If I could block out the castle, this view would be perfect—the tallest branch on the tallest tree, don't you think?"

Kayne cleared his throat. "Cadhla?"

She turned to see Kayne and Bram still clutching suitcases. "Sorry, boys. The room over there." She pointed to a doorway leading off the main area. "You'll have your own bathroom and there is a tiny kitchenette inside if you want to make coffee and snacks. I have a maid who cleans and a cook. I gave them the week off so you could settle in and get comfortable. Just put your things in there."

Ailidh hadn't moved from her spot. "Sister?"

Cadhla moved to her side again. "Yes?" "How can you afford such a place? In the forest, there is no need for gold, but I imagine you must need it here." Ailidh turned to her sister, the mirth gone from the forest green orbs.

Cadhla cleared her throat and avoided Ailidh's gaze. "Don't worry about that. It's handled."

Ailidh dropped her voice. "We can't stay without helping you somehow. I don't know what I can do if you already have someone to cook. Do you want me to clean?"

"No! That's what the maid does. Don't worry about it right now, okay? Just get settled in and we'll talk about it later."

Kayne had walked up behind Ailidh and wrapped his hands around her waist. "This view is magnificent."

Cadhla forced gaiety to her voice. "Isn't it? See, over there is the city hall and there is the oldest church in town…"

Ailidh watched as her sister rattled on about the buildings, streets, and history of Faetown.

Bram stood at the front door, his hand on the knob and cleared his throat. "Well, I'll be on my way."

Kayne and Ailidh trotted across the large room to the door where she hugged him and Kayne shook his hand.

"Give Silas our thanks for the great care and smooth ride he took in transporting us. Do drive carefully, Bram."

Ailidh watched as Kayne reached into his pouch for coins to pay Bram.

Bram held up a hand. "I will take payment when I have returned you to the woods. Let's just say this trip is only half over. I will convey your thanks to Silas. We'll wait for you to contact us about the return trip." He leaned closer to the two. "After all, you are Fae of the woods and that's where you belong." Nodding, he slipped out the door.

Kayne grabbed the handle, jerked the door open, and looked in the hallway for his friend. He was nowhere to be seen. A smile touched Kayne's lips. "Been a long time since Bram used his magic. Guess he wasn't too fond of that moving room."

He closed the door and drew Ailidh to him. "I will take care of you, my love. I promise."

He placed a gentle kiss on her forehead. "I'm very tired and the bed in the other room beckons to me. I'm going to lie down. You and your sister can catch up without me." Kayne slogged across the living area and disappeared into the room gently closing the door behind him.

Ailidh turned to find Cadhla gazing out the windows.

"I'm glad you took my offer to come to Faetown. The forest isn't safe any longer, Ailidh. I've heard rumblings about the destruction of the Ancients. I wanted to be sure you were okay and having you here with me is the best way."

"How can you know what is happening there when you live here?"

Cadhla turned to face her sister. "I have my ways."

"Oh, you're magicing."

"No. It's not allowed in most of the common areas of Faetown. I have… sources who kept me aware of the situation in the Fae Forest."

"Then you know just how frightening it has become. I don't know why someone would want to dig up and destroy the Ancients."

"It's more frightening than you can imagine, Ailidh."

Ailidh looked at the lines around the eyes of her sister. Something was not right about this place where Cadhla lived. Faeries did not show age and this human quality about her sister frightened Ailidh.

I must find out what is going on… but not tonight.

"There is much we need to discuss, and I urge you to take heed of my words. However, I suspect you are as tired as Kayne."

Cadhla moved to her sister's side and picked up the forest faerie's hand.

"Sleep well, Ailidh, for tomorrow, your world will change."

Chapter Eight

Gitty stood tall, pulling her shoulders back and holding her head high. She knew the human construction workers talked behind her back, but she paid them well enough that while she intimidated most of them, they stayed for the wages.

She'd learned from her grubbing gnome stepmother the value of money. While the faeries had no use for money and its power, the humans who were slowly taking over the fae forests put a high value on their paper with funny looking men's pictures on it.

Gitty had lived to see her stepmother try, and fail, to bleed her father of all his possessions. At the end of the last war when the fae and gnomes had succeeded in keeping the forest from the night elves, she swore she would get revenge. She'd gotten her half sister run out of the forest, but Gitty wasn't happy with that small victory.

Her father's wealth of lands and gold had been dwindling over the years, thanks in part to her narcissistic, spendthrift brother Morgan. The other culprits were these pestilent humans. Their belief that everything they saw belonged to them had eaten through the family's gold as Gitty had to buy back ancestral lands. She'd taken over the family wealth, sent her stepmother back to the underground hovel where her father had discovered her, and pulled the purse strings closed on her brother. The silence of her missing stepmother was filled by the constant whining of her brother.

If she had not stumbled across Thomas, *that obnoxious little leprechaun*, drinking himself to an early grave over the loss of some wayward faerie, Gitty might have been forced to sell the family's massive castle and surrounding lands.

But the gods had smiled on her. With a bit of the old leprechaun's magic turned on himself, she had been one drink from getting the *exact* location of his fortune. As it was, she was working from a poem muttered by a drunk, mere moments before his kin burst into the inn and rescued him.

She was nearing the end of her search. There stood only twenty more stands of oak between the treasure she sought and the titanium safe in her basement.

Gitty ran her hand along the brilliant, yellow earthmover. She trembled at the power the machine exuded as it sat rumbling, eager to start its path of destruction.

"What the hell is taking so long?" Speaking more to herself than anyone else, she stomped her work boots on the ground. Time was wasting while they waited for the inspector's go-ahead. And everybody knows—time is money.

She turned to give her crew the thumbs up when her messenger came running and yelling with each step.

"DON'T START THE EARTHMOVERS! DON'T START DIGGING!" He stopped in front of Gitty, panting and holding his side.

She crossed her arms and glared down at the underling.

"What do you mean, don't start digging?"

He had his hands planted on his knees, head down, gulping in great drafts of air.

"Like I said... don't start excavating."

Gitty bent over and locked her ice blue eyes onto his.

"Why the hell not?"

The young man gasped at the face before him. "Be... be... because there's been a 'cease work' order put on this site... on all this company's sites."

He straightened up and took a step back.

Gitty mirrored his actions. She watched his face drain of color.

"A cease-work order?"

The runner's mouth moved wordlessly reminding her of a fish on the riverbank. She pulled up to her full height and towered over him.

"Uh, uh. Somebody's filed a protest against this company. According to the inspector, until there's a hearing, nothing moves."

"Great!" Gitty smacked the side of the earthmover.

The young man jumped and started moving backwards.

"Ahhhh! Everybody go home!" She slammed both hands against the machine. The resulting boom echoed around the small valley. The human crew bolted to the four-door crew cab, the vehicle tires scattering rocks as they sped away. She checked the equipment, securing those machines left unlocked by fleeing workers, and trudged to her Hummer kicking pinecones with her boots as she walked.

How could anybody know who owned the company? She'd done her best to bury her name under layers of fake corporations just as she'd been shown. She was not going to let these human interlopers run her off land that had been in her family for centuries.

Gitty piloted the back road to her driveway and turned up the winding lane maneuvering the switchbacks until she drove through the gated entrance. Looking through wrought iron bars into the valley below as she closed and secured the gate, she spotted the roof of the building the faeries called the Lending Library. She parked the Hummer in the converted stables and strolled to the front lawn. Standing in front of the massive stone castle on top of the hill, she planted her booted feet and fisted her hands on her hips glaring at the nondescript rooftop. Her self-centered brother Morgan had pointed out the obvious—the only structure left in her search area was the Lending Library.

"Those little faerie pains wouldn't know how to use the Internet, would they? What of the woman they call the Librarian? Does she have some human magic?" Gitty glared trying her best to magic an answer determined to elude her.

She started when the thought struck her. "It can't be, can it? Is it possible my dear stepsister is behind this?"

A wicked sneer marred the flawless face and lit the ice blue eyes. "I can only hope."

Chapter Nine

Linda woke with a start. The work she'd done ferreting out the owner of the construction company, who seemed hell bent on tearing down the forest, haunted her sleep. Every labored step had led down one convoluted quagmire to another false lead. It was a labyrinth designed by an expert—but not as expert as Linda at getting to the center of the maze.

She'd found Black Catco was owned by someone named Gitty Saun. More research had provided her with another entity named Morgan Saun and a Lancelot Saun. Land ownership records of the early settlers showed vast chunks of acreage in the area had belonged to the Saun family. Recently plots seemed to have been sold off at an alarming rate. Linda could only guess at the reason for the sales.

This latest flurry of movement on the owner's part was haphazard and sloppy. Her search had turned up evidence the Sauns were carrying on covert negotiations and buying the land surrounding the castle on the hill overlooking the small valley. Battlements were rising around the fortress at an alarming rate. Meadows shared by the community were being fenced with razor wire and charged with electricity.

Linda shuddered. Why was no one asking questions? Had the family bought off, or worse, eliminated their detractors?

She was glad her husband Donald had forced her to learn the ins and outs of the legal system. When he knew his health was failing, he'd pushed her to take over their business affairs. She'd hated the endless paperwork bog at the time and with his passing swore she'd never touch another form again. However…

Maneuvering the legal alleyways, Linda had been able to get a sitting judge to issue a cease-work order to the Black Catco construction company effectively stopping the forest destruction—temporarily. She, too, had been forced to hide her identity under blankets of deception, but the final results had been to waylay the earthmovers for a couple months. After the hearing… Linda shook her head.

I'm not going to worry until the time comes.

She dragged herself from her quarters, her slippered feet hissing quietly through the empty rooms of her Lending Library. She looked around. The book-lined walls felt strangely cool and foreboding. Linda realized there was no sound coming from the kitchen. She tread lightly so as not to scare Chrissy and announced herself before peeking around the kitchen door.

The room was empty.

That's strange. Chrissy is always up before me. Linda decided to check on the nymph. Maybe she was ill and unable to leave her home in the oak tree. She grabbed a jacket from her room and headed to the front door. A quick survey out the window revealed no waiting patrons so she opted not to lock her door. She pulled open the windowed entry, turned left, and stopped in her tracks.

Beating her wings frantically against the wall of the house near the eaves was Chrissy. The expression of horror frozen on her delicate features stabbed Linda's heart. Reaching up as far as its black body would allow was a monstrous cat. At least that was what Linda figured it to be; whether it be wild or tame she wasn't sure. The creature was enormous and about to dig its claws into the aging wood siding on Linda's home.

"HEY! GET OUT OF HERE!" She stomped her foot on the wooden porch.

The creature turned slitted yellow eyes her direction and dropped front paws to the deck. It began to stalk toward Linda, a guttural growl growing louder with each padded step. As it approached, the animal barred gleaming, long white teeth as it wrinkled its nose and quickened its pace.

Linda kicked a foot in the animal's direction and, as the creature crouched to pounce, deftly sidestepped the subsequent attack.

The cat tumbled to the edge of the porch and, with her foot Linda shoved it over the edge, barely escaping the extended claws swiped at her.

"Chrissy! Quick!"

She opened the door and the tiny nymph shot into the house. Linda slammed the door shut and locked it. She peered to the front where the cat had fallen from the porch and noted the beast was sitting on its hindquarters licking the spot where her slipper had connected with its fur.

"What in the name of all faedom is that thing?"

Chrissy had fluttered to the nearest tabletop and was panting heavily. She pulled in deep draughts of air and closed her eyes. When her breathing had slowed, she opened eyes wide with terror and spoke.

"That is Lancelot Saun, the pet of Gitty Saun. "

Linda stared out the glass at the animal currently curling up in a sunspot on the driveway.

"That's a pet?!" Chrissy nodded. "That's Gitty's cat. Gitty passes herself off as human but she is elfkind. Her family used to act as though they owned all the land between here and the mountains."

"According to the records at the courthouse, they did." Linda checked the whereabouts of the black cat again. It had not moved from the warmth of the sunny spot.

"Well, whatever, they demanded payment from all of the forest folk for living on their lands. We've been here longer. When the Fae council convened and decided they would no longer pay the ransom, the Sauns hired rogue elves to make trouble in the valley."

Wrinkles creased Linda's forehead. "When was this? I don't recall reading about it in the news."

"You wouldn't have heard of this. Humans were so busy with something you called a world war that our small grievances were of no consequence to you." Chrissy stood on the tabletop. She crept to the window and observed the napping cat.

"My father and brother were killed in the ensuing battles. Many fae folk lost family. The treaty the two sides signed held a clause exiling Gitty's stepsister, Tiamoon. Gitty was furious the gnome warrior had taken up the cause of the fae folk. She made the demand mandatory, stating if it was not carried out, the elfkind would slaughter all but their living within one hundred miles."

Chrissy sighed and brushed unseen wrinkles from her clothing.

"I really miss Tia. She was a good friend and a ferocious fighter. I would feel much safer with her here and not off in some distant land. I've sent word with the mouse network to the last place I knew she lived. I can only hope she still lives there and cares enough for some of us to come back home."

The little nymph's shoulders sagged.

Linda felt her heart ache for the little fae. She knew the loneliness of losing your best friend. Movement from the driveway captured her attention. The monstrous black cat was stretching all four limbs and looking as if he were going to settle in for the day. Something about his actions felt—wrong—to Linda. She could see his body quivering slightly, muscles ready to leap at a moment's notice. His head rested on his front right leg, eyes appearing closed, but she could sense they were opened ever so slightly and focusing on the Lending Library's front deck.

She watched the constant movement of his ears twitching back and forth. Linda had been so intently watching the cat, she'd closed out all action except the movements of the black animal in her driveway jumping when the loud clang of metal rent the air. She clutched the table the little wood nymph stood on. "What the…?"

Lancelot jumped from his resting spot and arched his back, setting his hair on end, hissing loudly and baring his teeth.

Linda followed the line of his angry gaze to a small figure in full battle gear, a gleaming sword held high and to the right of its head in advance stance.

The cat hissed, crouched, and feigned attack.

The figure stepped forward switching the blade to the other side and advancing on the feline. The animal ruffled its fur to appear fuller, stood on the tips of its paws, and commenced growling.

The small warrior figure, body tensed, soft booted feet moving steadily forward, continued toward the creature.

Sensing the figure was not backing down, the enormous cat turned on its paws and fled across the driveway and through the meadow. The figure gave chase ,sheathing its sword behind it and pulled out a throwing knife.

Linda stared at the spot where the confrontation had just taken place. She couldn't wrap her mind around what she had just seen.

Chrissy strained forward trying to look sideways out the glass.

A face popped into the center of the window. Chrissy threw her hands over her face and screamed, the sound creating goose skin down Linda's back. Moving her fingers slightly from her eyes, Chrissy dropped her hands and screamed again.

"TIAMOON!"

Chapter Ten

Linda flung open the door and stepped back as Chrissy streaked past her to the figure on the porch.

The wood nymph threw her arms around a grim looking small person who grudgingly returned the hug.

"Tia! You came!"

Linda looked at her small friend. She'd never seen Chrissy smile so widely or beam so much as she was at this moment.

"Yeah, I came."

The voice from the small warrior was surprisingly soft, and Linda chose to stay where she was standing inside the doorway of the Lending Library.

"Come in, come in. You must be tired, hungry, and probably thirsty too."

Chrissy slipped her arm through the warrior's and led her through the portal to just inside the building.

Tiamoon stopped and gawked at the walls filled with books. Floor to ceiling on every surface were books; small books, large books, picture books, books of all shapes and sizes.

"When did this happen?"

Chrissy took Tia's arm and steered her toward a chair at one of the tables.

"Uhmmm, about 15..." she turned to look at Linda, her eyebrows raised in question.

Linda nodded.

"...years ago. The librarian and her husband lived here before that time but when he passed away, she started this." Chrissy waved a hand around indicating the shelving. "I've only been here for a year and a half in Other's time. My home was destroyed by the Other's machinery. They've destroyed homes of most of the forest fae and the meadow fae are finding themselves having a difficult time keeping their dwellings from being damaged. Kayne remembered the design on the yellow machine that tore up my tree and told the Librarian. She looked up the logo and discovered all the machinery belongs to a company Gitty and Morgan own."

Tia released the strap holding her sword and scabbard to her back and placed the gleaming weapon on the table. She divulged herself of two throwing knives and a hatchet she had worn on the belt of her hauberk. She hooked her thumbs on the collar of the protective shirt and pulled it over her head and off her body. Once divested of the warm, heavy gear she placed on a chair beside her, she sat at the table and looked around the room. After she had made a thorough reconnaissance of the room, she turned to the librarian still standing up by the door.

"This abode is yours?"

Linda nodded. "It is."

"How is it you can see us?"

Chrissy grinned. "She believes."

"Let me get you some water and a sandwich. Get comfortable and after you've eaten, we'll take your gear to my tree behind the house. It's probably the only oak still standing in the valley."

Chrissy winged to the kitchen and the sounds of water running and the refrigerator door opening and closing echoed in the empty library.

Tia watched the librarian.

"Why do you stand there?"

"I've learned to move carefully. I wait until invited before sitting with the forest folk."

"I've got a lot of questions. It's been many years since I left the forest and much has changed. Sit with me." Tiamoon nodded to a chair across from her. "My first question is why should I or any of the forest creatures trust you?'

"Tia!"

Chrissy flew to the table and alighting deftly near her friend, placed a container of clear water in front of the warrior. The gnome grasped the glass with both hands and gulped the contents in one swig. Chrissy raised her eyebrows. "Another?"

"Please."

Tia looked at Linda who sat examining her fingernails. "My question remains. Why should I trust you? Have you bewitched my friend into believing what you say?"

Chrissy returned with the refilled glass and a plate with a sandwich she slammed on the table in front of the gnome.

"Labhoise Tiamoon Saun!" Linda watched the face of the warrior darken.

Eyebrows knit together and eyes narrowed.

"What did you call me?" She stood slowly, the chair legs scraping against the wooden floor.

"You heard me." Chrissy fisted her tiny hands on her waist and tapped a foot on the floor as she faced the warrior. "You know how careful I am. Do you think I would live anywhere near someone who would harm me?"

Tiamoon stood with her hands at her side, clenching and unclenching her fists.

"How am I to know? I've been away a very long time. Who knows what these Others have learned to do?"

Chrissy glared at Tiamoon who was glaring back at her.

Linda could see neither of them was going to give an inch.

"Ladies?"

"What?" They answered in unison.

"I'm very tired so I think I'll take a nap. Why don't you take some time and work out this problem together?" She rose from her chair and made her way to her room at the back of the library. She really *was* tired. The confrontation with the monster cat had drained all her energy. A nap would feel good, and the two friends could discuss her at their leisure.

Chrissy crossed her arms, frowning at the gnome warrior standing across the banister from her. When the Librarian's door clicked shut, she huffed. "I would have thought you knew me better."

Tiamoon pulled a chair out and dropped into it. "Chrissy, how could you put trust into an Other?"

Chrissy rolled her violet eyes, flipped her light brown hair over one shoulder, and winged her way to the chair across from Tiamoon.

"You idiot. If the Librarian were a 'normal' Other she wouldn't be able to see us!"

Tia considered the nymph's comment. "Okay, so she can see us. That doesn't necessarily make her trustworthy, does it?" "No it does *not*. But I've been living here for a nearly a year, ever since my Ancient oak was destroyed. She lets me live in the one behind the building. Tia, she knows the customs."

Tiamoon found two deep violet eyes peering earnestly at her. Huffing impatience, she acquiesced. "Alright. If you trust her, Chrissy, I'll keep my mouth shut."

The nymph smiled.

"I didn't say I would trust her—just keep my mouth shut about her. Now, what's going on here?"

Chrissy shook her head.

"Tia, it's been a nightmare. After you left, things were quiet—lonely but quiet. Gitty and Morgan kept to themselves, adding to that enormous house on the hill where they live. Time passed, and all those machine inventions starting appearing everywhere. Our forest started shrinking when the Others moved in and built homes. For the most part, we've kept to ourselves and life has gone smoothly. That is until about eleven moons, sorry, months ago.

"Huge machines started coming into the forest and killing the Ancients. Just tearing them up for no reason. They weren't even cut up for firewood!"

"My tree was the first to go. I gathered what belongings I could find and came here. I'd heard via the fae this human was different, trustworthy, and I needed to see for myself. She was able to see me; extended me kindness and understanding. Never said anything about my size or try to talk stupid to me like so many of the regular humans do. I asked if I could live in her tree out back and she said yes."

Tia watched her friend's facial expressions change with the story she told.

"So why are you working here, Chrissy?"

"Keeps me busy, and I like the Librarian's company. She's smart and helps everyone who comes through her doors. She's a good person, Tia."

Tiamoon scowled. "No Other is good, Chrissy. Don't ever forget that. So what happened to cause you to contact me?"

"Remember Ailidh and Kayne?"

Tia nodded.

"Kayne's brother's home was torn down about four months ago. When their home was facing destruction, Ailidh and Kayne started coming to the Lending Library to learn about city life; Ailidh's sister lives in Faetown. About three weeks ago, they moved away. They're not the first, and I'm afraid probably won't be the last to leave the forest to the Others and..."

Tia looked up to see the hesitation on Chrissy's face. "And what?"

Chrissy slowly blew out a deep breath. "...Gitty and Morgan. "

Tia raised her eyebrows high on her forehead. "The night elves? My dear stepsister and brother?"

Chrissy nodded her head. "The Librarian got Kayne to remember the picture and name of the company on the side of the huge digging machine. It was Black Catco. She got on the Internet and researched the company finally finding the main stockholders and owners to be Gitty, Morgan, and Lancelot."

"Mangy creature."

"That's when I knew I had to get hold of you. If anyone can stop Gitty, it's you, Tia."

The warrior gnome smirked. "Thanks for the confidence, but I think I'll need as much help as I can get. Any reason for them destroying the forest?"

Chrissy shook her head. "No one has been able to figure it out. There is no pattern to the damage they do, but they're only tearing down the oak stands. Only a few remain. It was the Librarian who used the Other's laws to stop the digging up of the trees. She says this is just a temporary hold. If we can't do something quickly, Gitty will be able to continue digging up the Ancients."

Tia sat looking up at the ceiling and tapping a finger on the table. Finally, she looked at Chrissy.

"We need to convene the Fae Council."

Chrissy nodded her agreement.

"I'll use the mouse network to get the elders here then we can decide what to do from there." Tia nodded in agreement with herself. "I'll whistle for a messenger to deliver my requests."

She smiled at Chrissy. "Right after I eat."

Chapter Eleven

Kayne walked from the bedroom to the living area searching for Ailidh. He hated the long pants he was forced to wear and the leather shoes were causing blisters on his feet. However, he had promised Ailidh he'd try town living for three months. No more. If he hated it as much in three months as he did now, she had given her word they would return to the forest. He had to admit this penthouse, as Cadhla called it, did have advantages over the oak tree in the woods. He was getting used to warm showers and hot food on demand. Truth be told, he was also becoming quite fond of silk sheets. He felt himself stir with the thought of Ailidh naked on the soft sheets, her wings spread, hair cascading down the pillow…

Stop! We have to get to the job. He stopped on the step of the entry and turned to the windows.

There stood his mate facing the glass. Her shoulders drooped toward the floor. He noticed her beautiful, flowing hair seemed to hang limply and the sparkle from her wings was gone. In fact, she now kept her wings closed tightly against her body except at the job. Her delicate hand touched the glass and he heard a shuddered sigh leave her lips. He'd watched the fire leave her green eyes and her eyes had dark circles beneath them.

"Ailidh?" He spoke her name quietly.

The little faerie jumped.

Kayne watched her flutter her wings, lift her shoulders, and fluff her hair. She turned to face him.

"Kayne. How long have you been standing there?" she cocked her head to one side.

Danger old man. Don't push. "Not long my love. I think we need to get to the club. It's almost time for your first set. Are you ready?" He hoped the lie would go unnoticed.

Ailidh narrowed her eyes and pursed her lips. "Are you sure?"

He crossed the floor and gathered her into his arms. Placing a hungry kiss on

126

her delicate lips, he tried to relay the love he felt for her through this action. Finally, he pulled back and stared directly into her face. "I'm sure. Are you ready?"

The two turned to take a last look toward the forest they loved so much. A sigh escaped Ailidh's lips.

"Yes. Let's get going."

~ * ~

Kayne pushed open the entrance to the cabaret, halting as smoke roiled out the door. He coughed, pulled in a deep draught of fresh air, and plunged into the dark, stale smelling interior. He hated having to work. He especially hated the way the fae men of the city leered at Ailidh while she sang.

Gareth, the owner, made sure the lighting on the stage highlighted her tantalizing figure through her diaphanous forest dress. When her sister had brought Ailidh in to meet him, as she had promised, Gareth's eyes glittered greedily at the nearly transparent garment and had made Ailidh promise to wear the dress solely for performing. He knew his clientele would pay to see innocence and beauty in such a package. He'd been proven correct. In the three weeks since Ailidh had been featured at the cabaret, business had tripled.

Tonight was putting Kayne's patience to the test. Twice he'd had to pull men from the performing stage as they lunged at his mate during her performance. Ailidh was in tears the last time.

"Kayne, please," she'd wept into his shoulder.

He'd just tossed a drunken, swearing gnome out the door as the creature had gotten close enough to lay his grasping hands on his mate's delicate breast.

"Take me back to the apartment. I'll talk with Cadhla, and we'll find another way to make money to give to her. Please!"

Kayne had helped her from the stage, protectively holding her trembling shoulders, down the hallway to the performer's area when they encountered a furious Gareth, arms crossed over his muscled chest, feet wide and planted, blocking access to the rooms.

"Where the hell do you think you're going?" The faerie's face was crimson, puckered, and glistening with sweat.

"I'm taking my mate home. She's too delicate to put up with the rude actions of your customers. Aren't there other places for the things they insinuate to Ailidh?

I've heard you and Cadhla speak of such abominations."

Ailidh quivered beneath Kayne's grasp, a suppressed sob escaping her lips.

Gareth sneered at Kayne. "The only reason Ailidh is not working there is because her sister garnered my promise, on a 5-year contract, she wouldn't. How the hell do you think you and your 'mate' are able to stay in such luxury? Most forest fae who show up in the city eventually wind up living down by the river in hovels that make their oak trees look like castles. You are lucky your mate has a beautiful and willing, sister."

"Get Ailidh back on the stage before those blighters out there tear the place apart. Getting groped is part of her job, and she needs to act like she likes it!" Gareth dropped his arms to his side and clenched his fists.

Kayne glared at his opponent. Gareth's three-foot form towered over him and he was not in the position to take on the larger man. His mouth pulled to a single, angry slash, his jaw setting tightly. He felt his wings flush red. He drew himself to his full height and pulled a trembling Ailidh closer to his body.

"I'll not expose her to that humiliation."

"Oh, yes you will," Gareth walked up and placed his hands on the tiny faerie's breasts.

Ailidh gasped and stepped backwards, Gareth keeping pace with her. Kayne's arm was wretched from her shoulders.

"I own these and everything else that goes with them. I'll touch them, the customers will touch them, and if someone pays me enough…" he let the suggestion die.

Gareth fondled Ailidh as Kayne watched all color leave her face. Her wings quivered and several emotions crossed her pale face.

The tall faerie then placed his hands on her shoulders and propelled her down the hallway and back to the stage.

The crowd applauded and yelled lewd suggestions. The microphone crackled as Kayne heard Gareth's coarse laugh. His stomach rolled with the realization he'd been unable to stop Gareth and protect his mate.

"Isn't she something boys?"

There was thunderous applause.

"And look as these perfect domes of womanhood…" The floor shook with the beating of shoes on wood. "Why don't we get this little beauty into our spotlight and have her sing us a tune?"

Applause drowned out anything else the owner may have said.

Kayne felt the heat of anger flush his face. He strode to the wings of the stage and watched as Gareth's large hands stroked from shoulders down to the buttocks of his beloved. As he started to charge the stage, two pair of strong hands restrained him.

"Don't."

Kayne turned to glare at his mate's sister on one side and a muscular dwarf holding him on the other side. "She'll get over it and neither of you wants to live in the hovels down by the river. Gareth is crude but generous with his money when you understand he is the boss and his word is law. Once you resign yourself to that fact, everything gets easier."

Kayne strained against the hands.

"Please don't. He'll turn her over to the hospitality house owner." Cadhla shuddered. "She WON'T survive... the worst sort of lowlifes go there. Do you have any idea what they do to the likes of a faerie as beautiful as she?"

Kayne jerked his arms from the two as the breathy, whispering voice of Ailidh drifted through the microphone over the smoky room. The cacophony subdued and the sweet voice continued to strengthen with each sung note. He watched his delicate mate pull her shoulders back, lift and spread her wings wide, and stand straight, her chin held high. A strength he'd never seen in the forest seemed to fill her. By the end of the song, she'd stepped full into the spotlight, her diaphanous clothing disappearing in the strong glare.

A fae man weaving and sneering lopsidedly made his way to the stage. He reached a hand up to place it on the thigh of Ailidh. Kayne sensed rather than saw the shiver run through her but she leaned over, looked directly in the eyes of the drunk fae and spoke very quietly, her lips barely moving.

Kayne watched the drunk leer then, without warning or a visible move on Ailidh's part, he staggered backward.

Gareth scurried over to the customer. He frowned, nodded, and pointed a finger at Ailidh.

She stood tall, smoothing the fabric of her dress and tossing her hair over one shoulder.

Kayne, Cadlha, and the dwarf watched as the customer back stepped to the bar shaking his head and pushing Gareth away from him.

Cadlha turned to Kayne. "She is stronger than you can know. Someday I will tell you just how strong but not today. I told you she would do fine." She turned to her companion. "Turner, we have work to do."

Kayne watched his mate glide from the spotlight to the stage wings, a spark of fire dancing in her eyes as she caught sight of him.

Uh oh. I think someone is in trouble and I don't think it's me.

Ailidh strode with surety past him. "Come on. We've got packing to do. I won't be treated like this. It's high time I started behaving as my true self."

Kayne found himself scurrying to keep up with his mate. Something about the set of her mouth and forward thrust of her step kept him from asking the thousand questions in his mind.

Ailidh grabbed her few belongings in the dressing area. She burst from the door and marched to the adjoining room barreling her way through the portal.

Cadhla's started at the intrusion. "What…"

Ailidh held up her hand.

Kayne noted there was no quivering, no shaking visible.

"I need you to call the person in your building who will let us in the apartment."

Cadhla leaned back in her chair and cocked her head. "Now why would I do that?"

Ailidh placed her hands on the desk and moved to within inches of her sister's face. "Because if you don't, I'll invoke the ancient spell."

Kayne watch all the smug leave Cadhla's face. She picked up the phone and called someone at the building where they'd been staying. Hanging up the phone, he watched her eyes as they swept over his mate.

"If you leave, I'll be locked into this contract with Gareth for five long years, Ailidh. You don't want me to suffer, do you?" Cadhlas' eyes darkened with the question. She unconsciously twirled a wayward strand of dark curls around a finger.

Ailidh straightened and stared down at the only living sister she had.

"You chose this path not I. Nowhere in your flowering invitation to visit the city was there a mention of the degrading job you arranged for me." Stealing a glance at Kayne, she lowered her voice. "I'm a warrior, Cadhla, not a trollop. That was a role you chose during the wars, not I."

Cadhla rose so quickly from her chair it tumbled to the ground.

"How dare you! I chose not to fight because I didn't wish to die! I was never any good with a sword, and you know that. I was good at… at… making things run smoothly." Steel gray eyes flashed dangerously, the ceiling light highlighting her blue streaked hair now flying freely about her face. Ailidh planted her feet and crossed arms in a stance Kayne had not seen since he'd come into the tiny fae's life.

"I've been listening to the gossip from the customers these last three weeks. There is trouble in the forest and many fae are fleeing in fear of their lives. I will not stand by idly singing to drunken dwarves, city fae men, and what-all else while some outside force takes over my homeland. This life is yours, Cadhla, not mine. I belong in the forest—not this squalid mud bog you call the city. Don't get in my way, sister, or you will regret the day I arrived."

The tension in the room crackled, each sister squared off ready to battle the other.

Cadhla made the first concession. "I'll not stop you. I also won't stop Gareth if he seeks to find and bring you back."

Ailidh humphed at the suggestion. "You know of what I'm capable. Do you really think that gargantuan, lusting fool can capture me?"

"No. I'm just warning you he might try."

"Let him." Ailidh turned to find Kayne a step away from the door.

"We're leaving."

Ailidh blew past Kayne and strode out the side door to the street, Kayne hurrying to match her strides.

Getting in the apartment proved no problem, and the couple thanked the doorman for his assistance. Once inside they moved to the bedroom closet.

"Is there anything here you need?" Ailidh stood with the door open gazing at the clothing they'd needed for town living.

"The sooner I'm done with these city clothes the better."

She looked at the clothes hanging in the closet and the shoes she'd learned to walk in and nodded her head. "Me, too."

Kayne had moved to the balcony off the bedroom and leaned on the rail gazing at the view from this vantage point. He glanced down at the street.

"Ailidh!"

"What?"

"Are we ready to go?" "Yes, why?"

"Gareth just walked in the front door in a very big hurry."

Ailidh dashed to the balcony and peered down. Glaring up at her was Turner, the dwarf.

She pulled back and looked at Kayne.

"It's been awhile but we're going to have to use our wings."

Kayne took a deep breath and nodded.

Ailidh closed the sliding glass door, grabbed Kayne's hand and they jumped from the balcony spreading their wings and heading in the direction they had come from three weeks earlier.

Chapter Twelve

Gitty paced in front of the living room windows that overlooked the valley. Since Lancelot had come streaking back to their home several days ago, she couldn't get him to sit still long enough to magic what had made him so agitated. Seeing him on edge and not knowing why made her jumpy… and testy. All she could do was walk off the feeling until the wretched animal would allow her to see what had spooked him so badly.

Morgan breezed through the living area toward the front door his evening cape fluttering behind him.

"I'm going to use the Hummer today. I'll see you when I get back… whenever that is." He flipped a hand over his shoulder in a weak wave and made to grab the keys sitting in the crystal dish centered on the oak sideboard in the entry.

Gitty reached the bowl before Morgan had uttered the last word.

"No. You're not taking the Hummer, or the truck, or the Corvette, or any of the vehicles in the garage. You haven't earned the right to drive any of them."

He pulled himself to his full height and glowered down at his sister.

"I'm part owner of the company and because of that fact, I can drive any vehicle I choose. Move away from the sideboard."

Gitty distributed her weight evenly on her feet, ice blue eyes locked onto her brother's and fisted her hands on her hips.

"Our father was stupid enough to think you would actually learn to like working. He may have forced me to list your name as part owner of the business, but he can't force me to share the rewards of my hard work. When you put in a full forty hour week working, real work, not wooing some bimbo in a bar to take you home, then you'll get the privilege of driving. Not until then."

The siblings stood face-to-face, daring the other to make the first move. Morgan finally tossed his head, turned, and started toward the game room.

"By the way, I heard a rumor our stepsister is in the valley."

Gitty sucked in a breath. She bolted after him and, grabbing his arm, turned him to face her.

"What did you say?"

Morgan smirked at her. "What? I know something you don't? Well, well." She punched his shoulder. "Tell me what you heard."

He rubbed the spot where her fist had met his muscles. "Ow! That hurt. I'm not sure I want to tell you now." He feigned a pout until he saw the smoldering fire in Gitty's eyes.

"Oh, all right. I was at one of the taverns in town…"

Gitty rolled her eyes. "Morgan, just bottom line it for me."

He stopped, narrowed his eyes and stared at her. "This is my story. I'll tell it my way. Clear?"

Gitty huffed out an impatient breath. "Fine. Just get to the point sometime today."

"Anyway, as I was saying," he shot her a veiled glare, "at the tavern nearest the forest edge, I think it's called Dew Drop Inn or something stupid like that…"

Gitty closed her eyes and shook her head.

"…I wasn't having much luck finding a friend for the evening so I decided to move on from there. I stepped outside and nearly crushed one of those mice who work the message network they have. I wouldn't have known he was anything more than a common field mouse except he spoke to me. I wonder how he knew I'd understand?" Morgan frowned slightly.

Gitty stood looking at her 6'5" brother; his white hair glistening in the light from the front window, blue eyes framed by white eyebrows and lashes knitted together and shook her head.

He's such an idiot.

"Morgan?"

"Oh, yes. Well, he told me they were being kept very busy since Monday…"

Gitty whipped her head in the direction of the sleeping Lancelot. The cat opened one eye and turned his head from her.

"…running all over the valley delivering messages. I asked him if it was something I might be interested in, and he shook his head. Told me some gnome had just arrived in the valley and was in contact with family members, that's all. I mean; we know how they multiply like rabbits. After all, remember the family gathering when I was…"

"MORGAN!" He jumped at the shouting of his name.

"No need to get all huffy. I asked if he knew the name of the gnome and the mouse nodded, saying it was something about a moon. I deduced the rest. Tiamoon is in the valley and contacting her family." Morgan nodded his head and smiled.

Gitty pushed a big sigh through her lips. "You're an idiot but a useful one. Here."

She tossed him the keys to the Corvette. "Don't scratch it."

He allowed a sly smile to cover his lips as he walked toward the garages. "I wouldn't dream of it."

Gitty wandered back into the living room to stand looking out the picture window. She took in the view of the valley below and let her mind travel back to a time when the woods were full of fae folk. Her family had been generous enough to let them live in the woods they owned and what had it gotten them? Whining, gripping tenants who complained about a little rent. They'd even had the nerve to threaten a war!

On top of all that fuss, her father had moved a wretched gnome woman and her daughter in with Gitty and Morgan. Gitty never understood his fascination with the little creature. She was certain the blasphemous being had bewitched him at some gathering they were always having. Served him right when she left. Never trust a gnome.

So Tiamoon is back in the valley and networking with her family. Hmmm.

Gitty voiced her thoughts. "Thinking of starting another fracas, my sister? Feel free to try; it won't do you any good but please go ahead and try. It's been many a year since I was able to wade into the middle of a good fight. I'm actually missing the action."

Her hand ached to hold the sleek weighted blade, fingers wrapped around the handled designed specifically for her. Maybe, just maybe, she could rid herself of this stunted blight once and for all.

Gitty smiled. She rolled her head and shoulders trying to ease the tension that seemed to build daily. While the eflkind were superior to any other beings living in the area, the treaty which bore her signature along with her father and brother's signatures still restricted all the night elf community from using their magic to take over the humans. Tiamoon had just broken part of the original agreement by showing up in the valley. Gitty allowed a smirk to touch her lips.

"You set the ground rules, Tia. Only this time, I'm finishing the battle. You won't live to be banished. Once you're dead, the old treaty will only be good as fodder to start a fire. It's time for the night elves to move out of the shadows of the mountains and forests and take our rightful place in the world." Gitty gave the valley one last look before heading to the basement. She followed the steps down to a hallway that ended in a large room featuring three walls lined in mirrors, a floor with rubberized matting as covering, and the fourth wall of floor to ceiling windows allowing natural light to stream in and bounce off the silver and black gym equipment.

"The fools who idled my construction company may think they have beaten me, but I will make use of this time and turn their foolish decision against them." She glanced around the room surprised at the cleanliness of the area. Morgan was not known for picking up after himself. She wrinkled her nose at the faint aroma of stale sweat and wandered to the changing area. Once attired in workout togs, she moved toward the free weights. She lifted a 20-pound barbell in each hand and began curling them to her biceps. Physical labor always improved her thinking. At the moment, she was faced with two major challenges; one-finding out what her stepsister was up to and stopping her; and two-finding the leprechaun's treasure.

"If I dispose of Tiamoon, I might not need the leprechaun's treasure."

Gitty clunked the hand weights down on the stand and stared at her image in the mirror.

"Of course! With Tia out of the picture, the agreement is void releasing me from peaceful behavior toward non-elfkind. I won't need the leprechaun's treasure. I can grab all the property in the valley, and no one will be able to stop me."

She smiled at her reflection.

"Some days I amaze myself."

Chapter Thirteen

Kayne dropped to the ground on the balls of his feet then fell to his hands and knees. Ailidh floated down beside him.

"What's the matter?"

He panted heavily, his head bobbing with each breath.

"I—haven't—flown—that—much—in—several—years."

He pulled up to rest his weight on his knees and heels, toes tucked under his bottom. Forcing himself to pull in deep draughts, Kayne slowed his breathing and heart rate. "I'm so out of shape. I've gotten lazy."

Ailidh looked at her mate resting on the ground. "We've both gotten lazy. I allowed you to make all the decisions and think I was…fragile. I'm done with that. My home is in danger, and I'll not trust anyone else to protect the forest but myself."

Kayne peered sideways at his mate. Her arms were crossed defiantly, legs planted on the ground as she rested her wings against her shapely back. Her alluring figure was barely covered by her diaphanous dress. Even with the intimate knowledge of what lay beneath the flimsy fabric, Kayne realized his fragile flower of the forest was gone for good and the temptation to suggest a quick interlude withered in his mind. The creature that had pushed him from the balcony in Faetown wouldn't succumb to his male vanity with fluttering eyelashes and a shy smile. This Ailidh was one he'd never known. The strength she had exhibited in the crisis surprised him considering her timid reaction not but an hour earlier. Something about the drunken male fae staggering to the stage had triggered a power from deep within his mate.

He considered her profile. He was going to enjoy this strong female. But would it last?

"What about your sister, Cadhla?" Kayne rose from the ground and approached Ailidh.

Ailidh pushed out a humphing sound. "I have no sister."

Kayne raised an eyebrow. To this point, Ailidh had spoken continuously about the older sister who had succeeded in the city; how smart, bright, and wonderful she was. This turnabout was… unexpected.

"Any being who would sell another doesn't deserve respect or a family. As of this morning, my sister ceased to exist." Ailidh looked around and pulled in a deep breath. "The forest smells so clean." She looked at Kayne. "Let's go to the Lending Library. I'm sure the Librarian can help us find a new home."

She started down the road, Kayne trotting to keep up. Within the half hour, the two faeries spotted the familiar lane leading to the Lending Library. Ailidh stopped and gazed at the building, a mixture of elation and concern filling her.

"Do you notice anything?"

Kayne narrowed his eyes. "Not really. Why?"

"Where is everybody?"

He looked again at the front porch of the white building. Ailidh was right. Normally, on a day like today when the sun opted to appear from beneath the clouds, there were several fae outside sipping those coffee drinks Chrissy made, and the door was opened allowing fresh air to dissipate the closed-up smell. He couldn't sense his kind anywhere within a quarter mile radius. There was movement within the building and the essence of the Librarian and Chrissy wafted on the air. There was also another essence. One that was familiar but…

Ailidh snapped her head his direction. Her eyes were wide, sparkling with joy.

"Tiamoon! I sense Tiamoon."

She started to run then spread her wings and flew to the front door. Kayne followed, groaning with the ache his wing muscles produced. He touched down on the porch a mere seconds behind Ailidh. Her hand was already pushing open the Library door.

~ * ~

Tiamoon sat, her chin resting in the palm of her hand, staring out the window down the lane. Chrissy had made up a spot in the oak tree for her that she appreciated, but the inactivity of sitting around was irritating her. She really needed to practice her skills if she was to have a chance when facing Gitty. The thought put a smile on the warrior's face. She was sure she could convince the council to allow her the opportunity to face her detractor.

Movement at the end of the lane derailed her daydream. She strained her eyes to see if she could spot the movement again. At the beginning of the turnoff to the Library were two small figures trudging toward the building. Tia noted the two appeared to be fae in stature. She wondered if it were someone she might know. The figure wearing a flowing garment stopped then was suddenly flying up the road.

"Chrissy! Someone's coming up the driveway."

Tia stood up, feeling the rush of adrenalin pumping through her veins. Her fingers twitched over her knife blades, and she flexed her legs in anticipation of a confrontation. She could hear faint shouting from the flying figure. Her mouth went dry and she waited for the right moment to jerk open the door and meet the intruder head on.

She peeked out the window and saw two figures flying directly toward the Library.

As the two neared, Tia realized she was looking at Ailidh and Kayne. A gentle thudding indicated the fae had landed on the porch. Tiamoon opened the library door to find herself enveloped in the slender arms of Ailidh. Kayne dropped into the nearest chair on the porch, his wings quivering with exhaustion.

"TIAMOON!" Ailidh hugged the tiny gnome warrior tightly.

"Ailidh," Tia gasped for air. The little fae's small size belied her strength.

"Oh, I'm so sorry." Ailidh let go of the warrior and danced around her. "You're here, you're really here."

She clapped her hands in glee. "I'm so glad. Now everything will be just like it was before Gitty sent you away."

Tiamoon straightened her tunic and cleared her throat. "No, Ailidh, things won't be the same. Gitty has more knowledge of the magic and has had years to practice its use. She is more dangerous and cunning than before the war. I can only offer my help but will do my best to save our land. However, I have sent word for all the clans to gather. The decision to proceed must be made by everyone who has something to lose in the valley."

Tia turned to Chrissy. "Would the Librarian represent the Others?"

Chrissy thought for a moment. "I believe she would."

"Then what we must do now is wait for the mouse messengers to bring back replies to my requests for a council meeting. The decision for action will be made at that time."

~ * ~

Gitty stood at the front window staring down at the roof of the Lending Library. It seemed she spent a great deal of time in this spot contemplating her fate since the court had closed her work sites. The atmosphere of magic was building; she could sense it in the air, a light buzzing that tickled her ears.

"Tiamoon is back. Lancelot has finally allowed me to see his confrontation with her. But there is more to this than just her presence. This sensation feels more and more like the forest before the war." "What are you muttering about, dear sister?" Morgan sluffed into the living room and flopped on the couch, throwing one leg over the couch's arm. He bit into an apple. The pungent sweet aroma of the fruit combined with the loud crunch disrupted Gitty's attention.

She turned in time to witness juice running down her brother's cleft chin. He swiped at it with a sleeve and crunched away. His lackluster eyes and drawn expression along with the listless position he took on the couch grated Gitty's nerves. At the best of times, she could barely tolerate his presence but now, with the company shut down, she was ready to kill him.

"Don't you have some young thing to impress?"

"Naw. All the local girls know I don't have any money, and if I want to go out of town, I'll need to borrow some cash from you."

He shot her a lazy grin then bit into the apple again.

"When you put in a decent day's work, you'll get a decent day's pay. Since my construction sites have been closed down, you're just out of luck." She pushed him out of the way and sat on the end of the couch. "Have you noticed, brother, the magic level has spiked in the last few days?"

Morgan laid his head on the back of the couch and stared at the ceiling. "And this would interest me because…?"

"Because, you oaf, our dear stepsister is in the valley and must be gathering some of her little friends together. Can't you feel the difference?"

Morgan pushed out a sigh as he pulled himself to his feet. He turned to his sister.

"I've noticed, but why should we care? They can gather a thousand of those stunted, miniscule creatures and still not have the power we have. So what's your point? Are you afraid of Tiamoon?"

Gitty looked into the smirked face of Morgan. "Get real. That midget of a sister has as much chance of defeating me as you do of convincing the local tavern wenches you're wealthy without using magic."

She watched the sneer on his face morph into a scowl. *Point for me.*

She magicked a hundred dollar bill that she handed to Morgan. "Go play with your little friends but keep your inner ears open. I may call on you. Don't ignore me or you'll live to regret it." He raised an eyebrow in question, gave Gitty a nod of the head then bolted to his room to shower and get ready for an evening out.

"It's very strange how much magic is pooling around the Lending Library. The air is rippling with waves of enchantments. There is something going on and I need to know what it is. How...?"

Lancelot tread lightly across the floor and undulated around Gitty's legs. She started to scold him and stopped herself. Scooping up the large creature in one hand, she moved to the window at the front of the living room.

"Lancelot, my love," she cooed.

A rumbled purr was her answer. The cat had blanked its mind of all thought.

"Now, now, lovey. I want you to do a task for me. Capture one of the messenger mice."

The mind picture the cat projected was of a mutilated mouse disappearing down his throat.

"No, my love, not for eating."

Lancelot huffed his unhappiness.

"I need information from the creature. Once I have what I need, I don't care what you do with it as long as you don't do it in my house."

"Rrrrooowwwww."

Gitty watched the magic dwindle around the Library to small sparkles of light.

"I *will* find out what's happening, Tia. Then you'll regret leaving your safe, comfortable exile."

Chapter Fourteen

Linda slid quietly from her room to a chair she'd set against the back wall. Since the arrival of the small warrior and return of Ailidh and Kayne, life in the Lending Library had been anything but sedate. There were daily arrivals of faeries, wood nymphs, gnomes, sprites, and more wood creatures than she knew existed in this region.

On top of the daily arrivals, the sweet, shy, timid Ailidh who had left clinging to Kayne's arm had returned brandishing an attitude that rivaled the warrior gnome's own brashness. They had taken up sword practice behind the library and the clanging of metal against metal had become routine background noise. Kayne wandered around the first day or two looking lost but soon realized if he were to keep his ladylove, he'd just have to accept the change. Within a short period, he was offering his services as sparing partner for the two female warriors so one or the other of them could rest between practice sessions.

Linda realized her home, her library, had the feel of a base camp of operations during war. The thought frightened her a bit, but she wouldn't turn away any of the fae community. She was now, and always had been, a guest in their world.

The front door opened and several fae men wearing the trappings of clan chiefs entered the premises jostling for lead position.

"Innkeep!" The tallest fae thumped his sword on the wooden floor. "Innkeep! I need a room, a pint, and a willing wench!"

Raucous laughter rolled through the room.

Linda watched Chrissy dart from the kitchen to the front door, her wings a blur of movement.

"Behave yourself, you uncouth, loudmouthed, brute of a creature or I'll throw you out." The little wood nymph plunked herself in front of the two foot tall fae outfitted in chainmail and fawn leather shirt and leggings. His unruly flowing black hair fell loosely down his back. He placed his sword into the scabbard and faced the nymph.

Chrissy straightened to her full height, fisted her hands on her waist, and glared at the interloper, her violet eyes sparking wildly at the warrior.

Linda rose from her spot against the wall not sure how quickly she could cover the distance between her chair and the front door, but determined nothing would harm her friend. She edged along the bookshelves until she noted the sparkle in the deep brown weathered eyes of the fae chieftan.

"Will you now, Crystal of the Glen?" Chrissy was trying hard but losing the battle to maintain her frightful frown. She giggled then hurled herself into the arms of the faerie.

"Oh, Raghnall! Where have you been? I've missed you so much." She pulled the warrior's face to hers and locked him in a tender kiss that pulled a low moan from deep in his throat.

Breaking the kiss, he sighed and offered a tender, sweet smile to the little nymph.

"When the treaty was signed all those years ago, Tiamoon was not the only one to be exiled. I had to put my mark on the paper and promise never to return to the valley if I wanted my family and," he ran his forefinger down her velvety cheek, "my· love to remain healthy and alive. I've missed you so much, my sweet."

Ignoring the pandemonium that was quickly becoming the norm for the Lending Library, the two lovers gazed into each other's eyes. Linda eased her way back to her chair and felt the ache of loss as the sight of the two reunited lovers tugged thoughts of her husband from the recesses of her memory.

I do miss him so.

"What is all the turmoil I'm hearing? Someone is destroying the ancients?" Raghnall nodded at the troupe of men around him. "Rest. We'll camp in the meadow beyond the house tonight. I have business."

A few of the men snickered.

Raghnall turned an icy glare their direction. The sniggering stopped. As the clan chiefs fanned out around the room, he grasped Chrissy's hand and led her to a table.

"I have to get back to the kitchen."

"You what?"

"I work here, Raghnall."

"Why? You're faefolk. We don't need to work."

The corners of Chrissy's mouth tipped up. "I know but I needed something to keep me busy. Most of the other nymphs left after the war and the faeries tend to stick together." She looked at him, water pooling in her eyes, threatening to spill down her cheeks. "I had no one and when they destroyed my tree... well, the Librarian kindly offered the oak behind her house to me. She can see us, Raghnall."

"Who is this Librarian? And what difference does it make if she can see us? I can see you." "She's an Other?"

His eyes widened. "She's an Other?" He rose hurriedly from his chair knocking it over in his haste. He started toward the door. "I need to get out of here. I don't want anything to do with Others. The night elves..."

"AHA! That proves it!" Chrissy smacked the tabletop.

The noise in the room abated for a moment as all eyes centered on the furious wood nymph.

"It has been the Saun family and night elves all along! This is the first I've heard of you being exiled. Why did you feel you couldn't trust me with the knowledge of their treachery?"

Raghnall swung around, pulling his shoulders back and raising his head high.

"Because it was my choice and my burden to bear. I made the sacrifice for my family, friends, and the woman I love."

Chrissy narrowed her eyes at him. "You were the only family I had, Raghnall. Mine was all killed in the war. Remember?"

He opened his mouth to respond but was drowned out by the shouts of the other fae warriors.

"Food! Where does a man get some food around here?"

Chrissy looked at him. "We'll continue this discussion later. I have to work now."

She bustled over to a table of rowdy warriors and, dodging grasping hands and leering grins, took their orders.

Raghnall exited to the front porch. He stood, reconnoitering the surrounding meadow and woods. There was a sense of unease in the air that set his nerves to twitching. He felt certain someone was watching. *But who?*

~ * ~

Linda observed the increasing bustle in her home. There were fae of all sizes and shapes. She didn't know why but the realization the fae were as different in form as humans took her by surprise. Then she felt guilty she had presupposed what appearance faeries would take.

"Guess prejudice comes in all forms." She muttered more to herself than anyone else. The cacophony took on a pattern and Linda sensed liaisons were being formed throughout the room. The conversation around the tables appeared serious in nature. When the speaking ceased, each clan representative would look to the others sharing the table and, with a nod of the head, end the meeting. There would be back slapping and hand shaking then the appearance of little flasks let Linda know the faeries were magicking while she was present.

It was an honor she had never expected to happen. As the day wore on the seriousness of the meetings abated and soon the fae were relating tales of their time away. The atmosphere lost the seriousness of the morning and a relaxing joviality expanded around the room.

Linda noted Chrissy wander to the front porch where she siddled up to Raghnall. He slipped an arm around her waist and the two engaged in quiet conversation. Chrissy's face glowed as she looked up at the faerie warrior and Linda, feeling ever the voyeur, found herself wishing for one more time of feeling the same way. She got up and slipped into the kitchen to clean so Chrissy could spend time with her beau only to find the counters and workspaces spotless.

"You could've asked my help, my little friend…"

Turning on her heel, Linda stopped at the doorway then tiptoed back to her room. She was tired of sitting quietly away from the action. The need to feel fresh air on her face overwhelmed her. Slipping on her tennis shoes, Linda exited through a back door she seldom used anymore. She stood on her small back porch taking in the view of the valley. It had been many months since she gazed at the meadow and surrounding peaks. The mountains still rose majestically from the basin floor and groves of evergreens blanketed their sides. But all was not right with the valley. There was something… missing. Linda squinted at the expanse, narrowing her eyes to focus on the vast terrain in front of her. In the distance among all the green grass of the meadow and surrounding trees, sat a brilliant yellow machine. She started looking at the stands of trees more carefully and realized the oaks were missing in large numbers.

The recognition of this truth chilled her to the bone. If she had not stopped the dozers, they would soon have demolished every stand of oaks in the valley. *But why? What is so important about the oak tress?*

Linda strolled the back of her property until dusk darkened her path. She watched in amazement as the air around her home wavered wildly. *Must be more tired than I thought.* With each step toward her domicile, Linda's tiredness abated. When she stepped on the back porch, she experienced a lightness in her step she'd been missing lately.

The room hummed with activity and laughter smattered around the area. No one noticed her enter nor did her presence interrupt conversation. *They must be getting used to me.* She smiled and nodded at a couple fae chieftains who acknowledged her. She changed her sneakers and moved from her bedroom to the kitchen intent on fixing herself a snack when the metallic ringing of multiple swords being drawn stopped her. She snapped around to face the front door and sucked in a deep breath at the sight she beheld.

Looming in the doorway, a figure attired in a floor length, tan duster ducked under the doorframe standing erect once he entered. Short white hair, tanned skin, and eyes so blue they stood out across the room completed the image standing on her landing.

"If he stays, we go!" A warrior attired in all red stood, his sword pointed toward the figure at the door.

"Aye! We'll not stay in the same building as he!" Several others chimed brandishing swords and knocking over chairs in their haste to rise.

Raghnall stepped from behind the tall stranger and lifted his sword.

"This man was invited."

"Who would be foolish enough to invite a night elf to our gathering?"

The group muttered their agreement.

"I would."

All eyes turned to Chrissy.

Macartan, a river fae, walked to the nymph and hissed in her face. "And why would you do something so stupid?"

Raghnall sped to Chrissy's side. She looked at him and shook her head.

"Because this is a problem faced by all of us... including the night elves."

Macartan puckered his mouth to spit then thought better of it. He stomped to his table and began gathering his belongings. Many in the room followed suit.

Linda watched as the handsome, extremely tall, stranger stepped toward the center of the room.

"If I may..."

She felt her heart race and unconsciously ran a hand through her hair. The stranger put up a hand. "I know all of you feel we night elves were the cause of the last war between our races…"

The gathered crowd in the room bellowed agreement.

"…but I'm here to tell you the fighting was initiated and continued by the clan Saun. By the time the rest of our world heard of the war, the Saun's had secured the lands using rogue elves as soldiers and secured treaties signed by many of your clansmen. The use of brute force on another race is forbidden by elvan law. It's not our way."

"Tell that to my dead uncle!"

Chrissy faced the sea of angry warriors. "We *all* experienced loss from the war. It scarred every family represented in this room. I don't think anyone wants to experience the pain of loss again. That's why I asked Uther to join us. Maybe he can help find a solution to our problem that won't involve fighting."

Raghnall stepped next to her. "We have nothing to lose and Uther has taken the fae oath of silence. If he breaks that silence the penalty is…"

"DEATH!" The room roared.

Uther tipped his head in agreement. "Death. Frankly, I have many years left to live in my life. I don't wish to end it too soon."

Macartan dropped his belongings on the floor. "Then you will agree to anything we decide?"

Uther shook his head. "No."

Swords rattled and warriors snarled.

"I won't agree to anything that will end in the loss of life. I do think, however, I may have a solution to benefit us all."

Chrissy cast Raghnall a sideways look.

"If I might request a chair and something to drink? It has been a long journey this day."

Chrissy winged her way to Linda who stood in the doorway of the kitchen gazing Uther's direction. The little nymph smirked at Linda. "Is he not the most beautiful man you have ever seen?"

Linda felt heat flame her cheeks. "I, uh, guess so."

"Would you help me get him a chair and some water?" "Of course. How rude I am."

Chrissy giggled. "Uther has that effect on people."

Linda dragged the chair she normally used toward the front door. As she neared the night elf, her senses began to work overtime. She licked her lips and cursed the moisture forming in her palms. Her mouth felt dry and she knew she must look a sight. *Why didn't I run a comb through my hair after my walk?* She sighed in resignation.

A pitcher of water and a glass had been set on a table near the elf. Linda brought the chair and set it on the floor. As she was about to make her escape, a gentle hand on her arm stopped her. She turned to see who was holding up her progress from fleeing the room and long forgotten sensations.

"Thank you." Uther's deep silky voice vibrated the air around him.

"You're… you're welcome." She knew her cheeks were blazing red and she moved her gaze to the floor.

Chrissy flitted over to the table. "Uther? This is the Other I was telling you about. She's opened her home to us, given me a place to live, and agreed to help if there is anything she might do. This is Linda."

"Pleased to meet you Linda. I find it fascinating there is an Other who believes in our existence."

Linda squirmed. "My family is from Ireland, and I grew up with the tales of faeries and elves. I'm just luckier than most; I can see everyone."

An unseen force drew her gaze to the eyes she'd noted from the other side of the building. She looked into the cool blue orbs and found herself ensnared in their kindness. The hand resting on her arm halting her attempt to flee was strong. Well-formed fingers with calluses showing a practiced work ethic detained her escape but didn't clutch her in force.

"Your name is spoken throughout the magic community with respect. There are some in my clan who could afford to take a lesson from your actions."

Her lips moved but no sound emerged. Her cheeks flared hotly.

He smiled; a slow enveloping movement that lit the room with brilliance. His hand dropped from her arm to his side.

"You give no thought to personal gain. That's unusual in both our worlds. I hope to learn much from you during this meeting of clans." Linda cleared her throat. "I believe it is I who has much to learn. I hope I'm worthy of the privilege."

Chrissy smiled and winked at Uther. "I think so, Librarian, but then I know you."

Linda quickly escaped to the back of the library and disappeared into her room.

~ * ~

Uther gazed at the wood nymph. "Do you really believe she is worthy of standing for the Others in this meeting?"

Chrissy snapped around and stared at the night elf.

He watched her tiny body shake with anger, her wings rustling with the effort she was making not to explode into a tirade.

"I had to ask. Your reaction tells me what I need to know."

"Ahhh!" Chrissy streaked to the kitchen, the sounds of metal against metal letting all know of her anger.

Uther turned to look at Raghnall who'd been standing quietly back and observing the conversation. "She's quite outspoken, is she not?"

Raghnall shook his head. "You have no idea *how* outspoken. Had the Others' women not taken up the cause of equality first; our own would have demanded such rights a long time ago."

Uther flashed a wide grin. "Ah, but it puts spice in to life."

Dragging sounds of metal on wood interrupted the conversation. Tiamoon pushed through a throng of fae warriors congregating at the door.

"Where is he? I heard he actually had the nerve to show his face in these woods. Where is that devil Uther?"

She swung around to find herself facing the very soul she sought.

"Uther!"

"Tiamoon."

"So have you come back to try and finish what your kind started all those years ago? We're better armed now, and many of us have been practicing for just this occasion." "No, my fierce little warrior. I came to clear up some myths about the night elves in the last war and to make sure there is no war this time."

Tia narrowed her eyes at the creature whose kind had forsaken her to live near her family and friends. "Do *not* make assumptions based upon the size of a thing, elf. The sharpness of my blade doesn't judge the size of the thing it cuts."

Raghnall stepped between the two. "Tia, Uther. Let's not start on bitter ground. It's time for the clans to sit, discuss, and decide how we will handle the problem we all face. Uther says he may have a solution. Let's hear him out before we throw him out. What do you say, Tia?"

The gnome glowered at the elf. A barely perceptible nod signaled the beginning of the first meeting of the clans in nearly 80 years. Raghnall stepped outside to the porch and pulling a horn from his side, blew three short blasts. An hour later, the fae warrior called the meeting to order.

~ * ~

Linda peeked out at the roomful of clan chieftains and warriors of all sizes. The gleam of silver blades in the light set goose bumps on her skin.

Several of the higher clan chiefs spoke and were well received. Points were made about what was happening in the valley; homes being damaged, innocents nearly being killed, and Ancients being completely destroyed. The atmosphere was heading toward heated when the night elf stood and cleared his throat.

"I've heard enough to know what I'm about to propose is the best solution to rid this valley of the threat… permanently."

Chapter Fifteen

Gitty pulled the barbell up for one more curl before dropping it on the stand. She grabbed the nearby towel and wiped the sweat from her forehead. *I'm done.*

She'd found herself in the basement gym more often these last few weeks since the construction company had been closed down. *Temporarily, only temporarily.* She headed for the shower. Letting the hot liquid sluice down her pumped muscles, Gitty relaxed until the water ran lukewarm. A change of clothing and the growling of her stomach demanded an immediate response.

As she stood waiting for the microwave to finish heating her meal, Lancelot trotted across the flagstone floor.

"Where've you been, you mangy beast? I thought I told you to grab one of the messenger mice so we could find out what's going on in the valley. Well? What happened?"

Lancelot turned his back to her as he drank from his water bowl. Gitty, unable to see into his mind unless she looked directly in his eyes, walked over and picked up the cat. She held him in her arms and stared into his golden orbs. Once connection had been made she got the pictures she was seeking.

"What? No mice *anywhere*?" She unceremoniously dropped the cat to the floor. "Vermin infested monsters are in hiding. I can sense something big is happening, and I aim to find out what. Better to be one step ahead than one step behind."

The microwave dinged in response and Gitty retrieved her food. She sat at the kitchen table, microwave food container on a heating pad, fork held mid-air, staring morosely out at the woods below. She could see the glow of lights from the Lending Library and all day long she'd been feeling the light fingers of magic dancing across her arms. The warmth of the room and heat from food in her belly began to lull Gitty's eyelids downward. The muscles of her neck relaxed and her shoulders slumped. *A quick nap would feel so good.*

Leather boots thudding on the stone flooring interrupted the pleasant moment. The harsh sound drew closer, preceded by a wave of unpleasantness dispelling the magic's warmth. Gitty pushed her food away and looked up at the sour expression on the face of her brother as he stomped into the kitchen area.

"What's the matter, Morgan? Won't anyone come out and play with you?"

He growled at her. "What would you know about playing? No one can stand to be near you."

"My but we're touchy this evening. Did some gnome steal your best girl?" Morgan strode to the window and peered toward the valley, arms clasped behind his back.

Gitty began to worry. Morgan never let a chance go by to try and outdo her insults. His silence was unnerving.

"Morgan? What happened out there tonight? You're home entirely too early."

Gitty watched the broad back of her brother rise and fall with a deep sigh.

"We have a *very* large problem, Gitty."

She rolled her eyes. "For elves sake, Morgan, don't go drama king on me. What in the name of dragons and unicorns are you talking about?"

The tall night elf dropped his hands to his side and shook his head. He turned to face his sister.

"I hit a couple of my local haunts to see if any of my favorites were out with no luck. It was pretty quiet so I made my way north. There are a couple clubs near the university I've avoided because young Others are so—so…"

"Human?" Gitty raised an eyebrow.

Morgan narrowed his eyes and pushed out an exasperated sigh. "No. So unbelieving. The younger women still believe they're attractive to any and all men. They're harder to convince than the older ones who've had their hearts broken. Anyway, I strolled into several clubs and found myself welcomed for about an hour until the young girls got tired of buying my drinks.

"They informed me I wasn't anything like the 'other tall, white-haired guy with really cool icy blue eyes'."

"Like this is news?" She held her chin in the palm of her hand, her elbow resting on the tabletop. "So?"

Morgan glared at his sister.

"I decided to push a little and see who this guy was. I asked around to see if anyone could remember his name. A couple of the girls giggled and nodded their heads. They said he had an unusual name; something really medieval, like Geoffrey or Arthur or something like that."

"Morgan? Is there a point to all of this rambling?" "Gitty!"

"What?!"

"Quit being such an ass."

Gitty dropped her hand to the table and raised her eyebrows at her brother. "What did you call me?"

Morgan puffed out his cheeks in frustration. "Think! What tall, white-haired guy with blue eyes and a medieval name do we know?"

Gitty stood, the chair scraping the floor. "I'm done. This is a guessing game for children, and I haven't been a child in over 100 years. Why don't you go online and tell your tall tales to some of your Internet lovers? You can still magic over distances, can't you?"

She trudged from the kitchen toward the hallway and her bedroom.

"Uther."

The name, spoken softly, stopped all movement in the household; even Lancelot stopped eating, flattened his ears against his head, and growled.

Gitty stopped in the middle of the hallway and turned. Her face had drained of all color and her eyes were the size of the tea saucers in the cupboard.

"What did you say?" She whispered.

"Uther."

She walked back to the living room and fell on to the couch. "It—it just can't be."

"Why not? Because he fears the Sauns and the house of Saun? I doubt it."

"No, because I was sure I'd seen our father put a blade to him. He was sprawled on the ground; blood everywhere, not breathing. I was certain of it!"

Morgan moved to the wingback chair and lowered himself into the plush upholstery.

"Well, sister dear, apparently you were wrong. There is an elvan man in these parts calling himself Uther and being kind to everything and everyone.

"If he is the same Uther… we're in trouble." Morgan turned to his sister. "We need to find out what's happening in that library place before it gets out of hand and we lose everything." Gitty snapped her head his direction. "You *think*? I've been trying to get you to see what's been going on for the last month, but you've been too busy leeching off your girlfriends to see beyond your next free drink.

"Closing down our company was just the beginning," Gitty got up from the couch and paced back and forth. "The longer we're closed, the more chance there is someone will find the treasure Thomas talked about. If he told me in a drunken stupor, you can be sure he told someone else too."

She shuddered, stopping to cross her arms over her chest.

"I can't swear to it but it feels as if the magic level of the surrounding area has risen one hundred fold. I continually feel the buzzing of cast spells. Before, when it was just the two of us, the air was still until we used our own magic. Now, there's constant movement. The key to all of this lies inside the Lending Library."

The siblings turned and stared at the small rooftop. Light shown from the windows and the meadow moved with activity.

Gitty nodded her head. "I think it's time to make a neighborly visit."

Morgan frowned at his sister. "Why would we want to do that? You don't read."

She huffed out a breath, rolled her eyes, and shook her head. "You are such an idiot."

"What?"

"Think. What is the best way to find out what is happening?"

"I don't know."

Gitty dropped her head and let her hands drop to her side. Looking up at her sibling with eyes blazing, she gritted her teeth as she answered.

"How have you lived so long without being killed? The best way to find out what is happening is to *be* there when it happens. If we make a friendly visit to the Library, should Tiamoon or some of her pathetic little friends show up, we'd know about it because…"

"…we'd be there." Morgan brightened as he finished his sister's sentence.

"Uhhgg." Gitty shook her had and headed down the hallway. "I'm going to bed."

Morgan turned his attention to the light in the valley. "Maybe there'll be some women who don't know me there." The reflection in the window showed a lecherous smile spreading over his face.

Chapter Sixteen

Tiamoon sat in the child-sized chair and propped her legs, crossed at the ankle, on the lower slat of the porch railing. She made a visual reconnoiter of the surrounding area. There were a few spots of wavering air consistent with magic being used, but beyond that nothing was happening. The calmness made her uncomfortable. With her step- siblings so close, she didn't trust the serenity. She sensed the presence before noting his fawn colored boots standing next to her.

"Tiamoon."

"Uther."

"May I join you?"

"Still a free country."

The elf sat on the top step his long legs stretched languidly in front of him.

"Do you sense Gitty and Morgan nearby?"

Tia shifted her weight and recrossed her feet. "No. There's nothing here for them to gain. I know elvan magic is stronger than fae magic, one on one, but with so many fae present, the two would have to be out of their minds to attempt any confrontation. I also suspect they've felt your presence. Gitty may be bold, but she's not stupid. Everyone in the fae kingdom knows how powerful you are."

Uther smiled at the compliment. "Thank you, I think. I'm powerful but no more than any other night elf. I've just learned to utilize what's been given me. Two night elves in tandem against me could easily defeat me. I hope circumstances don't take that turn."

Tia snorted. "I can't see Gitty and Morgan *ever* doing anything in tandem. The only reason they live in the same house without killing each other is our father demanded it."

Uther raised an eyebrow and shot the gnome a side look.

"Yeah. We share a father, nothing more. When he was killed in the war, those two sent my mother away and exiled me. They wanted to make sure no one knew we were related. Hence, the stepbrother, stepsister verbage. It was as if anyone knowing we shared the same blood would taint them in your community. I couldn't have cared but it brought an early end to my mother's life. She idolized my father and willingly accepted his children. The feelings were not mutual.

"Anyway, I hope you know what you're doing with this party idea." Uther leaned himself back on his elbows stretching to his full length. "I've sensed them watching the building."

Tia's eyebrows shot up.

"Yes. They're keeping an eye on the unusual amount of fae traffic in and out of the house. They, too, can feel the spike of magic around the Library. If, as you say, control and power is foremost in their minds, they'll want to make sure they're prepared to protect what they have. Any attempt to overtake them will be met with brutal, deadly force.

"The party tonight will peak their curiosity. I'm surprised they haven't shown before now."

Tiamoon humphed. "Gitty likes to sneak up and ambush people. Walking up to the front door and knocking is not her style."

The two warriors sat quietly for a moment soaking in the smells and sights of a spring day in the forest. Sun filtered between the trees exposing new life on the forest floor. A gentle breeze wafted the sweet scent of early flowers celebrating the break from the constant rain and cold of winter.

"Has anyone figured out why the Sauns are killing the Ancients?" Uther sat up, placed his elbows on his knees, and stared down the driveway.

"No. That's the strangest thing of all. About ten to eleven months ago, seemingly out of the blue, they started tearing up the oak groves; nothing else, just oaks. The construction equipment appeared and a sign went up announcing a new subdivision of houses according to the Librarian. However, nothing was built, just the destruction of the oaks."

"Then our mission is twofold; stop the Sauns wanton destruction of the Ancients and finding out *why* they're killing the forest."

~ * ~

Ailidh and Kayne slowed their trek as they neared home. The tree still stood and she turned to him, a smile touching her lips.

"We may still have a place to live!"

Kayne looked around the meadow. He felt exposed and vulnerable walking in the open.

"Ailidh? Let's just check out the tree and get back to the library. Something is not right about this place." "Oh, don't be silly." Ailidh pushed open the door. Dust covered every item in the living area, but nothing had been taken or moved. It was as they had left it nearly two months earlier. She pushed a sigh through her lips, her shoulders relaxing, and smiled widely.

"We're home, Kayne. We're home."

Kayne had been backing into the trunk of the oak that served as home to the fae pair, watching the horizon for trouble. His magic sense tingled with danger warnings. He'd turned, gripped the door, and was pushing it closed when a large black paw clutched the side and shoved.

"Ailidh! Run!"

Enormous gold eyes gleamed dangerously as the cat tried to push its way into the hole. It swiped the air with one paw, pushing the door inward with the other.

Kayne tried to push back but the creature's size and weight made the battle an uneven match.

"Kayne! The incantation!" Ailidh drew her sword, closed her eyes, and pointed toward the door. She began chanting.

"I command you, I compel you, creature of Gitty, get out of my house now!"

Kayne added his voice raising it until he was shouting at the black intruder.

Chanting the incantation, Ailidh opened her eyes, glared at the enormous yellow-eyed monster, and pushed toward the door. A high-pitched keening began to rent the air. The cat dug its heels in pushing backwards from the tree and, yeowling in pain, fled. The two faeries watched the monster streak from their home in the oak.

Ailidh looked at Kayne a smug smile on her face.

"Welcome home."

~ * ~

Linda watched the activity in her lending library. The building was humming. She couldn't believe how many of the small magical folk were inside the walls of her home. Childhood dreams never included this many faeries in one place. The hub of activity was Chrissy's kitchen. The little wood nymph had taken control of the celebration planning and was barking out orders like a general planning a campaign.

"No, Rory, not there; near the doorway."

"What difference does it make? They're not gonna notice it anyway." "No, but I am."

Throwing up his hands, the warrior-turned-unwilling-room-decorator moved the floral display.

"Women!"

Linda couldn't stop the giggle that escaped her. Chrissy was a force to be reckoned with.

She'd been so busy watching the decorating, she'd not taken notice of where she was walking. Bumping into a muscular, wide chest, Linda felt the heat flood her cheeks. She immediately looked to the ground and apologized.

"I'm so sorry. My mistake."

A hand gently cupped her chin and brought her head up. She found herself looking directly into the stunning blue eyes of the night elf Uther. Again, her cheeks flooded with heat.

"Please don't apologize to me. The fae folk are notorious for not trusting anything they haven't invented or been around in the last 200 years. Frankly, I think they owe you a debt of gratitude for offering your home as a refuge."

"I agree." Chrissy interjected as she sped past her wings churning furiously. "Laughlin! Not there! *Why* didn't they bring their mates? Aaahhhh!"

Uther chuckled.

Linda felt the sound roll over her skin and tickle her ears. This beautiful man was reminding her of sensations she'd long put away. It made her uncomfortable on the one hand and happy on the other that she could still feel.

"I'm happy to have my house full of life again."

Uther smiled. "Yes, Chrissy told me of your brave fight to help your husband in his last days. He was a lucky man."

"I miss him." Linda looked horrified she had confided something so personal to a virtual stranger. "I'm sorry. That was very… rude. If you'll excuse me?"

She fled out to her backyard. Tiamoon was practicing her sword moves alone. Linda slipped past the gnome warrior and walked the fence line to the back of the property. A small creek served as the demarcation of the end of her property. Linda found her favorite stump and sat staring at the rippling water. "Are you okay?"

She jumped at the sound of the deep voice.

"No. I'm flustered, confused, overwhelmed… you name it. I had my life all planned out then my husband got sick and died. So—I changed my plans. I indulged my love of books and surrounded myself with items I knew wouldn't die or require me to do more than love them.

"Then Chrissy showed up. I couldn't believe all the tales my relatives told me were true and standing in front of me in the form of a wood nymph. I guess I got carried away thinking they would ever accept me.

"Then you showed up…"

Uther nodded. "And I stirred feelings you thought long dead."

Linda's mouth dropped. She put a hand over it and nodded her agreement.

He smiled. "No ,I don't read minds but you *are* fairly see-through. You don't hide your feelings very well."

She shrugged. "Yeah, Donald always did say I was an open book."

Uther knelt to the side of the stump and gently placed Linda's hand in his.

"If I may say… you are still a magnificent looking woman, Librarian…"

"Linda."

He tipped his head. "Linda. I would be honored if you would allow me to become a friend."

She turned her head and peered into his face. "I'd like that."

A grin touched his lips. "We can see where it goes from there."

Linda blushed. "Darn this blushing stuff."

Uther chuckled. "I find it attractive and honest. Would you like me to leave you to your thoughts?"

"Maybe for a little bit. Chrissy has everything so under control I feel in the way in my own home. I sure hope this works out for everyone." Uther stood, kissed the hand he held and placed it in her lap. "So do I."

~ * ~

Gitty walked the perimeter of her property noting the increasing activity at the Lending Library. She felt a pressing, unrelenting need to be there; so much so the need wretched her senses to the point of restlessness. Uther was there—she could feel his presence. Before this night is over, Uther, there will be a shift in power in *this valley.*

Gitty strode to the house and, upon entering, called for her brother.

"Morgan! It's time we met our neighborhood librarian. Get down here!"

She heard the laconic shuffle of feet and looked up to see Morgan dressed in a running suit and shoes ambling his way toward her.

"Oh, no, little brother. Get back upstairs and put on your best dress-to-impress outfit. For the most part you're useless, but unsettling the ladies with your first impression is what I need to give us the advantage. Move it!"

Morgan stuck out his lower lip and pouted as he turned around and trudged back to his room to change.

When he returned and received Gitty's approval, the pair climbed into the Hummer and drove to the Lending Library. The closer they got to the building the more agitated Gitty felt.

"There is a lot of magic being performed in this vicinity." She parked the car out front and exited her side. Morgan followed suit, allowing Gitty to take the lead. She walked up the steps of the quaint building and read the sign on the door—Open. Just walk in.

~ * ~

Uther shushed the noisy crowd as he watched the night elf pair ascend the steps.

"They're here. Shhhh!"

~ * ~

She pushed the door open slowly, unsure of what she would find on the other side. Once in the building there was a festive atmosphere, floral arrangements adorned walls and the tables had tablecloths and centerpieces. An older woman in a stunning blue dress came from the back room and jumped when she saw the pair.

"Oh! I'm sorry. You startled me. Welcome to the Lending Library. We're celebrating our tenth anniversary with a party. Her smile was bright and Gitty returned the gesture.

"Hello. I'm Gitty Saun and this is my brother Morgan." She turned around and grabbed him by the coat muttering under her breath. "Get over here, you idiot."

From behind the tall, white-haired woman's back, stepped a man with waist-length white hair and deep blue eyes. Linda sucked in a breath, smiling to cover her surprise. Uther had warned her Morgan was handsome, but his warning paled in comparison to the reality. The man smiled, showing a set of dazzling white teeth, but Linda noted the smile didn't reach his eyes.

"Pleased to meet you."

Linda subtly stepped back and slightly to the side. "I'm Linda and this is…"

"UTHER!"

The brother and sister spoke in unison. Their faces were locked in an expression of shock when Uther pulled his staff and pointed it their direction.

"FREEZE!"

The two forms were trapped in the positions they had been standing when the night elf had cast a stunning spell on them. Linda watched as their eyes blinked.

Uther lifted each of the night elves separately and carried them to the center of the room standing them side-by-side. Once in place, the room filled with fae warriors, wood nymphs, gnomes, and forest creatures.

Tiamoon walked from the back porch to face the elvan pair.

"Gitty and Morgan Saun."

Linda swore she could see hatred radiate from the pair's eyes.

"You have terrorized this valley for many decades; killing many of our relatives, stealing from those who remained, and banishing others as you saw fit. Your actions have indicted you. The fae clans, along with Uther representing the Night Elves and the Librarian representing the Others, have decreed that as long as you wish to act like the humans, you will live like the humans and die like the humans."

Tiamoon nodded and the elvan pair watched as clan chieftans came from various parts of the room and stood in front of them. Uther and the person they called the Librarian moved to the back of the fae. The group looked directly into the eyes of the two rogue night elves while Tiamoon spoke. "Guardians of magic, your hearts have strayed, You seek wealth and power and have chosen the dark way. This council has voted to speak as one, We withhold your powers from this day on. No longer will you use the Old Magic ways, A human life you'll live for the rest of your days. All the room pointed at the elves and spoke in unison. Gitty and Morgan Saun: It is over, it is done. Gitty and Morgan Saun: It is over, it is done. Gitty and Morgan Saun: It is over, it is done."

Uther moved to face the elves and lifted his staff pointing it their direction.

"FREE!"

The startled expression on the two faces turned to frowning snarls, and the two began to flex muscles and move around.

"Don't think this is over, you little freaks. You've just made the biggest enemy you could have in your lifetimes." Gitty lifted a hand toward Tiamoon. "Destroy!"

Silence filled the room.

Tiamoon stood tall, her right hand clutching the handle of her sword. She looked at the woman who'd exiled her and smiled.

"Like to try that again?"

"MORGAN! Help me!"

The two elves stood pointing at the gnome and yelled together. "Destroy!"

A ripple of laughter passed through the room when nothing happened.

Gitty's face blossomed to a bright red. "AAAAHHHHH! I still have the construction company and I'll bulldoze every stand of trees in this valley!"

"I don't think so." Uther moved to face Gitty.

She glared at him, her fists clenching and unclenching. "Oh? Do you really think I care what you think? My crews will make matchsticks of this building then I'll dig until I find the blasted treasure that drunken leprechaun babbled on about."

Linda stepped forward. "Treasure? There's a treasure in my house?" Morgan had slinked to the door and attempted to leave. Several fae chieftans held him at sword point inside the room as Tiamoon walked up to face him.

"You're not going anywhere, brother dearest."

She watched him flinch at her use of the word brother.

Gitty narrowed her eyes and spit her words out through clenched teeth. "Yes, treasure, as if you didn't know."

Linda looked at her. "What leprechaun?"

Gitty rolled her eyes. "Others. You're all so stupid."

Uther moved toward Gitty. "Watch your mouth."

"Or you'll do what?"

Linda stood, finger tapping on her chin. She looked at Uther and a smile spread to cover her whole face. "Is he a short man with an Irish accent and bright green eyes?"

Gitty shook her head. "That describes three quarters of the men in this valley."

"A little man who speaks of enough gold bricks to build a mansion?"

Gitty stopped and turned to Linda. "That's the one."

Linda bit her lip to keep from laughing but gave into the urge. Soon she was holding her sides and guffawing.

The effect soon had the room responding the same way.

"WHAT IS SO DAMN FUNNY?"

Linda stopped laughing long enough to look directly into the eyes of the angry female night elf.

"Thomas always told me my books were worth more than any monetary fortune. In fact, he made up a little ditty just for me.

A stand of oaks That all can see, Hides the fortune Most seek from me. Linda watched the vein in the elf's neck throb. Her face turned purple and she screamed as she ran from the room grabbing her brother in her escape. Linda looked at Uther.

"She's quite upset. Are my forest folk really safe from them?"

He nodded. "Yes. They've lost their magic. Right now, they don't understand what that means, but next time they try to magic something away, nothing will happen. They wanted the power and life of humans, now they have it until they die."

Linda shook her head. "How sad. For something as fleeting as power, they gave up the most important thing of all—they sold their heritage."

Uther slipped her hand into his. "It's their loss. Now, let's not worry about them and celebrate. This week has resulted in a gathering of clans that hasn't been seen in many decades. The valley now has its rightful owners back, and I have a new friend I intend to visit often.

"Is there any cake?"

Linda felt her cheeks flush. "I believe I can arrange that."

Defying the Odds

Chapter One

In a meadow east of Eugene, Oregon

Bram ambled up the roughly hewn stairs to the willow lounge chair located at the front of his home. He pulled the scrimshawed pipe from his pocket and filled the bowl with his favorite blend of black cherry tobacco. The paced routine of loading the ivory bowl with fragrant leaves and tamping them firmly into place was one of his favorite after dinner rituals. Withdrawing a matchstick from the inner pocket of his vest, he struck the sulfured end against a river rock he'd placed on the root of the towering oak that served as his home.

The fading evening sky showered the mountains in hues of gold and red. Pushing away the light, a blanket of dark blue velvet sprinkled with luminous star points soon prevailed. Bram puffed smoke rings at the darkening heavens.

"Evenin'." A scruffy black and tan terrier mix meandered up and, after circling three times, lay next to the chubby gnome.

"Evening, Silas. How's the family?"

"Well, thank you. Daisy announced we're expecting—again."

Bram chuckled into his beard. "Congratulations."

"Humph. I'll be glad when we're both too old to care. I came over to ask if there are any jobs in sight. I'll need to be working as much as I can now."

It seemed he got one batch of kids out of the house and another was on the way.

Silence stretched between the business partners. Bram pulled deep draughts on his pipe, blowing the smoke away from his friend. His eyes were drawn to the large block of light spilling from the picture window of the behemoth on the hill. The Saun clan, night elves whose callous actions nearly destroyed the fae population of the meadow and surrounding forests, owned the out of place monstrosity.

Bram squinted his eyes to focus his vision on the methodical movement that broke the beam of light. He could just make out a figure pacing rhythmically in front of the casement. Unable to ascertain which of the night elves was engaged in the determined striding, Bram was sure of only one thing…if the night elves were restless and unhappy, the rest of the valley was in trouble.

~ * ~

Gitty paced in front of the picture window, ignoring the expansive view of the green valley below. The thick carpet covering the hand selected hardwood floors muffled the angry stompings of her boots. At the end of each turn, she jabbed the air with her finger.

"Think you can take away my magic, do you?" She spun on the ball of her foot and stamped to the other side of the room. "We'll see about that!" Jab, jab.

Morgan, the younger of the two siblings, stretched his limbs languidly across the fine leather couch, watching the angry display being played out in the living room, a smirk residing on his lips.

"What has your knickers in a twist?" His leg, hanging over the arm of the couch, swung slowly back and forth.

Gitty broke her tirade for a moment. "I'm surprised yours aren't. How can you tolerate not having magic to use?"

"Because, dear sister, I don't *need* magic to get my way. I have my," he waved a hand up and down his body, "*obvious* attributes."

Gitty grimaced. "Please. Don't make me sick."

Pulling to an upright position, Morgan stretched his long legs in front of him, tucking his hands behind his head.

"You're just jealous."

"Hardly."

"Then what's your problem?"

"I don't fancy living my life in pubs among the scum of the valley sponging off the pity of strangers. My plans include owning all I see."

Morgan rose from the couch and faced his sister.

"Good luck with that. Even the Others are wise to your quest for power. I'm going out. See you later." He moseyed out of the living room and down the hall.

Gitty gritted her teeth. Morgan might be her brother, but he was useless when it came to thinking beyond his next good time.

She glared at the source of the fingers of light stretching over the meadow.

The owner of the Lending Library was an Other the local fae had embraced with open arms. Even Uther, the one-time leader of the night elves and her uncle, had taken a personal interest in the older female. "Must be losing his sanity."

She spotted a pinpoint of red light glowing in the far distance. As hard as she tried, she couldn't sense the origin of the light.

"I hate not having my magic!" She smacked the wall with her hand, immediately regretting the action. Bolts of pain shot up her arm.

"Damn it!"

Turning on her heel, she tramped out of the room.

Chapter Two

Linda Brown, Librarian to most of the fae, peered down the entry lane, the cinnamon coffee exploding on her tongue. Spring was evident by the riot of color lining the road. Mist settled gently on the new foliage stretching to greet the sun. She sighed, a contented sound followed by a slow-forming smile. Her keen hearing picked up the subtle flutter of tiny wings.

Chrissy, the resident wood nymph, languidly made her way to the edge of the chair and, back-winging furiously, settled on the arm.

"Librarian?"

"Yes?"

"Would you like a refill?"

"Thank you, no. I'm doing fine. Your new coffee drink is heavenly. I think we need to create a name for it. What about *Cinnamon Chrissy*?"

There was a quick flapping commotion as the little nymph moved to face the librarian. Her deep violet eyes were wide with excitement.

"Really?"

"You did suggest and create it."

The nymph flew a loop-de-loop.

"Whohoo!" She buzzed around, settling once again on the arm of the chair, humming a tune the librarian recognized as an ancient Celtic song of celebration.

"Librarian?"

"Hhmm?"

"What are we going to do about May Day?"

"I'm not sure. What do you normally do?"

"We have a celebration of several days with dancing and feasting."

"I'll let you handle the planning. Just tell me what you need, and I'll do my best to provide it."

Silence stretched between the unusual friends. "Chrissy?"

"Uh-huh?"

"You okay?"

"Uh-hum. Just trying to figure where to start."

Librarian smiled. The nymph had come such a long way from their first meeting when she'd tumbled into the library, disoriented and trembling in fear. The coffee shop and restaurant portion of the library ran smoothly under her guidance. A faint rustle of wings interrupted the librarian's thoughts.

"I think I'll start setting things in motion. If you need me, I'll be in the kitchen." The tiny figure zipped through the door, disappearing into the building.

Linda opted to stay on the porch and enjoy the sweet smell of the valley as the spring showers commenced to lightly sprinkle the earth. Through the mist, she spied a figure hiking up her driveway. Something familiar about the gait tickled her memory; the stride so confident, head held high.

Night elf?

Heat rushed to her cheeks, coloring the fair complexion. Stirring from her chair, she stood and stretched her legs. Her view of the traveler was better from a standing angle. There was no doubt as to the identity of the lanky man who assuredly strode to her front porch.

"Beautiful day, Librarian. Don't you think?"

"Yes, it is." Her cheeks glowed a healthy pink. "How've you been, Uther?"

"Well, I have a great hunger and thirst. Have you bread and drink available?"

"Let me speak with Chrissy. Please…" she indicated one of the chairs near a table, "…rest your feet. I'll be back soon."

Uther allowed a smile to cross his lips. This lovely woman whom the fae community had taken to their ranks so loyally made his heart pound. Removing his cape, he lowered his tired frame into the offered seat and leaned back to admire the scenery. His eyes threatened to close and would have had Linda not brought him a glass of water and several slices of fresh made bread. He could smell the delight before she placed the plate in front of him.

"Oh, my. It has been some time since I sank my teeth into the likes of fresh bread." "You can thank Chrissy. I don't know why that little wood nymph is so determined to learn all the human tasks there are to living, but it's been a blessing in disguise. She really does make the best bread in the valley."

Uther slathered butter on the still warm slice and bit into the concoction. His moan of appreciation tickled Linda's heart. Sensations long forgotten started to make her uncomfortable.

"Would you like to try one of her coffee drinks? They're really quite good."

He held up a finger and slumped against the chair. "How anything can be as heavenly as this bread I don't know, but I'll try one of her coffees."

Linda noted the relaxing of his shoulders and settling of his body.

Good. Maybe, he'll stay longer than a day or two. Wait! Where did that come from? She hurried to the kitchen, slowing as she neared the door. A gentle knock to alert the nymph to her presence was given.

"Yes, Librarian?"

"Could you make one of your Cinnamon Chrissy's for Uther?"

The little fae buzzed to face Linda. "Uther's here?" Her violet eyes danced with delight.

"Yes. He just arrived and is tired and hungry. I thought he could do with a tasty pick-me- up."

"Where's he staying?" Her wings shook with excitement.

"I...I hadn't asked him." Linda's brows knit together. "Why?"

"He used to stay with the Sauns when he came to visit. But he can't stay there now."

"Hhmm, you're right. I suspect the welcome mat wouldn't be set out for him."

"I'd offer my tree, but I don't think he'd fit." Chrissy tapped her finger on her chin, forehead crinkled in thought.

Linda burst into laughter.

"What?" Chrissy frowned.

Shaking her head, the librarian settled into a warm chuckle. "The picture of Uther trying to squeeze into your home just hit me as funny." The little wood nymph tried hard to hold her serious look but was soon giggling.

"It would be funny, wouldn't it?"

Linda nodded. "What say we brew up some of your magical coffee for our night elf?"

Chrissy set to putting her talents to use, whipping up her cinnamon specialty. Linda carried the steaming mug to the front porch. Toeing open the screen, she headed toward the table Uther occupied.

Legs stretched in front of him, the night elf sat with his head against the building. His arms were folded and his platinum eyelashes rested on his tanned cheek. Linda stopped in her tracks and sucked in a deep breath.

He's magnificent; so long and muscular. She set the steaming coffee cup on the nearest table and retrieved his cape from the back of a nearby chair. Gently, she covered her sleeping visitor.

He stirred and blew out a deep sigh.

Linda froze. When Uther shifted and his breathing deepened, she backed away.

"What am I going to do? You can't sleep on the porch for the next couple days. There's a real possibility of the temperatures dipping." She muttered gazing at the form of the man whose looks made her heart pound. *Wait a minute!*

The cup of coffee trailed cinnamon scented steam into the library.

"Didn't he like my coffee?"

Linda recognized the hurt tone of the wood nymph. "He didn't even take a sip."

"What!"

"Hold on, Chrissy. I went out to give him the coffee and found him sleeping in his chair. Who knows how many days he's been traveling? I didn't see a vehicle or horse, so I can only assume he was walking. I'll bet he's just exhausted."

Chrissy winged to the window and peeked out at the slumbering night elf.

"Too true. Where's he going to stay?"

"When Donald, my husband, was alive we used to go camping in the Three Sisters Wilderness area. Somewhere in the shed out back I think I still have some down filled sleeping bags he brought home with him from his time in the service. I can air them out and provide some comfort from the elements for Uther. He'll be able to use the floor of the library after we close up at night."

Chrissy winged to face the librarian. "What if he says no?"

Linda shrugged her shoulders. "I don't know."

~ * ~

She wrapped her grey woolen sweater to her body and shivered. "Feels cool." The librarian hadn't been down the trail to the shed in several years. When her husband died, she couldn't face the memories stored in the eight by ten building. Placing her hand on the lock of the hasp, she pulled in a deep breath and turned the handle. Squealing unhappily, the warped door opened with difficulty.

Linda covered her nose to ward off the pungent smell of mildew. "Whew! I should've done this ages ago." She leaned in and grasped the thin string hanging from the socket of the bare bulb Donald had installed. The glare from the fifty-watt light momentarily blinded her. Recovering from the brightness of the light, Linda took a second look and groaned. Cobwebs blanketed everything in sight. She'd need to give the place a good cleaning before she'd be able to find anything.

Sighing in resignation, she turned out the light and closed the door. At the moment all she wanted to do was wash her hands in the stream and pull clean, crisp fresh air into her lungs. A hint of mildew clung inside her nostrils. Her throat tickled from the dust and everywhere she looked at her clothes she saw dirt. The path to the stream ran past the property line to the east of the shed. The proximity was too much for her to deny the pull and heeding her heart and not her head, she strolled through the woods admiring the spots of wild flowers exploding in spring color. Clear water tumbled wildly through the rocky riverbed. Linda stopped. By summer's end, this mad, rushing torrent would dwindle to a gentle, meandering brook.

She knelt down and dipped her hands in the closest pool. Chills exploded on her arms, and she fell against the mossy bank from the shock.

"Wow! I knew this was snow runoff, but I figured by the time it got here, the water would've warmed a bit." Linda furiously rubbed her hands together then stuck them under each arm for warmth. Rays of sunlight streamed through the forest canopy and speckled the riverbank, enticing her to lean back and close her eyes. A gentle breeze ruffled her hair. Muscles unaccustomed to relaxation betrayed her. For the first time in many years, Linda felt calm and at ease. Quieting her mind would prove more of a challenge; however, the roar of water exploding over rocks and rushing to the ocean soon gentled her overactive brain. As the rumble of water faded to background, Linda began to pick out the songs of robins and scoldings of bluejays nearby. Swishing grass tickled her arms and the new leaves on the overhead branches rustled. The scene was bucolic, but deep in the pit of her stomach, Linda felt a nagging. Something was off. She realized the birds had stopped singing. Opening her eyes, she looked around as she lay on her back. When she couldn't find the source of her uneasiness in the treetops, she propped on her elbow and reconnoitered the landscape around her.

The bank on the opposite side of the stream appeared barren of life. No swaying branches from the few bushes near the water. Linda's gaze moved south in the direction of town passing over a downed tree. She'd started to turn to her right when her brain registered what she'd just witnessed.

In front of the log, crouching low to the ground, sat an animal the size of a bobcat. This creature, however, was completely black with glowing yellow eyes. And worse yet, the animal had her in its sights. The eyes didn't blink. Linda looked away and turned back to find the creature crouching lower. She could swear the pupils had enlarged. The cat appeared ready to pounce.

Linda clamored up, turning to bolt back home as quickly as her legs would carry her. She ran square into a muscular chest. A piercing scream left her mouth as she fainted.

~ * ~

Uther swept the librarian into his arms before she could hit the ground. His heightened senses detected a presence across the stream. He narrowed his eyes and spied the black cat crouched on the bank. The malevolent eyes took him in, and Uther heard a low growl from the same general direction.

You are the traitor of your own kind.

The animal's thoughts jolted Uther. He kept a steady watch on the animal as it rose and slipped into the brush at the edge of the river.

"Ooohhhh." Linda was gaining consciousness. "Where am I?" She tried to focus on the nearest object. When she registered the fact she was in Uther's arms, her fair complexion disappeared beneath a rosy wave of color.

"Ple-please put me down. I can manage."

She wiggled in his grasp, causing him to let down one arm. Linda's feet dropped to the ground with a thump.

"What happened?" The worry in his eyes sent her to blushing anew.

"I went to the shed to find a cot and sleeping bag for you. I didn't realize just how long it had been since I'd been inside. When I emerged, I felt a desperate need to wash the dirt from my hands and, I guess, I sort of…"

Uther spared her the embarrassment she seemed to be experiencing. "With the cat?"

"Oh, I was enjoying the beautiful day and realized I could no longer hear any birds. When I looked around that…that huge animal was glaring at me. I thought it was going to attack me. I'd gotten up to head back to the house when I bumped into you and, well, you know the rest."

He chuckled, a warm soothing sound bubbling from deep in his chest.

"I can't say I blame you. That creature is the biggest house cat I've ever seen."

Linda furrowed her brow. "Are you sure that's a house cat?"

Uther nodded. "I can be fairly certain it's not a wild cat. I've never seen a black bobcat in my life; not that there couldn't be any, but I've not seen them. What say we go back to the house? I'm fine sleeping on the floor. I've spent the last six months or so sleeping in places not as warm or as comforting as the floor of your home."

Linda felt the warmth of a blush touching her cheeks. *I'm too old to be blushing like a schoolgirl.* She tromped up the path toward the Lending Library.

Uther stifled the urge to chuckle. *She looks so determined.* This Other had captured his interest when the clans of the valley had gathered and stripped the night elves, Gitty and her brother Morgan, of their magic. She'd not backed down against the formidable pair. Knowledge circulating in the fae community spoke that she willingly opened her doors to any who needed assistance, asking for naught in return.

He opened his mind and issued a warning. *I'm not sure what you're up to, Lancelot, but if you or your master, Gitty, bring harm to this Other, I will string you up and use you for target practice.*

The air before him wavered slightly and he knew his message had been received.

Chapter Three

The lithe figure gave a flip of the tail and caught the current of rushing water to beyond the spot occupied by the large black creature. Finding her favorite lichen covered boulder, Trickle tucked behind the stone barrier and watched the action above her. The wicked, black cat was in the hunter mode and crouched to attack another victim. She ran a delicate webbed finger down the jagged white scar marring the beauty of her scales. The vitriolic beast had caught her off guard and nearly made her the object of a meal. Had it not been for— *His voice! He's close by.*

She poked her head from behind the rock and noted he held the female in his arms. Trickle allowed a wrinkle to mar her porcelain forehead. *Is she dead? Did that monster feline claim another victim?* Movement in the man's arms answered her query. Trickle watched the woman stomp off toward the building where her cousin worked.

Must be the one Chrissy calls The Librarian.

He stood on the bank of the river and she jumped when the sound waves carried his issued warning to all who could comprehend.

Lancelot. That is the name of my enemy. Swishing her tail, she moved to the center of the manic flow of water and peered at the bank where the cat had stood. *He's gone— good.*

~ * ~

Uther caught the flash of tail and undulation of golden hair.

"Trickle, my friend? Is that you?"

The tiny creature wiggled her way to his side of the river and peered up at him.

He held his hands in front of him as he spoke. "I've no net and I promise on my honor as a reformed Night Elf of the house of Saun, I intend you no harm."

The brown speckled green eyes regarded him suspiciously.

"If I had meant harm, would I not have kept you after the attack?"

He tried his best to give her an earnest look of honesty. He could only hope it would work.

The water fae slipped a delicate hand on a rock near the bank and pulled up, flipping around to sit in the best position to afford her a quick escape. "How are you, night elf?" The words from the mermaid flowed eloquently over Uther's ears.

He smiled. The first rule to speaking with a merperson was to be armed against the bewitching tone of their voice. He murmured lowly. "Block."

The mermaid giggled. "Ah, but you are wary."

"Indeed, my watery friend, and still dry on the bank. How is your side?"

Trickle gently moved her hair, exposing the wicked white scar she bore from her attack. "It hasn't disappeared." She traced the route of the mark.

"Why don't you magic it away?"

"It's a reminder to me each time I pass my hand over the hard line to be more alert in my daily life. If you hadn't come along at the right time…well, I won't allow myself to become anyone's lunch."

Uther nodded. "A very wise move. Be careful. Lancelot appears to be hunting these woods, and I know he hates losing a good catch."

"I shall, night elf. *You* be careful. If my cousin Chrissy is right, you are next on the list of targets." She flipped water with her tail and spattered him. A giggle escaped.

Brushing off the droplets from his breeches, he rose from the bank.

"I will, little one, I will. Until next time." Uther watched the selkie dive under the turbulent rapids and disappear. Turning from the river, he made his way back to the Library.

~ * ~

He was aware there were selkies in some of the local rivers but hadn't seen one. On a hunch after the clan meeting where his niece and nephew had been stripped of their magical powers, Uther had followed them out of the building. He'd sent Linda the Librarian off to get him a piece of cake to occupy her while he slipped out the back door. Using his enhanced vision, he tracked the pair as they crashed through the woods to their home. They still believed their magic was viable and arrogantly issued spells to clear the pathway to walk. On many an occasion that evening, Uther was forced to cover his mouth so he wouldn't burst into laughter as the two night elves stumbled over bushes and tree stumps which didn't magic away.

When he'd decided the pair was well on their way to their home, he turned around and headed back. His senses were overwhelmed by fear. Following the path of the terror, he came upon a scene he would not soon forget. Clutched in the paw of the massive animal Gitty Saun kept as a house pet, was a limp figure. One side appeared to be covered in scales while the other showed bare flesh and flowing yellow hair. Uther acted on instinct and blasted the animal with a magic command.

"DROP HER!"

The cat pulled in the paw, bobbling its prize and growling as the creature fell to the ground. It started to reclaim the booty when Uther threw a lightning bolt above the animal's head. Yowling in anger and fleeing as fast as the padded feet could move, the cat vanished into the dark night.

Uther dashed to the river's edge and was amazed to find a miniature mermaid bleeding profusely from a slash the length of her body. He knelt and lightly placed a finger on the open wound while uttering a healing spell. He had to repeat the spell twice before the slash closed completely.

Her body fit neatly into the palm of his hand and he was careful not to jar her as he carried her to the river. Water slowly filled his palm as he lowered her into her element. His heart pounded as he prayed this unique creature wasn't dead. Her eyes fluttered and she opened her mouth to scream.

"Ssshhh!!! We don't want that monster to know you survived."

Affirmation from the mermaid was all he needed, and Uther released her completely, watching her swim slowly on the river's top then, with a flip of her tail, slipping beneath the water.

He'd not seen her since that time. Spying the little selkie was a pleasant surprise. However, viewing the black monster, Lancelot, was not.

Uther groaned. He just knew Gitty and her brother Morgan were up to something, and the rest of the valley would be caught in the backlash.

Chapter Four

Large golden eyes observed from the foliage the interaction between the fair mermaid and the night elf.

So she survived. Not for long. I'll have that tasty treat before the next moon.

Employing all the lessons his mother had instilled in him, Lancelot moved through the underbrush with stealth. He needed to get home and communicate with his master, Gitty. Time was of the essence. It was imperative she be told Uther was in the valley again.

Breaking into a gallop, the sleek black cat sprinted through the forest. He stopped to reconnoiter the meadow when he reached the edge of the copse of trees. The air teased him with hints of mice nearby, but he couldn't stop to indulge his love of the hunt. The mice would be there in the early morning hours.

Tall grass whipped against his face as he raced up the hill. The sun cast golden shafts of light through the windows as he entered the house by means of his cat door. A quick stop at his water dish then he marched into the empty living area. The air hung in angry waves.

I'll check her room. He padded down the hall, skittering to avoid being kicked as Morgan burst from his room.

"Get out of the way, you wretched animal," he scowled at Lancelot.

Growling lowly, the black animal bared his fangs then continued on his mission. He flicked his ears when the door to outside slammed and slowed his pace as he neared his mistress' room. Cautiously, he surveyed the scene. Clothing was haphazardly strewn over the furniture, and the dressing table chair lay on its side. Lancelot eased his way into the space and hopped up on the overturned piece. He sniffed the air and twitched his ears forward and backward to catch the sounds of his lady, but his efforts were met with silence. Straining his neck and focusing his concentration, the wavering of air and clanging of steel crashed against his nerves. There could only be one place from where these sounds could emit.

He jumped off the chair and bolted to the basement gym. He must get to his mistress and make her aware of the enemy in the valley. The crashing of steel against steel muted his thundering paw steps.

"I HATE not having my magic!" Crash! The metallic clang echoed around the practice area. Grunting and thrusting with barely contained anger, Gitty attacked the dummy again. Crash! Lancelot flattened his ears. The noise permeated his head and made his fur stand on end. Yowling, he tried to get her attention.

"I hate this." Crash! "I hate this." Crash! "I hate this!" Crash!

Sweat rolled down the sides of her face, and Gitty swiped at her forehead with the back of her free hand. Out of the corner of her eye, she spied Lancelot.

"What are you doing here?" Something about his presence rubbed her the wrong way. *What good are you if I can't use magic to talk with you?*

She ambled to the window and peered at the valley below. The sword clattered from her hand to the floor.

Lancelot cocked his head as she tried to choke back a sob. *Crying?*

"Yes. What's it to you?" Gitty barked.

Just haven't seen it before.

"Well it happens to everybody so—" She stopped and whipped around to face him.

"I can hear you."

Yes.

"Ho...how?"

Humph. You lost your magic, not your telepathy.

Gitty watched Lancelot roll his eyes. Then she started to chuckle. Soon she was laughing and dancing around the gym floor.

"Whohoo! This is just the beginning! I'll get my magic back yet." She wrapped her arms around herself and began to hum.

There's a reason I wanted to talk to you.

Gitty looked at the black creature and smiled. "What?"

Uther is back.

The smile disappeared from her face. "Are you sure?"

Lancelot narrowed his eyes. *Of course. He threatened me.* "He threatened you? Where is he? Why is he back?"

He shook his head. *I don't know why he is here, but he's staying with that Other in her lair. He threatened me when I was watching her by the river.*

"Really? Hmmm. This might work to our advantage. We'll let Morgan have his little play date tonight, but tomorrow, we need to come up with a plan to regain our rightful place in this valley—and get rid of Uther in the process."

She reached down and ran her hand over the fur on the back of Lancelot's body. "This turned out to be a *wonderful* day. Come on, big boy. Let's get you a treat."

~ * ~

Gitty stretched her legs to the mahogany coffee table. Lancelot had curled up at her side and napped by his mistress. Save for a haunting melody she quietly hummed, the room was silent. When the backdoor slammed, Gitty jumped and Lancelot raised his head and emitted a low growl.

Morgan stormed into the living room and started down the hall.

"Home a bit early, aren't you, little brother?" She glanced at the wall clock, noting the time was only a few hours later than his departure.

"Yeah, well, maybe I missed my loving family."

Gitty noted the acrid tone and sneer on his face.

"Pray tell what happened?"

"Don't feel like it."

"Fine, but don't come crying to me when Uther walks in to your favorite watering hole and sweeps the ladies off their feet." She stared at the retreating back and smiled when Uther's name stopped him in his tracks. She watched in fascination as he slowly turned her direction, noting the loss of color in his face.

"Uther?"

"Yes, dear brother, Uther. He's back in the valley and staying with the Other who's captured his eye." She watched the normally icy blue eyes of her brother darken to a cloudy grey.

Visibly shaking and gritting his teeth, Morgan measured his steps as he entered the living area. "He's the reason my nights have become so miserable." The faint whisper of a smile touched Gitty's lips. "I thought you said you didn't need magic."

His brows knit together. "I say a lot of things. Doesn't always mean they're true."

She feigned surprise. "Really? Why, Morgan—I thought you to be a man of honesty and integrity."

"Save it. How can you know for sure Uther is back in the valley?"

"Lancelot told me."

He opened his mouth to answer then snapped it shut, rolling his eyes. "Sure. And the cow jumped over the moon. How can you talk with the monstrosity of a cat without your magic, sister?"

Lancelot raised his head to glare menacingly at the male night elf.

Morgan took a step backward.

Gitty inspected her nails. She allowed the ticking of the clock to fill the silence for five minutes before answering.

"I may have lost my magic but not my ability to use telepathy. And Lancelot saw Uther on the riverbank behind The Lending Library."

Morgan groped behind him to locate the chair. Once having found the leather seat, he dropped into the buttery cushions. "Uther...here in the valley again."

Gitty hid a smile. "Yes. A bitter fact we have to live with; however, dear brother, what would you sacrifice to have your magic back?"

Morgan snapped his head up and stared at his sister. "How?"

"That's the question to answer before the rising of the next sun. I think a pot of coffee with sugar and cream is in order. We need a foolproof way to implement this plan. And this time, *Uther* will pay with his life."

Chapter Five

Chrissy tumbled wings over toes backwards, throwing out her arm to grab the microwave handle. Wildly swinging from the chrome grip, she caught a flash of grey barrel past her, leaving a faint whisper of pine in the wake. Librarian's sun streaked haired danced in the wind caused by her rush through the kitchen. The crash of the door against the frame set the little wood nymph's teeth on edge. She winged into place on the kitchen counter and listened to footsteps skitter across the hardwood floors of the library's main room. A slammed door followed by silence ended the abrupt interruption to the tiny nymph's afternoon routine.

The small fae spread her delicate wings and loped across the main room to the closed door on the opposite wall. She hovered in front of the portal and keened her hearing to pick up sounds behind the barrier. Odd sounds of shuffling assailed her ears. She raised a tiny fist to knock on the door when Uther burst into the room.

"Linda! Linda! Where are you? Are you alright?" He searched the aisles of the bookshelves and opened the front door to check the porch. Spotting Chrissy, he moved toward her.

The fae whipped around and crossed her arms over her chest pinning her most fearsome glare on him.

"What have you done to her?" She cocked her head to one side.

Uther shrugged his shoulders. "Nothing."

"Really, Chrissy. He's done nothing."

The nymph zipped around to stare directly into the steel gray eyes of her Other friend.

"Then why were you making such funny noises in your room?" Violet eyes widened as the little fae cocked her head.

"It's, well, it's not Uther's fault. Just my own issues that have taken me off guard."

Chrissy shook her head. "What?"

Linda clutched a book in one hand. "Would you set the water to boiling? I feel the need for some tea."

"Sure. What kind, Librarian?"

"Chamomile. The calmness of the brew will help to set my mood. Uther? Would you care to join me on the porch? We need to talk." He raised his brows at the fae and dipped his head in acquiescence to the librarian. "Of course, my Lady. After you."

He held the door open and followed Linda to the table and chairs on the porch.

When she bent to sit in the chair, an item fluttered from the book to the deck.

Uther leaned over and picked up a photograph. Pictured was a beautiful raven-haired maiden attired in a long satin wedding gown. A crown of tiny crème-colored roses perched atop a black mass of curls falling loosely about her face. Her delicate hand was slipped through the arm of a striking, fair-haired young man in Navy dress whites. Both young faces were glowing. His hand covered the small fingers resting in the crook of his arm. She smiled shyly at the camera. His eyes were tenderly locked on her face.

Uther handed the photo to Linda. "This is yours, I believe."

Linda snatched the photo. She felt heat crawling up her neck. "Darn it!"

He settled in the chair next to hers. "I'm sorry. Did I offend you?"

She pushed out a big breath. "No. It's why I wanted to speak with you." She turned to face him.

She held the memento in her hand and examined the two young people.

"This is a picture of me and my husband on our wedding day. Donald had received permission to come home before he was shipped overseas to Vietnam, and we put together a rush wedding and reception. We had three days for a honeymoon, which we spent in Bend at a ski resort then he left for the war. For eleven months, I lived on pins and needles dreading every phone call, watching the road for the car that would bring the officials to my door to tell me he'd been killed. When he walked through the door of our home in Eugene two months early, I fainted. He picked me up and carried me to the couch.

"Your actions this afternoon took me back to that day so long ago.

"I've been embarrassed about my reactions to you when we're near each other. I'm too old to be blushing like a schoolgirl, yet every time you speak to me, I explode in waves of redness. I'm an old woman, Uther, and I don't have time to waste playing silly games. That's for very young people."

He looked into her steely gray eyes. "You are a beautiful woman, Linda."

"Was." "*Are.* The bloom of youth isn't all a true man searches for in a woman; kindness, intelligence and courage are just as important. I listen to the tales of the woods and the fae who dwell there. Your acts of kindness are spoken of throughout the valley and into the mountain ranges as well. You've protected many of the lost fae and guided others who aren't sure where to go. You open your home and food stocks for all who would ask. What more could a man in his right mind ask?"

Her cheeks exploded with color. "Damn it."

Uther leaned toward her and ran his fingers down the soft skin of her cheeks. "It is a beautiful sight to see a woman who is still humble and appreciative of a compliment.

"As far as the game playing, I have entered into many a contest but don't toy with affections. When I gaze at you with caring in my heart, it's because I wish you to know how I feel. I, too, am too old to engage in the foolish deeds the young seem to feel necessary for their courting rituals.

"And, yes, my Lady, I intend to court you. I have but a few decades more before my time to leave arrives. I intend to enjoy those years with a companion of my choosing."

Linda looked up to find teal eyes searching her face. She allowed herself to act without hesitation and placed her hand on his.

"I'd given up on the idea of finding a companion to spend my time with when you arrived for the counsel meeting, and I lost my heart. However, you left, and I was bereft; happiness was slipping through my fingers—again. Many a year has passed since my Donald lost his battle with cancer. Most Others believe you get one chance at a forever love. When you arrived, my heart told me once-in-a-lifetime was a fallacy. Sometimes, just sometimes, life pulls a fast one on you."

Linda ran a finger down Uther's hand, noting the musculature of his fingers.

"Courting is an old word and concept." She allowed a blush to color her cheeks. "But one I love. I like the idea of being wooed."

Uther raised a delicate white eyebrow. "Wooed? Whew! What a sexy word." The hint of a smile touched his lips. He gently lifted her hand to his mouth and placed a kiss on the back.

"I, too, have waited another lifetime to find a suitable companion. I was beginning to lose hope until the counsel meeting. Your reputation made you an interesting person. However, you are an Other and usually we don't get along. Your beauty intrigued me, but I believe what won me over was how you stood up to Gitty and Morgan. No one has laughed in Gitty's face and lived to tell the story. I knew then I had to get to know this Other who, first of all, believed and was able to see the wee folk and second, could stand her ground with a power hungry female Night Elf." Linda had been staring at the floor as Uther spoke. He placed his fingers beneath her chin and lifted her eyes to meet his.

"So, yes, I plan to woo you and, if the gods favor me, make you my companion until the end of our lives." He leaned toward her.

"Librarian! Librarian!" Chrissy buzzed past Uther and hovered directly in front of Linda.

Pushing a wistful sigh from her lips, she replied. "What, Chrissy? What has you in such an uproar?"

"That wicked black cat is in the back yard prowling around."

Uther pushed up from the chair and bolted to the back yard. "He'd better not be."

Linda stood and stretched her legs. "Are you sure?"

Chrissy gave a delicate shrug of her tiny shoulders. "Well, the animal sure looked like that wicked creature." She caught the corner of her lip with her teeth as she brushed her light brown locks away from her face.

Uther returned with a smirk on his face. One hand was behind his back as he climbed the porch steps.

Linda gave a wary look his direction.

"This…" he brought his hand around to the front. In his palm snuggled a tiny black and white kitten, mewling noisily. "…is the wicked black cat."

Linda felt her heart melt. "Oh, my goodness. Somewhere a mother kitty is searching frantically for this little bundle." She held out a hand to Uther.

He placed the little cat in the center of Linda's hand and slipped his arm around her shoulders. "To the best of my ability, I searched her memories and discovered this little girl was born nearby, but her mother went out to hunt for dinner and never returned. This little thing wiggled her way to your backyard because, even in the world of animals, you're kindness is widely known." He ran his finger across the downy soft fur of the kitten.

Linda let a gentle smile light up her face. "Well, I guess I'll make sure she has a home. Did you get a name?"

Uther chuckled. "She says her mom calls her Piggy because she's always hungry. How do you propose to feed her?" "You can't!" Exploded Chrissy.

"And why not?" Linda noted the crimson color of the nymph's face.

"That...thing will grow up and eat us."

"I don't think so."

"Fine. Then I'm leaving." Chrissy started to wing back to the kitchen.

Linda heard Uther mutter beneath his breath.

The little wood nymph stopped mid-air, her wings flapping furiously.

"UTHER! Let me go!"

"Not until you come back and apologize to Linda."

"I won't be eaten!"

He withdrew his arm from Linda's shoulder and walked to face the little fae. Crossing his arms, he set his face in a fierce scowl.

"Do you think the librarian or I would allow such a thing?"

Chrissy stopped trying to escape and slowed her wings to a hover. "And just what can you do to stop the animal from eating me?" She stuck her fist on a hip.

Linda stifled a giggle.

"Are you or are you not a wood nymph?" Uther slightly tilted his head as he asked the question.

Chrissy huffed. "Well, of course, I'm a wood nymph." She swept her hand up and down. "Duh! Tiny person with wings?"

"Yeah, I can see you and so can the librarian. Why can the librarian see you?"

The little nymph threw up her hands and rolled her eyes. "Because I'm not using magic to cloak myself."

Relaxing his expression, Uther stood back, allowing the statement to hang in the air, a slow easy smile replacing the scowl.

The thunderous frown Chrissy had mustered slipped away. "Oh, yeah. I can do magic." "Um huh."

"So I can stay invisible as far as the creature is concerned."

"Yup."

"Oh. But..."

Uther reached out and placed his two fingers around the fae, breaking the spell. He carried her to Linda and stood with the fae facing the kitten. The tiny creature trembled in his grasp.

"This is an extremely young cat. Her memories are faint about her life lessons. You have the ability to perform magic and can be seen by the creature or not as you so choose. Imagine, if you will, training this creature to protect you."

Chrissy wiggled in his hand. "What? These are wild animals that hunt birds and small creatures to eat. I'm smaller than most birds. How could this beast be trained to protect me?"

Uther lowered her closer to the kitten. "Right now, this little one is desperate for love. She'll imprint on the person who gives her the most love. Pet her, go ahead."

The nymph cringed and opened her mouth to scream.

Uther shook his head. "You survived much worse in the woods. Try it. If the creature looks as if she'll try to eat you, I'll snatch you away and keep you safe."

Grudgingly, Chrissy reached out an arm and quickly slid her hand across the nearest section of fur. The tiny kitten began to purr.

"SEE! It's warning me to stop."

Linda smiled. "No. That's the sound they make when they are happy. It's called purring."

Chrissy glanced at the sleeping creature. She had to admit it was attractive, but so many years of fear couldn't be wiped away in five minutes.

"Okay. I'll give it a chance, but the first time it lunges at me, I'm setting its tail on fire."

Uther nodded. "Fair enough. Now I'll release you. Stay or go as you please." He opened his hand.

Chrissy shot him one last look of disgust and buzzed into the library.

"How are you going to keep it from eating her?" Linda chuckled. "I believe after this one has had some nourishment, I'll sit down and let her know who's the boss around this establishment. We both know it isn't me. After a few weeks, I'm sure Chrissy will have Piglet dancing to her tune."

"Piglet?"

"Yeah. I like the sound of it better than Piggy. Shall we take this new member of my household inside and make a nest for her?"

Uther dipped his head. "After you, my lady."

Chapter Six

Morgan lolled his head to one side of the couch cushion. His eyes hurt from tracking Gitty's march back and forth across the living room floor.

"What is your problem, sister?" Yawning, he set his booted feet on the coffee table. "Unable to hatch a winning plan?"

"Some input on your part would be helpful." Gitty stood at the window and glared. The pair had been kicking ideas around most of the night and nothing had struck her as feasible.

Morgan dropped his head forward, his eyes glazed by lack of sleep. "Just kidnap the librarian. Tell Uther you'll kill her slowly unless he gets the clans together and gives back our magic. I'm tired and going to bed."

Dropping his legs to the floor from the coffee table, Morgan rose from the couch and trudged down the hallway to his room.

Gitty watched his retreating back and glowered. "Kidnap the librarian, indeed." She moved to the window to stare morosely at the valley below, Morgan's ridiculous suggestion ruminating in her mind. She hated to admit it, but the idea was beginning to have merit.

"Well, why not? The plan has viability. Two birds, one stone; Librarian is gone and Uther will be too once his lady love is out of the picture. But how?"

Gitty worried her bottom lip, lines forming above her brow as she turned over one plan of attack then another. Morgan's idea was a good one, but she was stumped on the execution. Lancelot wound his way around and through her legs.

Why not kidnap her while she sits on the riverbank?

"Riverbank, uh, what?"

I said why don't you kidnap her when she goes to sit by the river?

"That's a great idea if we can guarantee she'll be out there when we're ready to move ahead with our plan."

She will be.

"How can you be so sure?" *When you were pouting because you didn't have*

189

your magic, I started watching the library from the opposite bank for a chance to get even with those miserable little faeries. Every day when the light has started to dim, she sits by the river for a while.

"I don't pout."

What would you call stomping around the house muttering to yourself and ignoring the rest of the world?

Gitty graced the black animal with a cool stare.

"I was...thinking."

*Same difference. You were acting irrationally—even for you. It's time you regained your rightful place in this valley. Sitting and...*thinking*...won't move the situation to where it needs to be.*

"How can I guarantee the librarian will be there?"

A daily walk appears to be in your future. We're able to keep contact within the length of a meadow, but no further. If you stay back a couple of your long steps in the brush by the river, I can let you know if she's there.

"That's all well and good, but the moment she sees me she'll start screaming and our plan will be for naught."

Then we need to recruit Morgan to be part of the action. If he appears on our side of the river, she'll be so concerned with him she'll lose track of what's behind her. You can subdue her and we'll bring her to the shelter in the woods.

"Won't Uther be able to sense her?"

Not if we place enough sensory camouflage around the shelter. We can send a note to Uther with subtle references to a warehouse in town. Maybe he'll believe it, maybe not, but it'll buy time.

Gitty gazed in amazement at the black feline sitting at her feet wrapping his tail around her legs. "Where did you learn all this?" She could swear Lancelot was smiling.

I listen and learn from the best. He doffed his head to her then began to lick his front paw.

For the first time in many a week, Gitty smiled. "I do believe we have a plan of action that will work." Standing up and gracefully stretching his legs, Lancelot moved to the warm spot in front of the heater vent. Circling three times, he finally lay on the floor and proceeded to go to sleep.

The she-night elf flipped off the lighting in the room and let her eyes roam over the landscape of the valley and surrounding mountains. She rolled her neck and dispelled the feeling of dread that had hung over her for the last few months.

"Retribution."

Gitty liked the way the word rolled off her tongue. She allowed a small smile to blossom and humming a Celtic war song, wandered down the hallway to her room. With any luck, tonight she would have the best night's sleep she'd had in longer than she cared to remember.

~ * ~

Morgan heard low humming and the soft swish of Gitty's house boots pass his door. The sound of silence followed a snick of the latch. An involuntary shudder passed through him. Whatever she and her wretched cat had cooked up would wreak havoc on the valley and further alienate him from the local inhabitants. Light from the scented candle on the nightstand next to his bed flickered across his chiseled features.

He leaned against the rosewood headboard and watched the changing shadows on the ceiling. There had been a time in the highlands back home when he and Gitty were inseparable. She'd been the only opponent to best him at the sword, and her skills at the Longbow were touted throughout the highlands by the bards. It wasn't until they came to this wretched country with its backward farmers and huntsmen did Gitty's temperament morph.

The bonnie lass from Scotland who could drink, fight and cuss with the best of the boys became a shadow of her former self. When the love of her life, Glade, was killed in a battle between the fae and night elves, Gitty shut down completely, turning into the miserable elven being who currently lived in the room next to his.

As her attitude declined into sarcasm and scorn, she quit seeking his company for sword practice preferring to set up her own obstacle course and workout haven in the basement.

It didn't take Morgan long to come to the realization the way of life they'd been taught to live was fading into the past. He frequented the local pubs and, with his striking looks, developed a reputation as a ladies' man. After a fight or two with the farm boys, his position was secured in the community. That is until Gitty felt the need to tear apart the old oaks in the meadows. "There was the dandy with the heavy Irish accent I dueled who lost, but I'm sure that had nothing to do with my getting kicked out of the pubs." Morgan checked the clock on the nightstand and blew out a breath.

"Morning will arrive too soon."

He blew out the candle and crawled beneath his covers. His stomach was lurching with the anticipation of what scheme Gitty had hatched.

Chapter Seven

The clatter of metal against metal woke Uther from a lovely dream of a fair-haired maiden with cloud grey eyes who was lavishing a great deal of attention on him. He stretched his lanky form. Despite his statements about not needing anything but a blanket, Linda had scrounged a cot, his feet hung over the end, and several sheets and blankets to cover the canvas bed. Somewhere in the area behind her door, she'd located a pillow. The cover smelled of fresh spring days with a hint of warm spice. Sleep came easily within his warm cocoon between the aisles of the library.

The noise increased with the hour, and Uther gave up and crawled out of his bed. Rubbing his eyes, he pulled in a deep breath. The pungent smell of mountain coffee raked across his taste buds. He stumbled into the facilities and completed his morning routine.

Replacing the gentle warmth and sunshine of the previous day were light showers.

"Coffee?"

Uther had been staring out the front windows of the building and started when Chrissy spoke.

"Yes. I'd love a cup of black coffee."

She buzzed back to the kitchen and Uther heard the metallic clatter again. Curiosity got the better of him and he tiptoed to peek his head around the door. The little nymph was cooking by dancing in the air and on the tops of the pots and pans. The food on the stove was bubbling and hissing as she danced her magic to prepare breakfast.

"Oh!" She stopped when she spied Uther peeking in the doorway. Pointing at the cup on the counter, she muttered. "Warm."

He watched the steam rise from the mug. "Thank you." Grabbing the mug, he strolled through the aisles to the front door and went out on the porch. There was coolness to the air punctuated with moisture, sending a shiver down Uther's back.

"Damp." The coffee cup rested on the rail of the porch as his gaze was pulled to the road. Raindrops splattered on the asphalt creating a patchwork of lights and darks, rivulets of water racing to the sides.

"Yes, but good for the garden."

Uther jumped. "I didn't hear you walk up." He could feel the warmth of her smile.

"You were so intent on something down the road I really didn't want to scare you. Guess I did anyway, didn't I?" The abashed expression on Uther's face let Linda know she had guessed correctly. "What has you so serious this morning?"

He took a sip of the cooled coffee. "I can't explain it very clearly, but I have a very bad feeling the Sauns are planning something. We both know nothing good comes from that."

Linda nodded her agreement. The last time the Sauns had planned something, they came close to eliminating all the oak trees in the area. Chrissy had fled from the demolition of her ancient home and stumbled into Linda's home library. It was a meeting of destiny as the two were closer than ever.

Uther faced Linda. "Please promise me you'll be careful."

She took a breath to protest.

"I know of what I speak. As much as it pains me to admit it, my thinking was very close to theirs until I met a few Others who changed my mind." He leaned in and brushed a soft kiss across her lips.

Linda felt her knees wobble and she closed her eyes. His touch set her ablaze. Her stomach flipped. Parts of her body she thought long dead were reacting in ways she'd forgotten. White spots appeared before her closed eyes, and she realized her need to breathe.

Heat swarmed up her neck and across her cheeks. She pulled away. "Oh, my."

Uther picked up her hand and with his thumb rubbed across the soft skin on the top. "You, my lady, are special, not only to me, but to many others through out this valley. Should any harm befall you, I'm not sure anyone could stop the fae from declaring all out war on the Other inhabitants of the meadow."

"Baloney. The Others of this valley are ignorant of the magical population who live here. They choose not to see what's right in front of them. They couldn't be blamed if anything happened to me because we both know the anger comes from the hill above us."

"You speak the truth, my lady. Please give me your word you'll take care with your daily routines and should you wish to venture away from the house, you'll allow me to accompany you."

Linda frowned. "I think you worry too much. I'll be fine but just to make you happy, I'll get hold of you if I feel the urge to take a stroll in the woods. Will that make you happy?"

Uther smiled. "Yes. I know asking you not to go outside are fruitless, so this will give me some peace." Before either of the two could speak again, a tiny figure buzzed out to face them.

"Enough talk. Breakfast is served."

The night elf and Other stared at the wood nymph hovering between them. Crossed arms and a ferocious scowl convinced them argument was futile. Uther offered his arm and Linda slipped her hand through the crook of his elbow, strolling inside to the café.

On a table covered in an ivory tainted linen cloth, sat a sumptuous feast; eggs and bacon were accompanied by toast and pancakes. Fresh butter and warmed syrup were placed near the pancakes. Real porcelain plates and silverware resting on linen napkins that matched the cloth finished the picture. Gracing the center of the table was a crystal- cut vase holding a single daffodil.

"Wow." Uther pulled out the chair for the Librarian.

"You can say that again." Linda pulled the napkin from beneath the silverware and placed it opened on her lap. "You've outdone yourself, Chrissy. This looks amazing and appetizing at the same time."

Linda observed the nymph's face color a deep pink.

"Thank you, Librarian. Now, no more talk—eat."

"Yes, ma'am." Uther winked at Linda as he reached for the eggs. "Don't have to ask me twice."

Linda watched him shovel several eggs onto his plate as he grabbed for the bacon. The hint of a smile dimpled her left cheek. *Haven't seen a man eat this well since before Donald got sick.*

"Don't tell me you're one of those Others who pretend not to eat until after the man has left." Uther snagged two slices of toast and with his knife slathered big globs of butter on each piece.

"Nope. Just didn't want to lose a finger or get my hand stabbed." She slid one egg and a couple pieces of bacon to her plate. Quickly snatching some toast she used her spoon to cover the top with homemade blackberry jam.

Silence filled the room as the food disappeared. When both plates were clean, Chrissy magicked her special coffee blend for them to top off their meal.

"I think you should tell Chrissy." Uther stretched his legs in front of him and took a sip of the cinnamon concoction. "No. She worries enough without adding to it." Linda absently stirred the liquid.

"If you don't, I will. I want this land protected by as many entities as possible. I know how devious the Saun clan can be when they feel they've been wronged. Unfortunately, my lady, you stand in the center of their target right now."

"Fine. If you want to tell Chrissy, go ahead, but I won't put anything more on her."

Uther watched Linda gather their plates and stop at the kitchen door, knocking gently.

"Chrissy?"

"Yes, Librarian?"

"I need to get the dishes done and I believe Uther wants to speak with you."

The little nymph peeked around Linda's shoulder to the table. "Why?"

"I think you should ask him."

"Okay." She fluttered casually toward the table stopping just in front of Uther. Turning, she glanced at the librarian.

Linda made a shooing motion with her hand. She watched the tiny fae straighten her back and hover in front of the night elf.

Faced with such a show of courage, Uther cleared his throat in an attempt to keep from chuckling. "I would like to ask a favor of you."

"Why would I grant you...anything, night elf?"

Uther tipped his head in agreement. "Point taken. However, what if the favor had to do with the librarian?"

"Well, that's different." Chrissy rolled her eyes.

"As I thought. I fear for the safety of the librarian. I have an unsettling feeling the Sauns will attempt to harm the librarian in some way."

A wrinkle marred the forehead of the wood nymph. "Why would they do that?"

"They are aware I have...feelings for her. As they no longer have magic because of something I did and the Librarian supported, what better way to get back at me than by harming her?"

Uther watched the wings of the nymph tremble. "They wouldn't DARE!"

"Ahh, but they would, and I'm afraid they will. That's why I need your help."

"What can I do?"

Uther watched the worry on the little face turn to fierce determination.

"Put the word out. If any of the wee ones see the night elves from the house on the hill acting…odd, even for them, please let me know. I'll do what I can to make sure the librarian is safe. Any help your people can offer will be greatly appreciated."

"I'll leave the rest to you. I need to find a permanent place to stay." He unfolded his frame from the chair.

"If the librarian is in danger as you state, would it not be better for you to stay and guard her?"

Uther watched a tiny eyebrow raise in question. *Linda is right. This little wood nymph is very quickly adapting to human ways.* "You're right. I just wanted to spare her from the gossip of having a single man living in her home."

Chrissy humphed. "As if our people ever worried about the rumors and gossip of the Others."

Uther had to agree. The fae community worried very little about the moral boundaries set by the Others. He dipped his head in acknowledgement at Chrissy and went about the task of clearing up his sleeping area. The doors would soon be open to the Lending Library, and the place would come alive with the flurry of tiny wings. The fae in the community used the building as a safe haven to gather and update each other on the activities within the local population.

From the corner of his eye, he spotted Chrissy streaking out the back door. *Wouldn't want to get in her way.* He could only hope she was carrying out the task he'd asked of her. His instincts set his nerves on edge and he was certain Gitty and Morgan would be planning some retaliation in the near future.

The silence from their household defied the nature of the two spoiled night elves and it worried Uther. Anything concerning the Saun clan concerned him. As a former active member, he knew the mindset of the family. They didn't tolerate defeat well and he found himself disquieted at the thoughts lingering in his mind.

"I can only hope the fae will band together again to protect the librarian."

Chapter Eight

Soft leather, moccasin-styled boots hugged the feet of Morgan muffling his footfalls down the hallway to the kitchen. His only thought this morning was of a rich hot cup of coffee. Aromatic whiffs of the potent bean drew him closer to the counter and his reward.

"Morgan!"

The tall night elf groaned. When his sister bellowed, he was usually in trouble. He set a mug from the cupboard on the counter and poured precious brown liquid inside.

"MORGAN!"

Throwing caution to the wind, he didn't answer but took a swig of the life giving fluid. Searing pain racked his throat, sending him into a coughing spasm.

"What?" he croaked.

Gitty's measured gait put him on guard. Her normal mode of travel was to barrel her way through, heedless of anything in her way. Most valley folk had learned to step back when they saw the statuesque blonde headed their direction.

"Good. We need to talk about the plan to get back our magic."

Blowing across the top of the cup, he lifted his eyes to stare at this sister. "What plan?"

"Again, I've had to come up with everything. So sit there and listen while I explain how we're going to accomplish our plan."

Our plan? He'd not submitted any input into the plan. How was it *our* plan? He could guarantee if anything went wrong he'd be the only one to pay.

Gitty filled a mug with coffee, adding sugar and milk to the dark brew. Beckoning her brother with a finger, she moved to the living room and sat on one end of the couch. Morgan followed her into the high-ceilinged room choosing to sit in the tufted leather chair near the fireplace.

"Your suggestion last night got me to thinking…"

"What suggestion?" Morgan furrowed his forehead.

"The suggestion about kidnapping the librarian."

"Wha? I, I, I didn't make any such suggestion." Gitty watched the color drain from his face. She pushed an exasperated breath between her lips. *Constitution of a jellyfish.*

"Right before you skulked off to bed you said, 'Why don't we just kidnap her?' The more I thought about it the better I liked the idea."

"I was being sarcastic. I didn't really mean it." Morgan's hand shook as he lifted the mug to his lips.

"Of course you were being sarcastic. It's one of the things you do best. However, the idea took root. I think we have the means, without magic, to take back what's ours."

Morgan stared at his sister. She'd hatched some pretty wild ideas to get what she wanted before, but this was—insane! Without magic they risked being caught and taken to the Others jail...for life.

"Well, I think I can safely say you've lost your mind. I need more coffee." He pushed up from the chair and snatching his mug, disappeared into the kitchen.

Gitty ground her teeth but waited for him to return.

"What makes you think we can pull off taking the Librarian from under Uther's nose while all those miserable little fae people are meandering around her?" Morgan set his coffee on the side table and dropped into the chair.

Agitation drove her to stand. It took all her restraint not to start pacing.

"I have it on good authority the librarian goes to the river around the same time every day...and she goes alone; no fae, no Uther."

"Right. Who is this good authority?" A sneer began to form on Morgan's face.

"Lancelot."

"Ha! Now I know you've been into the liquor cabinet. We don't have our magic, so how can you communicate with your...pet?"

Because you both still have your telepathy. The aforementioned animal padded in and started rubbing against Gitty's legs.

I'm hungry.

Morgan sat, blinking his eyes in disbelief. "It's a trick. You've learned to throw your voice." He pointed a shaking finger at his sister. Gitty shook her head. "I can't believe we have the same parents. You're an idiot, you know? Mental telepathy isn't magic. That's why we can still talk with Lancelot. I'm going to feed him then we'll continue this discussion." She strode to the other room.

Morgan heard the banging of silverware against the cat's bowl and clatter as the spoon was dropped into the sink.

Gitty strolled into the lounge and dropped to the couch.

"I think you need to take up a hobby."

"Do you now? And what would that be?" He cocked his head to one side and proceeded to cross his arms.

"Fishing." A sly smile tilted Gitty's lips.

"Okay. That's it. I hate fish. I hate fishing. I won't put squishy wiggly worms on a hook and throw it in the water to stand around for hours doing nothing. I can't stand the thought of cleaning them, and if you don't eat them, what's the point of fishing?" Morgan scowled at her.

"You won't actually be fishing."

"What?"

"You'll be observing the librarian and waiting for a good time to let me know when to grab her." She watched a puzzled expression replace the scowl. "You need to start appearing on the opposite bank of the Lending Library for the next week to ten days. Once you become a fixture, she'll give it no thought whatsoever. Observe the time she comes out and when she leaves. Once we have her pattern established, we can choose the optimum time to grab her and slip away."

"Yeah, but won't she recognize me?"

"Not if you wear fishing gear and a big hat to cover your face."

"Just where are we going to put her? This is the first place they'd look."

"Eons ago, after the war in the valley, I took the time to provide myself an escape from the insanity of this house. My cabin is five miles due north from this location."

She watched the wrinkle in Morgan's forehead reappear as he contemplated this information.

"How do we get there? The area you're talking about has no roads." "That's right. The only way in or out is on horseback."

"Right. So we drag this Other, on horseback, to some cabin in the woods until…what? She dies of starvation? Or are we going into the business of murdering people?" Morgan pushed up from the chair to refill his mug. He wandered back to the chair and took up his position.

Gitty shook her head and sighed. "Again, I have to wonder how we can have the same lineage. No, we won't starve or murder her. That would defeat our reason for kidnapping her. We'll put her across one of our saddles carrying her to the cabin, which by the way is continually stocked with a month's worth of food and water. One never knows when the need will arise to take some 'alone' time."

"Just how are you going to take her without a ruckus?" Morgan lifted a brow in question.

"If you'd stop interrupting me, I'd be able to lay out this plan and fill in all the details."

He held up a hand and settled back in the chair. "Please…educate me."

"We don't have enough time for that. I'll just fill in the blanks so you can stop whining like a little girl. Each day you go to the riverbank to fish, Lancelot will accompany you until you've seen the librarian come out and go back into her library. After a week or so…"

Morgan groaned.

Gitty shot him a withering glance and he refrained from making further noises.

"As I was saying…when you've established a routine of fishing on the bank, the librarian should relax. During the second week, you'll need to ride your steed down the hill. I'll be out for an afternoon ride waiting for Lancelot to tell me when the time is right. I've devised a way to knock her out without leaving any physical marks. Once I've accomplished that feat, I'll throw her across my saddle, and from there we'll head to the cabin avoiding any contact with the locals.

"At the cabin, we can restrain her. I've located one of the old cameras that spit out pictures to use in making our demand. One shot of her tied up and gagged and we'll have Uther eating out of our hands. By my calculations, we should have our magic back by the end of the month."

Silence followed the detailed explanation. Gitty watched her brother mull over the plan.

"What's the issue? I've contemplated all the possibilities and worked out things so neither of us will get caught. What's taking you so long to agree?"

"Do I have to wear those stupid looking waders?" "What?" Gitty jumped up from the couch to face her brother. "You're worried about how you'll look!" She stomped to the kitchen and slammed her cup on the counter.

"Complete idiot. The fates are against me. First, a total brainless wonder like Morgan as a blood brother then our father goes and marries a gnome. A gnome! And I'm saddled with that miniature female wanta-be-warrior, Tiamoon. What a joke. I should just liquidate the assets we have here and move back to Emerald Isles." Scrubbing the cup, she muttered between clinched teeth.

"Uh, Gitty?"

"What?" She turned to glower at her brother.

"I think your idea is really great. When do we start?"

She stared at him; a nervous smile attempted to blossom on his face. He shuffled from foot to foot and kept pushing his long hair behind his shoulder.

"Truth be told…I've been miserable without my magic. It seems I've overestimated my attraction to the Other women. Once they discover I have no income, they melt away. I'd love to have my magic back."

Gitty realized his reason was shallow, but whatever it took to have him work with her was fine. "We'll start tomorrow." She watched his shoulders drop as he relaxed.

"What time?"

"Lancelot says she takes a break around three in the afternoon. You'll need to be on the bank a little before. When you get there, pretend to be setting your line then monitor her actions. You might want to nod her direction so she isn't alarmed by your presence. Check the time she goes in then stay for thirty more minutes and pack up and leave.

"We'll continue this for the week, and about Wednesday of the following week, we'll make our move."

Morgan nodded and drifted off toward his room.

Gitty watched his lackadaisical shuffle and mentally kicked herself. *If we pull this off, I'm leaving this offensive valley and all the inhabitants behind.*

Chapter Nine

Chrissy zipped through the door Linda had specially made for her. She flew as fast as her wings would allow and arrived at the riverbank breathless. Slowing her speed, she surveyed the river, trying to recall the outcropping her cousin Trickle had described to her. About to give up, she caught the flash of flowing golden hair. She winged to the top of the water then hovered.

Trickle. The gold flash moved nearer her position. *Trickle, it's Chrissy.*

Rising from the water, the golden hair undulated down her back as the mermaid immerged from the depths of the river.

Cousin. What can I do for you?

Long ago the cousins had agreed to communicate nonverbally to keep eavesdroppers at a minimum.

Uther has asked me to convey to you the urgency of keeping an eye on the river.

The mermaid swished her tail and her eyes lulled seductively.

You mean the handsome, gentle night elf?

Chrissy huffed an impatient breath. *Yes, the same one. Could you keep you mind off your tail? Anyway, he's afraid his niece and nephew might try to harm the librarian.* She watched Trickle's eyes light up.

Nephew? Is he as handsome as Uther?

Come on, Trickle. Yes he's as handsome as Uther, but don't you... Chrissy stopped and stared at the flow of golden curls waving in the current of the stream.

That might just be the answer.

What? Trickle rolled a backward somersault coming up in the same place.

If you happen to see the very tall, very handsome Morgan, feel free to charm him the best you can. You might not be successful as he was once of the fae community but...who knows?

Trickle cocked her head and narrowed her eyes. *What do you mean was once of the fae community? Isn't he any longer?* A smile touched the lips of Chrissy, exposing a small dimple in her right cheek. *He and his sister sought Thomas' gold and were willing to kill all the Ancient Ones in the forest to find the treasure.*

Trickle chuckled. *Everyone knows Thomas is a braggart and liar. Why would they believe him?*

He told them the treasure was around The Lending Library. When they arrived to dig up the fortune, the clan Chieftains were meeting, having banded together to find the culprit in the killing of the Ancients. So many fae had lost homes and been forced to move to Faetown, the elders were willing to put their differences aside until the mystery was solved.

Gitty and Morgan threatened to use their magic and, consequently, it was taken from them. They are as vulnerable as the Others.

Trickle fluttered her tail and giggled. *Ooo, a mortal for my very own. I've wanted to come out of the river, but only for a good reason. This might be fun. Maybe I'll just keep him.*

Chrissy started an ascent. *Have fun. Let me know if you see him.*

The little mermaid zipped around the river singing, *A man of my own, for my hearth and my home.*

Chrissy couldn't stop the blossoming smile. The night elves were in for a big surprise if they thought they could outwit the fae. *A big surprise.* She loped along the path to the Lending Library stopping every so often to admire the new growth of spring. This year the rain had fallen, just enough, to ensure spring and May Day would provide an explosion of color for the festivities. She spun around, lope-de-loping, before entering her door.

Time was quickly slipping away and she had so many things to do. With Trickle on the alert for the night elves from the back of the property, she needed to get the word out to the community to keep a watch on the nefarious two from the hill.

~ * ~

Uther had watched the lithe wood nymph zip from their conversation out the back door. A chuckle bubbled up from deep inside his chest and he marveled at the determination on the little one's face.

"I'd sure hate to be on the wrong side of that little fae." He stretched his arms above his head before standing and reaching for the ceiling. "Need to get some fresh air." Stepping out the front door, Uther meandered to the porch railing and surveyed the scenery. There was light chatter from the surrounding birds as new hatchlings tried their shaky wings in flight. A gentle breeze ruffled his long locks, and he pulled in a deep breath of the rain freshened air. The clouds last night had wept on the landscape but dissipated this morning, leaving a light layer of moisture over the budding earth. Everything felt…new. Uther smiled and straightened up. As he was about to turn and return inside, a movement on the driveway caught his attention. He stood watching in fascination as the black spot moved closer, revealing a small donkey cart pulled by some sort of wire-haired dog. In the driver seat, he recognized the being as a gnome.

Bram held the reins in his hand and let Silas take the lead. The two had been partners for all of Silas' life and could predict what the other was thinking a majority of the time. Silas, a terrier mix, was panting heavily as he slowed and positioned the cart in front of the Lending Library.

"Bram, my friend." He panted and folded his legs beneath him.

"Ahhh! Silas! Let me know before you do that." Bram grasped the front rail of the cart. "You nearly threw me over you."

"Sorry. I think you might want to, uh, cut back a bit on the mead. I do believe you have increased your girth." The terrier stood, leveling the cart.

"I think you, my friend, are too tired due to the Mrs.' condition. However, I'll take your advice into consideration. We have business to conduct. We can discuss this after we have spoken with Chrissy."

The terrier waited for his passenger to disembark before lying on the ground. "I don't recall getting a message. When did you hear from her?"

"I received a message from the Sky Network. The bluebirds were busy gossiping as I cleaned the cart this morning. Sorry I didn't let you know." Bram realized Silas was fast asleep. He shrugged his shoulders and shuffled to the steps.

"Morning."

Bram snapped his head up and lost his balance, tumbling backward off the steps.

Uther scurried down the steps toward the gnome.

"Don't touch me! You've already scared the life out of me. Don't make it any worse." Bram scowled dangerously, lifting his gaze up to stare into cool, blue eyes sporting a twinkle set in a tanned complexion. Long silver hair fell forward around high cheekbones and an amused smile touched the stranger's face. Yet, Bram knew this face was…familiar.

"Uther?" The angry frown disappeared as the stranger extended a hand. "When did you get back?" Bram allowed himself to be assisted off the ground. "I returned within the last few days. I've been feeling anxious about the librarian's safety. How have you been?"

Bram dusted the dirt from his breeches as he climbed the steps to the porch. "I've been just fine. Work has been a bit slow in coming, but it's the time of year when most everyone is hunkering down in their homes. And you, friend? How is life treating you?"

"Mostly I've been traveling the back roads, keeping tabs on the fae community."

"While I would love to sit and chat, I need to speak to Chrissy. Will you excuse me?"

Uther extended a hand. "Of course."

Bram reached up and shook the night elf's hand and dipped his head moving through the Lending Library's entrance. He stopped to get his bearings within the building and allow his eyes to adjust to the darker room. Humming directed him toward the kitchen.

Poking his head around the doorframe, Bram ventured a foot over the sill.

"Uhm, Chrissy?"

"AHHH!"

The clatter of dishes and silverware reverberated throughout the library.

"What the...Bram!" The flustered wood nymph fisted hands on hips and glared at the cart driver. "Watch where you're going! Look at the mess you made."

The gruff gnome furrowed his brows, the bushy slash marks of hair forming a dark sinister line above his eyes. "You're the one who called me. What do you need that is so important you'd use the Sky Network?"

Chrissy waved a delicate hand over the broken bits of dinnerware scattered upon the floor. Rising from their location, each piece found its corresponding mate and cleaved together, hovering above then lowering to the countertop.

Bram had to admit he admired the nymph's magic. Her temper, on the other hand...

"You saw Uther?"

"Aye."

"Did he fill you in on the reason for his visit?"

"I believe he mentioned something about the librarian." "Good heavens,

Bram, don't you ever get excited?" The little fae rustled her wings in agitation.

"What's the point? It's useless energy. What is it Silas and I can do for you, Chrissy?"

Pulling in a deep breath, the fae slowed the flutter of her wings to a hover before the gnome. "Uther believes the night elves, Gitty and Morgan Saun, will try to harm the librarian. He asked me to get the word out for the community to keep a watchful eye on them. If you see or hear anything that seems out of place for them, use the Sky Network to warn us as quickly as possible."

Bram lightly ran his fingers down his beard, trying to herd the coarse hairs into place. "I can make sure the word is spread. How will I be paid? I have a family and Silas' Mrs. just announced they're expecting—again."

"You're joking, right?"

"No ma'am. My services cost. You can try the Sky Network and see how well that works, but Silas and I are dependable."

Chrissy felt the urge to throttle the meadow fae with her bare hands but kept her irritation under control. "You, Silas and your families will be the guests of honor at the May Day celebration; all your food and drink will be furnished for you by the community. Fair enough?"

Bram rolled the idea around in his head. "Sounds good. I'll be shoving off. We've got lots of work to do and not much time. Miss Chrissy." He saluted the wood nymph and spun on the ball of his foot, marching through the rows of books to the porch.

Chrissy magicked the silverware to the sink where she worked with the water and dish soap to again wash the utensils clean. Gone was the contented humming replaced by muttering and banging of the forks and spoons. Once she'd cleaned everything, she ordered the items to put themselves away. She needed to take a break and rest her magic. Slipping from the kitchen, Chrissy winged her way to the windowsill and settled in the high heel shaped recliner the Librarian had given her. The sun streamed through the boughs of the tall pines warming the spot where her chair sat. Chrissy considered contacting the Mouse Network to ask the animals to keep watch for any unusual behavior on the part of the night elves. She'd be certain to set the plan in action...tomorrow. Before too long, the sound of gentle snoring filled the corner of the room.

~ * ~

Bram nudged Silas from his nap with the tip of his soft boots. "We have work to do."

The dog yawned and stretched his front legs. "Going far?" "Yup. All around the valley."

"Big payday?"

"Not quite."

Silas had stood and was stretching his back legs. He stopped and turned to Bram. "We're not doing this for free, are we?"

"Nope. We'll be the guests of honor at the May Day celebration. Everything will be provided for all our families."

Silas used his back leg to scratch behind his left ear. Spring always made his skin dry and itchy. "Guess that'll do. We ready to go?"

Bram climbed into the cart and grabbed the reins. "Let's head out."

"Where to first?"

"We'll start going west then circle the valley. Should be back home in a couple days."

Silas tugged against the weight of the cart and Bram, getting his footing and setting a walking pace he could maintain for the long haul.

Bram saluted Uther and turned his attention to the road. He pulled out a pipe and lit the bowl with a quick flash of fire from his fingertip. *Chrissy isn't the only one who has magic.* He settled in his seat and pulled in the sweet taste of his black cherry tobacco. This job was going to test the flint of both he and his friend Silas. *We can do it.*

"Silas."

"Yes?"

"Stop when we come to the fae community of the lower meadows. I need to speak with the clan chieftain. It's important."

"You got it." Silas knew this was Bram's way of saying he was going to nap.

The easy pace set by Silas eased the tension Bram had felt at the Lending Library. He puffed on his pipe. Silas' nails click-clicked on the road, lulling Bram's eyelids toward his cheeks. He slid the pipe from between his teeth and knocked the smoldering tobacco into a tin can he carried for just this purpose. Once he secured the pipe inside his vest, he gave in to the urge to snooze. He could rely on Silas to wake him when they arrived at the fae community.

~ * ~

Uther watched with amusement as the odd pair disappeared down the driveway. He wasn't sure what had transpired, but glancing in the window he noted the little wood nymph lay out in what looked to be a reclining chair. Her tiny wings were tucked beneath her form. Eyes closed, her face glowed with serenity. She was indeed a beautiful creature.

Venturing into the library, Uther scanned the area, his stomach clenching when he couldn't locate Linda. His stride quickened as he moved from one aisle to another. Using his last resort, he knocked on the door he knew led to her private area. The response was a hollow unanswered sound. *Where is she?* A clock tolled from within her room alerting him to the time. Eleven times he heard the bells chime. *Where is she?* The slamming of a door sent him charging into the kitchen area, knocking Linda askew. He reached out and grabbed her arms as she started to fall backward.

"I—I'm so sorry."

She narrowed a look his direction. "What is *wrong* with you?"

"I said I was sorry. Worry clouded my thoughts when I couldn't find you."

"Why?" Linda put the overflowing basket on the counter, removing dirt-encrusted carrots from the top of the pile. She ran water from the faucet over the orange roots and used her hand to loosen the mud.

"I'm really serious about you being careful. I have a bad feeling you're in danger."

Linda continued to wash the fresh vegetables. "I've lived this long in my home with no problems, and I'll continue to live as I please. I'm not stopping my life because you have a *gut* feeling I *might* be in danger. Since Gitty and Morgan no longer have their magic, what can they do?"

Uther ground his teeth. "My lady, I hate to be a pain, but I know this family, and I know how devious they are when they feel threatened. Your involvement in taking away their magic is paramount in their thinking of you as an enemy. *Please* be more careful."

Placing the carrots in the sink, Linda turned to face Uther.

He noted her stormy eyes take on a softness, reflecting a light dove gray color.

"I've been on my own for so long, I've become quite adept at taking care of myself. It's…difficult for me to realize someone else might care if something happens to me." Linda stepped toward Uther and rose up on her tiptoes to place a kiss on his tanned cheek. She watched him slowly turn a ruddy pink and lower his eyes. "Well, someone does care. Will you take care—for me?" He raised his gaze to her amazed expression.

The sincerity and—angst—held within made Linda's breath catch in her throat. "I—I'll try to remember." A tremulous smile touched her lips.

"That's all I can ask." He straightened and glanced at the basket of vegetables. "Need help?"

Linda glanced at the cornucopia of greens. "Nope. This is women's work. Now, scoot out of my kitchen." Giggling, she'd grabbed a dishtowel and snapped at him with it.

"Don't have to ask me twice." Uther hustled from the room and made his way to the porch.

His gaze fell on the back of the cart disappearing down the driveway. Birds merrily called to each other across the greening meadow and the sun peaked through the tiny sprouts of new growth on the pine trees lining the lane. Serenity appeared to be the weather of the day.

Uther felt a shudder travel his body. It was quiet—too quiet. Everything in him screamed of trouble brewing, and the cause had two names, Gitty and Morgan Saun.

Chapter Ten

Trickle lay on her back, slowly swishing her tail and watching the birds above the water arguing over placement of a nest.

"Silly beasts." She turned and swam to her cove. Wedged behind two rocks was a mirror she'd found on the side of the river. She gazed at her reflection, noting she was getting a bit thin and pale.

"Need to go top side for a day or two." The thought brought a smile to her face. She wiggled to the mirror and feeling along the backside, pulled an oblong piece of paper encased in plastic and a drying spell from behind the reflective glass. The paper had a picture in one corner and Trickle was amazed at how much it resembled her. She'd asked Chrissy to have the librarian tell her what it said, but her cousin had clucked her tongue in disgust, reading the black lines to Trickle. This piece of special paper was; what had Chrissy called it? Oh yeah, a driving license, whatever that was.

Trickle found the paper at the edge of the water and, on an impulse, dragged it back to her secret cove. She knew at some point it might come in handy. She was right. The last time she'd opted to go *above,* the paper had helped her to go where she wanted. She thought maybe there was magic in the paper because all the doors opened for her.

When she'd returned from her land adventure, she'd bargained a bit of simple magic for a small valise to store her human clothing. One of the few oak trees not bulldozed by the she night elf's company served as a storage and changing place, Trickle deposited the case deep in the hollow of the tree. She hoped it was still there. She'd have to ask Chrissy to help her come up with something to wear otherwise, and right now she wasn't willing to include her cousin in her plans.

~ * ~

"Really? I mean, really?" Morgan looked at the dark green, rubber wading boots, fishing hat and pole displayed on the couch. "You really expect me to wear these…hideous things? Not on your life. There's got to be another way."

Gitty was trying to keep from chuckling and not doing a good job of stopping herself. She burst into laughter.

"Oh my god, you should see your face. Ahh ha ha…" Rolling on the couch, clutching her abdomen, the she night elf was caught up in waves of hilarity. "I have to get a picture of this."

Morgan pulled up and straightened his back. "Then do it yourself." He turned and stomped to his room. Gitty lay on the couch sniggering and trying to catch her breath. She'd better apologize to the drama king or they'd be back to square one and still have no magic. Sighing with exasperation, she moved from the couch and headed down the hallway to soothe her brother's ruffled ego.

She knocked on his bedroom door. "Come on, Morgan. Don't be such a baby. It's only for a week or two, no more. Just think…when you're done and we have the librarian, you'll get your magic back and everything will be the way it's supposed to be."

The door creaked open an inch. "I'm not wearing those hideous— whatevers."

Gitty backed away. "Fine. But take them, anyway. They'll be good props. Anyone passing by will think you're actually fishing."

He ventured out of his room, keeping a wary eye on his sister. "If this works and we get our magic back, I want a proper apology."

She turned on her heel and strode to the living room. "I'll write it in the sky with my broom."

Fitting. Once in the living area, Morgan stood in front of the picture window, ignoring the view of the valley below. He turned his back to the glorious sunshine and faced his sister on the couch.

"When is all of this to happen?"

"I'd like to ride to the area today and give it a look-over to see how much camouflage you'll need. Lancelot will lead the way. Once we've seen the stream and the foliage on the banks, we'll have a better idea exactly where you need to stand to get the best observation point. That alright with you?" Gitty cocked her head and hitched her right eyebrow.

"Fine. I'll change and get my horse ready. I'll be in the stables when you're ready to leave." Morgan marched out of the living room and back down the hallway.

Gitty blew a breath between her lips. "My brother, the drama king." Shaking her head, she got up from the couch and ambled to her room to change to her riding leathers. The weather was a bit cool so she grabbed her insulated jacket and quilted leather gauntlets. Her horse could do with a good brushing.

She was at the back door when Lancelot appeared. "Where've you been?"

Napping. It's what I do. Where are we going? Gitty opened the door, letting the cat out first. "I thought we'd ride to the stream behind the Lending Library and you could direct us to the best spot to keep an eye on the Librarian. I'm going to brush my horse first, if you care to join me."

No thanks. I'll lay here in the sun until you're ready to leave.

"Suit yourself. I'll call you." She turned to the black creature only to find him sunning himself on the step of the back porch, his eyes tightly shut.

The brisk walk to the stables energized the night elf and she entered the barn with vigor. Her most recent acquisition was a mahogany brown stallion bursting with spirit. His haughty manner and rippling flanks caught her attention the moment she saw him running through the fields of a local farmer in the valley. Buying the animal involved a great deal of bartering on her part, and she knew the man overpriced the animal to discourage her. What he didn't know was once Gitty decided she wanted something, nothing could dissuade her from that goal.

Glade whinnied the moment he caught wind of her scent.

"Hello, my beauty. How are you today?"

The stallion threw back his head and pawed the ground in his stall.

"Ah, good to see you're anxious to get out and run. We're going on an adventure, but first I'll give you a good brushing so you sparkle in the sunlight. What do you think?"

The animal, seventeen hands at the shoulder, lowered his head, allowing Gitty to scratch behind his ears.

She stood on her tiptoes and whispered. "I miss you so much, Glade. If I had to do it over again, I'd let you catch me this time." Gently rubbing the horse's nose, she gazed into the dark brown eyes. "I know you're in there. I can feel it."

Brown eyes blinked at the night elf and the steed pushed his nose against her hand. Gitty grabbed the brush from the shelf. She put Glade on a lead and freed him from the stall, tying the lead to a center post. With determined slow strokes, she brushed him from the tip of his nose to the end of his tail. She felt the ripple of his muscled body and sensed the excitement building within him. It had been too long since the two rode from the grounds. They were about to resolve that problem.

Clip clopping of horse hoofs broke Gitty's rumination as Morgan and his horse headed toward the exit of the stables. She gave one last swipe to the mane of her steed and preceded to place the hand-tooled, black leather saddle on his back. Completing the task of readying her ride, she swung up and trotted out the stable door as she donned her riding gloves. "Get that, would you, Morgan?"

He glared at her as he moved to close the entrance. "I'm not your personal servant, sister. If you want my help on the project, you'd best stop treating me as though I am."

"Fine." Gitty removed a glove from her right hand and, placing two fingers to her lips, whistled for Lancelot. She pulled Glade to a stop to replace her glove and wait for the third member of their troop to arrive.

Strolling up to the mounted elves, the black cat stretched his legs in front of him and yawned.

"You ready?" Gitty touched her heels to the stallion's flanks.

Yes.

Morgan snapped his head around to stare at the cat. "I can hear him!"

"Bravo. Now let's get going. I want to find this place and get this reconnaissance over. I have other things to do with my time before we set this in motion."

The odd party of large black cat and two night elves on horseback cantered out of the stable yard and down the hill toward the valley.

Chapter Eleven

Linda slipped out the back door and followed the trail from her garden to the bank of the stream. The sun was blessing her favorite spot, and she needed time alone to let her mind wander. Uther's intentions were pure, but he was being a bit of a pain about implementing them. After all, she was well over twenty-five and caring for herself was a daily ritual. She could spot danger the moment it appeared. As she sat and argued with herself, she succumbed to the warmth and peace of the moment. Linda laid back and closed her eyes—for *just* a moment.

~ * ~

Gitty let her body roll with the rhythm of Glade's easy gallop. The spring was in a teasing mood, providing sunshine and warmth to bath the valley. She allowed a moment of contentment to color her outlook—for a brief time. Her cat, Lancelot, sprinted through the tall grasses of the valley looking over his shoulder every so often to make sure she was still following.

His frantic gait slowed to a walk where upon he undulated behind a large bush.

"Lancelot." Gitty pushed an angry whisper between her teeth. "Where are you?"

Come on. Use your mind. I'm right behind the bush staring at the librarian across the stream. That is what we came for, right?

Gitty reined back on Glade's bit and dismounted in one smooth movement. Morgan brought up the rear, reining his horse to a walk before flipping his leg over the saddle horn and dropping to the ground.

"Shhh!" Gitty shot a nasty look Morgan's direction.

Straightening up, he tied his horse to a nearby bush. Morgan measured his gait as he inched toward the stream's edge. Rounding the mulberry, he spotted the form of the female the fae called Librarian. Bile rose in his throat. This being is the one who doomed him to a life of banality. Heat rose up his core and Morgan's vision blurred red around the edges. He took a determined step toward the stream.

Gitty watched her brother's slack features harden. His eyes locked on the human opposite their location. She'd never seen him so focused. When the color of his neck started to turn a deep pink, she knew Morgan had crossed the line of logical thinking. He was running on emotion alone and the consequences would be disastrous. She shot out a hand, grabbing the back of his duster to restrain him.

"WHA…!" Tugging with all her strength, Gitty yanked him behind the bush and clapped a hand over his mouth.

"Ouch!" She snatched her hand to her chest. "Why did you bite me?"

His blue eyes were glacial. "You put your hand over my mouth. Why?"

"You were headed to the stream with blood in your eye. That's not the way I want this to go."

"I, what?" The surprise on his face was genuine.

"Little brother, I think it's time to go. I'll explain it as we head home."

Morgan leaned his head to look around the mulberry bush. The prone figure hadn't moved from the sunny spot. As he started to pull back, the glitter of gold flashed in his eyes.

Lancelot rushed the stream. *Mine, all mine!*

Lancelot! You can fish later. It's time to go home and finalize our plans. Gitty ground her teeth. If it wasn't her brother testing her limits, it was the single-minded cat.

Grumbling with each step, the black feline stomped his feet as he moved away from the stream. *I'll have that half fish yet.*

"Half fish?" Morgan untethered his horse and swung into the saddle. "What is the other half?"

It resembles one of those dreadful faeries.

"Really?"

Gitty turned and sneered to the lagging parties. "Get a move on. We don't want to be discovered because the two of you decided to have a leisurely conversation about fish. Move it!"

Hmm, half fish and half fae. Morgan's face brightened. *A mermaid.* He urged his horse on and was soon rolling the thought of mermaids around in his mind as he galloped toward the stables of home.

~ * ~

Trickle's scales itched. Something wasn't right, and she could sense an ominous force nearby. Swimming against the current near the rock-strewn bottom of the stream, she located a niche in the rocks by Librarian's favorite spot. Chrissy had entrusted her with the duty of keeping an eye on the human, and while she'd rather play in the currents, she had made a fae oath and was bound by the laws of the fae community to keep her word. She wiggled down behind a rock and clutched the lichen growing on the sheltered side. The nasty black animal skulked about the shoreline, concentrating on the area where Librarian usually sat. She crouched down. That's when *he* appeared.

His hair shimmered in the sunlight and his skin was pale—like hers. She wiggled to the top of the water and flashed her tail his direction. Maybe he'd look at her and she could whisper sweet words to him. She liked what she'd seen so far. As she was about to jump out of the water in joy, the form of the black cat materialized dangerously close. Gazing her direction, it moved with determination, stopping short of the river's edge. She felt the animal's disappointment as the dark figure slinked away.

Wiggling free of the rock confines, Trickle caught the current back to her home.

A talk with Chrissy is in store...and soon. She shivered with excitement. It had been quite a while since she'd walked on dry land. *I wonder if I'll remember how?*

Chapter Twelve

Bram and Silas trudged down the back road toward Bram's home. Silas had listened as Bram snorted and snored for the last two miles. Being just as tired as the gnome, the noise was grating on his tender ears.

"Bram. Bram. BRAM!" When yelling at his friend didn't work, Silas resorted to the old fashioned way of alerting and barked his high-pitched yap.

"Wha…what!" Bram yanked his head off his chest, whipping it from side to side. "Why did you bark?"

Silas plunked down. "Because we're at your house and yelling didn't work."

Bram stretched his arms above his head then rubbed his eyes. He lumbered from the cart and trudged to his front door.

"BRAM!"

"What, Silas?" Bram's voice took on a dangerous edge.

"Unhook me."

"Oh—yeah." He sloughed back to the cart.

The terrier rolled his eyes and huffed his impatience at his friend's negligence.

"My apologies, Silas. I can't remember when I've had so much mead and heard so many tales."

"I hope it was worth it because my pads are blistered. Think I'll go home and stay off my paws for a couple days." The terrier waited while Bram unhooked the harness and rubbed the chaffed spots on Silas' fur.

"Rest, my friend. We earned this payment."

Silas limped off and disappeared in the tall grass of the meadow. Bram watched him go.

"Funny, I've never seen his home." He shrugged his shoulders. "I'm sure he'll invite me one day. Now to a soft bed after a good meal." He pushed open the door to his home. Holding up his hand, he fended off a barrage of questions from his wife.

"Enough. I'll give you a detailed account of my journey after I've eaten and slept in my bed." Igrayne narrowed her moss green eyes his direction. "Don't hush me. You take off for a week then stagger into my home reeking of mead and road dirt and tell me not to ask questions? If you want a home cooked meal, Mr., do it yourself."

Igrayne stomped into the bedroom, slamming the door behind her.

Bram blew out a deep, weary breath. It wasn't in his nature to argue, and he was bone tired. Tapping gently on the door, he acquiesced.

"I promise I will tell you all of the travails if you will honor me with a bowl of your marvelous stew, my love."

The door squeaked open an inch. "Really? All the things that happened?"

This time he held the hand to his chest. "I give my oath."

She pulled the door open and strode into the living room. "In that case, I'll warm the pot." She padded to the kitchen and lit the stove. Turning to ask Bram a question, she noted the empty room. She retraced her steps through the living area to the bedroom and found her husband planted in the middle of the bed on his stomach, snoring loudly.

"I guess I'll wait until the morrow for those details." She closed the door and turned off the stove. In the front room she picked up her embroidery to pass the time until he woke up or she fell asleep—whichever came first.

~ * ~

Uther was feeling a restless sensation wash over him. Being so long in one place was not in his nature. He gazed longingly down the lane, jumping when the gentle voice spoke in his right ear.

"You don't have to stay."

He turned toward the light smell of fresh meadow grass. "No, I don't but I wish to. I've many years on the roads wandering the land. It's time I settled and shed my nomad ways."

Linda moved to the railing of the porch on Uther's left side. "I think you'll be very unhappy and restless. You are very much the rolling stone, Uther."

He turned to look down on her. "Don't you want my company? I'll depart if you wish me to."

Time slowed as he watched her face mirror the thoughts roaming through her mind. First, she was terrified then hurt by his statement. "I'm sorry. Did I offend you?"

"No."

He watched her face morph into a calm façade. Her stormy gray eyes took on a flinty hue and shuttered to the outside world.

"I simply meant once a man has traveled extensively, settling in a small community will kill his spirit. That's what happened to my Donald. Oh, they called it cancer, but he was never the same after we put down roots here. Eventually, the stagnation, as he called it, took his life."

Uther placed his hand on the small of her back, his fingers sensing the tightness through her chambray shirt. "I am truly sorry for your loss. Your Donald must have been quite a man to have captured your attention and love for so many years."

Linda felt her breath catch in her throat. Tears were pushing to escape her eyes. She pulled in a deep breath.

"He was very...special. I'm afraid I wasn't able to fulfill his dying wish to remarry. There just wasn't anyone I cared to spend time with," she turned eyes Uther's direction, "until now. I find myself hesitant to share my feelings. Being left alone and lonely is something I've already experienced and don't wish to do again."

Uther turned her to face him. "I *choose* to stay here. I made the decision long ago not to couple when I saw how miserable my brother, Aethel, was. He married the daughter of the clan chief, a beautiful ethereal creature with flowing silver hair and ocean blue eyes. Unfortunately, she had the heart of an iceberg. It was almost a blessing when she died in childbirth with the second child, a son.

"He met the love of his life in the heat of battle. She was as opposite as his wife was like him; a gnome." Uther chuckled. "She was spunky, talented with a blade and took no foolishness from my brother. He was so smitten with her that..."

Uther hesitated knowing the information he was about to impart was privy to very few.

"...they produced a child."

Linda's eyes popped open. "Wow. The idea boggles the mind. The child must've been very—odd looking."

"No. I don't think he ever learned of the child. By the time his love was deep into the throws of pregnancy, Aethel was bound by his family's word to marry his night elf mate. "So, you see, Linda," he tucked his finger beneath her chin to raise her face to his. "My family has a history of breaking the norm. When my eyes beheld you for the first time, I knew if I stayed I'd not ever leave."

She reached up and ran her hand down his face, hesitating lightly on his dimpled chin.

"Yet, here you stand." She rose up on her tiptoes, slipping her hand around his neck and pulling him to her. "Stop me anytime."

Uther groaned. "My lady, I would be a fool."

He lowered his head and allowed their lips to meld together. His heart pounded so hard he felt the pressure in his ears and realized other parts of his anatomy were responding in kind.

Linda pressed her body against Uther. She wasn't sure if the pounding she felt in her chest was her heart or his. He'd slipped his arms completely around her and drew her as close to him as possible. She sensed his passion against her stomach, momentarily confused by the pressure. *It's been too many years.* Sensations lost to time began to surge through her limbs, and she allowed them to overcome her.

The lovers pulled back to stare at each other.

"I never had this much emotion for another being. I fought it, believe me. That's why I left before. I couldn't face feeling the kind of loss Aethel did. I saw love tear him apart. Yet, I had to return when I heard my niece and nephew were being so vocal about the loss of their magic. I know them. When they start talking, it isn't too long before they put actions to their words. I…"

Linda pressed her finger to his lips. She stepped back and gently took his hand in hers, leading him inside the Lending Library to the door of her room.

She opened the entry and gave him a quizzical look. "Join me?"

Uther looked into the warmly decorated interior. A smile started to spread on his face.

"Yes."

The two passed the threshold into the Librarian's private sanctum. When the door closed, both knew the life they'd experienced before this day was about to change.

Chapter Thirteen

Trickle tugged at the piece of magically sealed paper. The time had come for her to get her feet on dry land. For the last three days, the handsome night elf Chrissy had called Morgan appeared on the bank in some very odd clothing. He threw line in the water, but there wasn't any bait or even a hook on the end. She watched him pace back and forth. Around the same time every day, he'd back away from the bank and disappear. She noted the librarian appear on the bank under the tree about the time the night elf would vanish.

Dragging the paper with her, Trickle cruised up stream several oak trees from the library before exiting the water. The oak roots created a cove on the bank where she could make the change from water creature to land creature. Maintaining her small size until she was done dressing, Trickle entered her land home beneath the oak. Beneath a tangle of moss covered roots sat a small dressing table fashioned by the fae workmen, a piece of mirror hung above. The two drawer sides held the slab of wood Trickle used to hold her brush and comb. She set the paper against the wall to dry as she looked beneath the cot for the valise and her clothing.

"Ahh, there you are." Pulling the brown case out, Trickle sat on the rug-covered floor and popped the latches. She ran her hands over the clothes inside before lifting out the top item. The simple, long-sleeved shirt was deep green with white mother-of-pearl buttons. The next item was a pair of fitted black jeans. She pulled the rest of the clothing from the valise and laid them across the small bed. Closing her eyes she murmured words learned during her childhood. The material wrinkled then straightened, all evidence of being locked away for several years gone.

Noting sunlight outside her tree, Trickle opted to take a nap until the sun left the sky for the day. Tonight was the beginning of her hunt for the night elf called, Morgan. The less magic she used to locate him the better. While the two cursed night elves may not have their own magic, she was sure they'd be able to spot the use of magic better than humans.

Grabbing a blanket of moss, Trickle covered her legs, drifting into a dreamless slumber.

Cold. So cold. Teeth chattering. Cold. Daring to open one eye, the merfae felt panic grip her throat. *Where am I? This doesn't look like my stream.* Feeling the panic creep up her spine, Trickle magicked a low yellow light orb sending it to the middle of the room. She clutched the moss blanket to her chin as she surveyed her surroundings. Slowly the terror subsided as she realized she was in the oak tree she called home when she walked. The cold continued to plague her so she conjured a heat orb to warm the room. The area outside the tree was dark and she heard crickets starting their nightly concert.

"Time to start my quest to find my night elf." Humming as she moved about, Trickle put together an outfit from her valise she felt would gather attention her direction. She brushed her golden locks one hundred strokes as her mother had instructed and fetched a cape of silken spider's web. A quick glance at the figure in the mirror and she headed toward the opening of her home. At the doorway, she turned to extinguish the light orb catching sight of the paper.

"Almost forgot." She returned to the dressing table to retrieve the item. She hurried to the door, closing then uttering a covering spell to camouflage the tree.

Trickle pulled in a deep breath as she stepped away from the base of the oak. Pulling a perfect pearl from her pocket, she held the smooth pebble in her hand and started to chant:

"Size is but an illusion,

Make this small form,

Become the human norm,

To create confusion,

And bring me the solution I seek."

The air wavered and a glow began at the base of the oak. A rainbow colored cloud plumed up and drifted across the stream. From the center of the light and color display stepped a tall, willowy blonde clad in figure flattering dark jeans. The tailored man's shirt was worn with the hem outside the jeans, collar opened at the neck and flipped up in the back. A black patent belt emphasized the tiny waist of the ethereal creature. The belt matched black, patent three-inch heels the blonde carried in one hand; the other hand carried a matching clutch bag carrying the driver's license she'd tended so carefully. As of this moment, Trickle was now Katherine Lee from Springfield, Oregon. She wasn't sure why this particular piece of paper was so magical, but in previous outings, it had opened all kinds of doors.

Trickle—Katherine closed her eyes and imagined the most likely location she would find her target. With a snap of her fingers, she disappeared.

Appearing at the side of the building, Katherine put on her shoes and flipped her hair behind her shoulder. A quick smoothing of the shirt, and she walked to the sidewalk and up the steps to the gathering place for humans and those who enjoyed their company. She opened the door and was hit with the pulsing of bass guitars thumping out a bottom line to a rock and roll song.

"This is for the fae and Librarian." There was a change since the last time she'd walked on two legs. This was one of their drinking places, but the air wasn't choking with cigarette smoke. She could actually breathe!

"I really need to get out more often." "No kidding, babe. Let me buy you a drink."

Katherine shrank from the leering, weaving man leaning against the bar. She hurried past him and headed for a booth in the rear of the room. She slid into the leather bench seat facing the door. If the night elf showed, she'd have an eye on him first.

The hours ticked away with Katherine keeping a watchful eye on the door. Her sixth sense had never failed her before. *Why now?* As her patience wore thin and the bar emptied of patrons, she decided she'd made a huge mistake trusting her instincts. She grabbed the clutch and scooted to the end of the bench seat when the door opened and there he stood.

His hair took on the blue hue of the beer sign over the door.

Trickle, Katherine, noted his shoulders were slumped forward and he shuffled to the bar. According to her cousin Chrissy, this night elf was supposed to be so full of himself no one could bear to be near him. He'd left a trail of broken promises throughout the valley. The being she was looking at certainly didn't reek of confidence, quite the opposite. This might prove easier than she'd been lead to believe. A quick thought and she scented her skin with night musk. Plucking up her determination, Katherine stood and walked to the bar a couple chairs from the night elf. She caught sight of him in the mirror at the back of the bar. It was indeed the handsome face she'd been studying from beneath the surface of the stream.

She raised a hand to get the attention of the bartender. "Excuse me?"

The dark haired young man smiled and sauntered her direction. "Yeah, beautiful. What can I do for you?"

Trickle watched hazel eyes take stock of her. She started to speak and stopped. Enchanting someone was on her agenda but not this someone. She graced him with a smile.

"Yes. I've been waiting for a friend and," she shrugged her shoulders, "it looks as if I've been stood up. Can you tell me how to get transportation to Golden Meadows?"

"Wow. You're quite a way from there. It's too late for the buses to run and, truth be told, the cost to take a taxi is exorbitant. You'd be best to stay at one of the local motels and take the bus tomorrow."

Katherine did her best to look disappointed. "Okay. Can I get a cup of coffee and the phone book?" She glanced toward the morose figure occupying the bar stool to her left. The air around him wavered oppressively. His waist length silver hair was confined to a braid down his back. Pulling in a deep breath for courage, she turned to face him. "Excuse me, but would you know of a nearby motel? I'm new to the area and it appears I've been stood up."

Listless blue eyes stared at her for a moment. Trickle saw the effect of her voice beginning to work on the night elf. The gray tint of his skin receded, and she noted vitality appear in his light orbs.

"What? I'm sorry. I didn't hear you." He motioned to the large black speakers overhead. "Too much noise. Could you repeat that?"

Got you. "Just wondering if you were familiar with the area."

The man turned to face her. Animation appeared in his actions and, relaxing his posture, he graced her with a brilliant smile.

Whew! He's good looking when he smiles.

"I'd love to help but I'm an infrequent visitor…"

Katherine caught the bartender rolling his eyes in her peripheral vision.

"…so I'm afraid my knowledge is limited. However, if you'd like a ride…I can offer to take you anywhere you'd like in my vehicle."

She graced him with a shy smile. "Thank you for the kind offer, but I make it a policy not to get in vehicles with strangers."

The fair-haired man feigned hurt, clutching his chest and swooning with his other hand to his forehead.

Katherine giggled. "You, sir, are a drama queen."

A flicker of…something dark passed over his face.

"Too true, my lady, but I'm fun to be with, and if you'll allow me but an hour to make your acquaintance, I can promise you an entertaining time."

She thought for a moment and checked the clock at the back of the bar.

"You have one hour to change my mind."

She had him. By the time the hour was up, he'd had her laughing and blushing. She made sure she departed at the time set—one hour later. Stepping around the corner of the building, Trickle removed her shoes and snapped her fingers, picturing the front door of her oak home. She removed the door spell to enter her dry retreat. As she neared the cot, clothing fell to the ground where she'd peeled it off. Tomorrow she'd magick the items from the floor and clean them. Right now, all she could think of was sleeping. She flopped on the cot.

"I've hooked him." *He wants to meet in a few days. I'll have to use all my tricks to reel him in. We'll just see who wins this fishing contest.*

Yawning, she closed her eyes. All scheming was shelved as the merfae tumbled to sleep.

Chapter Fourteen

Morgan stood in front of the window gazing on the valley below. A smile curled the corners of his mouth. He couldn't help it. The lady he'd met the night before at the pub made him feel the way he had before he'd lost his magic.

"What are you grinning at, you fool? You should be getting ready to go to the stream bank." Gitty stood next to him at the window. "Good heavens. You have on cologne. You'd better not be planning on leaving me in the lurch."

"I'm not, your highness. Don't get your panties in a bunch. I decided to shower and put on cologne. So what?"

"So, fishermen don't wear cologne." Gitty narrowed her eyes and leveled them his direction. "You've got a new girlfriend."

"What?"

"You have a new girlfriend. We can't deter from our plan. Dump her. When you have a girlfriend, you're absolutely useless."

Morgan faced Gitty. "I don't have a new girlfriend. I felt like cleaning up and putting on cologne. Why is it necessary for me to continue this charade of being a fisherman? We've established the librarian comes out every nice day around two-thirty pm. She takes a quick nap then heads back to the Library. How many more days do I have to waste my time?"

Morgan watched the color of Gitty's face slowly turn to crimson.

"Until I tell you to stop!" She punched his shoulder and stomped to the kitchen.

As Morgan sat rubbing his shoulder, his mind wandered to the previous evening. The mysterious blonde entranced him. In the hour he was given, he'd pulled out his best stories and tamed his boasting. For some reason, he really wanted this enigma to like him for himself.

"I think I succeeded, but she disappeared so fast I won't know for sure."

"Won't know what for sure?" Gitty carried a bottle of water in one hand and a glass container full of some white powder in the other.

"Nothing."

"Right. I've considered what you said, and I think you're on the mark."

Morgan jerked around. "What?"

"Okay, little brother. I'm only going to repeat this once. You are right. Let's move forward. I've decided today is the day we'll complete our plan. You'll go to the stream as you have for the last few days with Lancelot at your side. When the librarian relaxes to take her nap, Lancelot will let me know and I'll subdue her. You'll need to have your horse ready to receive her. Bring mine as well, because I'll be taking us to a safe location to stash her."

Morgan gawked at her.

"Did you think this was a joke?" Gitty was in his face, eyes wide, teeth clenched.

He leaned back, putting distance between he and his angry sister. "N...no but I didn't think this would happen so soon." *I have unfinished business I wanted to complete tonight.*

"It is. Your impatience gave me the push I needed to move our situation closer to the resolution we want. It's time to act instead of waiting or talking."

Gitty shoved past him toward the back door. "Grab your stuff. We're leaving."

Morgan sloughed to the kitchen to rinse his cup.

"NOW!"

He trotted to his room and grabbed the fishing gear he used as camouflage.

"MORGAN!"

Good Lord, she's pushy. "ON MY WAY."

Double-timing his pace, Morgan snatched his sunglasses and bolted to the back door. The pair readied the horses and took off in a flurry of hoofs.

Silence punctuated the ride to the stream behind the Lending Library. Morgan set up in the spot he'd been all week with Lancelot hovered in the closest bushes swishing his tale back and forth. Morgan could feel Gitty's eyes burning a hole through his back. Sweat trickled down his back as the sun beat on his fishing vest. *Damn hot for spring.* Movement across the stream caught his attention.

The Librarian had a book in hand this time and settled in the sunspot verses the shade. She opened the text, turning to a specific page and started to read. Five minutes passed before the book teetered from her hands and rested on her legs. Morgan tensed. Things were about to get bad. Lancelot let out a low growl. *Time?*

Morgan pulled the line from the water and made as if to button up his fishing. "Yes. She's sleeping."

The large cat trotted back to Gitty. An apparent conversation ensued between feline and night elf. Morgan heard the scuffle of hooves and turned to see Gitty walking her stallion away from the bank.

Maybe she's changed her mind.

Lancelot trotted up to Morgan. *Mistress says you are to follow her and be ready to follow her orders.*

"Great." Morgan set his fishing gear under a tree and mounted his steed. There was no turning back now.

Follow me.

He kept his eyes on the waving black tail pointing straight up in the air until they stood next to the slumbering Librarian. Gitty dismounted and pulled the water and white powder from her saddlebags.

"What are you doing?" Morgan whispered.

"Shut up and watch. This will guarantee cooperation and no damage to her."

Gitty scattered a bit of white powder on a washcloth she'd previously packed in the bag. She then sprinkled water droplets on the powder. White smoke start to spiral but quickly dissipated. She placed the cloth over the nose and mouth of the Librarian. In less than a minute, the form on the ground was limp. A fact Gitty proved by picking up and dropping the Librarian's arm to the ground.

"Get your butt over here and pick her up." Her voice was dangerous and low.

Morgan dismounted his horse and moved to the supine figure on the ground. He slid his hands beneath her shoulders and knees, lifting her from the grass. She was surprisingly light, barely one hundred pounds. His next stop was to slip her on his saddle before mounting up. The form leaned back against him and he noted the compactness of the woman.

Gitty swung up to her saddle and wretched the reins to the right.

"Follow me. Don't ask questions and don't lose me." "I thought you were going to take her on your horse." Morgan's eyes narrowed at his sister.

"Things change. Just try to keep up and don't ask stupid questions."

Morgan nodded. When Gitty was this brusque, any deviation from what she said could bring dire consequences. The odd traveling companions galloped around the open meadows, keeping to the wooded areas away from prying eyes. Gitty stopped to let the horse drink from the upper section of the stream before plunging the riders into the forest on the opposite side of the valley.

For two hours they rode through wooded acreage. When the Librarian would start stirring, Gitty would repeat the process of putting the white powder on the washcloth, adding water then placing over the librarian's face.

Just when Morgan thought they must be getting near Eastern Oregon, Gitty slowed the pace of the ride.

"Stay here." She slipped off her horse and vanished into a dark copse of pines.

Morgan sat on the fidgeting horse that started pulling up tufts of stray grass nearby. Gitty emerged from the woods and waved him over.

"Don't go any further until I get my horse." She jogged to where she'd left her stallion and swung up to the saddle. "Follow me."

The pines closed around the small caravan as they moved deeper into the woods. Light beamed through the canopy of pine boughs. Five minutes into the ride, Morgan noted an area ahead where the forest thinned to expose a cabin. Gitty dismounted her horse and tied the reins at the porch railing. She motioned Morgan over. He nudged his mount forward.

Gitty lifted her hands. "Give her to me."

Morgan slid the sleeping form off the horse with ease.

"Tie up your horse then help me secure her."

Morgan did as he was bid, ducking his head under the doorway as he entered the shelter.

"When did you find this?"

Gitty dumped the limp form on a couch facing the stone fireplace. "I built it."

"What?" She turned to find his eyebrows raised and shock on his face. "Don't look so surprised. I'm quite handy with a hammer and nails."

"I—I have no doubt. I just don't remember you being gone long enough to do this."

"Well, I was. Can we make sure she's securely fastened so we don't have to worry if we go outside?"

He moved to her side and assisted as she bound the Librarian's hands together at the wrists and feet at the ankles.

"You going to put something over her mouth?"

Gitty looked at the prone figure. "No. She can yell all she wants. No one will hear her. We're too far from civilization. I'm going to put a blanket on her so she doesn't get too cold."

"That's rather kind of you."

Gitty turned to him. "Not really. She's no good to us dead."

Morgan nodded his agreement.

His sister rummaged through the closet nearest the front door and brought out a battery powered camp lantern. "Use this until I get back. I'm going to locate dinner. Don't let her talk you into anything. Right?"

"Right."

Gitty shut the front door behind her. She'd planned this to the last detail but didn't want Morgan to know. He was the loose cannon in this formula. Who knows what he would blurt out given enough alcohol? She rode the quarter mile to the storage barn she'd constructed to house food supplies. Dismounting Glade, she pulled a set of keys from her vest pocket. Finding the appropriate key, she inserted it into the lock and turned. The lock opened easily and once removed, the door was easy to slide. Gitty stepped into the interior and stood still for a moment, adjusting her eyes to the darkened interior. Her breath caught in her throat as the light from the opened door featured an etched, wood portrait of Glade, the male night elf and love of her life, in a shadow box she'd created. She'd commissioned a member of his clan to create the likeness for her. Next to the portrait were his forest green, leather hauberk and broken blade. He was gone but not forgotten. Gitty's heart ached.

"Who knows my love? I may join you soon." She went about the business of gathering supplies to feed three for a week. The food wasn't exotic but would keep them alive. After loading the supplies on her horse, she locked the door and headed back to the cabin.

Morgan walked around the large room. He was having a difficult time imagining his sister sawing wood, banging nails, installing windows or anything related to building. The sofa faced a stone fireplace complete with mantel. Framing the hearth was wood and stone shelving and two small windows, one on either side. The hardwood floor was a deep red brown in color and emitted a warm glow adding to the cozy feel of the room. To the right of the room, Gitty had installed a half wall that divided the sleeping area from the sitting area. Opposite the fireplace was a galley style kitchen with the fundamentals, nothing more. A bathroom had been built off the sleeping area. All in all, Morgan had to agree, this was an amazing retreat.

In his reverie Morgan failed to notice the librarian sit up. She groaned.

"Oh, my head. Where am I?"

He jumped. "What?"

"You! What have you done to me? HELP! HELP!" Linda tried to stand, only to fall forward and cut her lip.

"Great! See what you've done now?" Morgan grabbed the woman and hoisted her up, plopping her on the couch. "Sit still. You can yell as loud as you want. Hell, you can yell until you're hoarse but no one will hear."

Linda glared at him with blood running down her lips. "You're Morgan Saun, aren't you?"

"Lady, be quiet. It doesn't matter who I am. You can try to get away if you want but trust me, the effort will be futile. I'm getting a cloth and some Band-Aids to stop your lip from bleeding." He strode to the bathroom and opened the medicine cabinet door. An unopened box of the adhesives sat to the right. Grabbing a clean washcloth, he ran cool water over it and snatched the bandages from their spot in the cabinet.

Linda ran to the front door, both hands on the handle, trying her best to open the barrier. Her face dropped in surprise as the door opened and she stood facing Gitty.

"I should have known. You."

Gitty sneered at her. "Yeah. Me. You and your merry little band of fae friends ruined my life with your stunt of taking my magic. It's been nearly a year, and I think it's time I got back to being myself again. Don't you?" She pushed Linda back to the couch without consideration of her captive's stumbling. "I have no love lost for you, Librarian." Gitty leaned over to look at Linda's face. "What the hell happened here? Morgan!" He bolted from the back of the cabin carrying bandages and a washcloth. "What?"

"What did you do? She's bleeding."

"Yes, I know. She tried to get up from the couch, tripped and fell." He sat next to Linda and placing his fingers either side of her head, turned her to face him. Linda fought to break free of his grasp.

He dropped his head to his chest. "Please. I really don't want to hurt you."

"Right. That's why you have me trussed up in some god forsaken hut in the middle of nowhere." Linda's eyes radiated hate his direction.

Gitty leaned down level with Linda. "Let me tell you something, Other. Morgan here is a lily livered coward who happens to be very adept with a blade. He's happiest carousing with you mortals in some pub, trying to impress the women. He probably wouldn't hurt you.

"Me, on the other hand, I have no love for the human population as a whole.

As I'm going to live to be two hundred fifty years old or older, I'm more than willing to cut you to pieces to get my point across to the people I need to convince. I'm the one you need to fear."

Backing away, Gitty spoke to Morgan. "Fix her up. I'll put something together to eat in the meantime. I don't want her dead—yet." She turned a glare Linda's direction.

Linda shrunk back and looked at Morgan. He shrugged his shoulders.

"She means it. Now, please let me clean up your lip and put a bandage on it." He put the cloth to her face and very gently cleansed the blood from her lip. Once he dried the spot, a bandage was applied. Morgan checked his handiwork and rose from the couch.

Gitty was slamming pots and pans on the stove and grumbling. "I didn't sign on for this. All I wanted was a simple snatch and grab with a compliant body. Who the hell knew this *old* Other would have such—spunk? I don't need this."

Morgan waited until she quit ranting. "I have an idea."

Gitty whipped around with a large spoon in hand. "Great." She shook the spoon as she spoke. "This was your idea in the first place. What now? Let her go free?"

Morgan stepped backward with each shake of the spoon until he felt the couch back hit his thighs. He gingerly took the spoon from his sister. "Let's go outside. Turn off the stove and let's take a minute."

Gitty tossed a look Linda's direction. "What about her?" "Use your sleeping potion."

She crossed to the counter and grabbed the cloth, sprinkling crystals and adding water. As she came at Linda, her captive tried to wiggle away. Winning the battle, Gitty had her prisoner unconscious within a few seconds.

"We may have to tie her to a chair. Let's go." She nodded toward the front porch.

When the brother and sister stepped on the precisely crafted boards of the front porch, they opted to leave the door open.

"Okay, what's your bright idea now?" Gitty placed the cloth over the porch railing and crossed her arms.

Morgan held up the washcloth smeared with blood. "What was going to be your next move? You're heading up this production."

She leaned against the support. "A note saying she's being held until the council convenes and agrees to reinstitute our magic—one hundred percent."

"How far do you think that will get you?" Morgan lifted a brow.

"As far as I need it. I don't think Uther will be happy about his lady love being held captive."

"True. But all he'll do is employ his magic to locate our whereabouts and come rescue her."

"So you have some idea that will inhibit this ability?"

Morgan smirked and held up the washcloth. "This."

Gitty huffed disbelief. "Get real. How's a bloody washcloth going to stop Uther from using his magic?"

"By seeing the bloody cloth, he'll know we're serious. There's enough blood to make him question how bad his lady is hurt. We can suggest if he tries anything, she'll be returned in pieces. How do you think he'll react to that?"

She stood looking at her brother. A smile slowly began to turn up the corners of her lips.

"I was beginning to wonder if our mother had been fooling around with the stable boy before you were born. That is a truly *wicked*, devious plan. I love it!" She unfolded her arms and headed for the cabin, humming a Celtic victory song. Morgan smiled. Finally. His sister was actually appreciative of his plan. He'd have to remember this day; they came so seldom.

Entering the building, Morgan went to the kitchen to search for a storage bag. He dropped the bloodied cloth inside and sealed it. Rummaging in a small desk placed against the wall, he located paper and a pen. He sat at the two-person table and created the ransom note.

We have the Librarian. If you want her back alive and in one piece, send your reply via the Mouse Network to the family warehouse in Springfield for further instructions.

"Gitty, what do you think?"

She read the two-line note and nodded. "Excellent. For once, I can say I couldn't do better myself. How will we get it from the warehouse?"

Morgan chuckled. "That's the best thing about the Mouse Network."

Gitty raised an eyebrow. "What?"

"They have no loyalties. Given enough payment, they'll go anywhere to deliver a message. I've been working with one particular messenger who'll go pretty much where I ask."

"Well, well. Aren't you the devious one?" Gitty stood. "Can you contact your messenger and tell him to meet me at the house with the response?"

"WHAT?"

"Yes, little brother. You get to baby-sit the hostage."

"Great." Morgan grumbled.

"Just remember, when this is all over and you have your magic back, you'll thank me. I know if that—Other—tried anything with me, I'd have no problem eliminating her."

"Fine. But I have a...date in a couple days."

"If all goes well, you'll be able to charm her and get lucky with your magic." Gitty smirked. "I should be home in about an hour. Have your messenger meet me there in two hours."

"How am I supposed to do that since you have tied me to this house?"

Gitty glowered at him. "Get a messenger to find your messenger." "How?"

"That's your problem not mine."

Morgan grumbled and watched his sister leave on her horse.

"Open my big mouth and wind up babysitting. Some day..."

Chapter Fifteen

Uther checked her room. He walked the path to the stream and checked her favorite spot along the bank, finding her book opened to her favorite poem but no other sign of Linda. He trotted back to the Lending Library and hunted until he found Chrissy.

"Have you seen Linda?"

The tiny nymph smiled and looked at him, a twinkle in her eye. "Lost your lady love?"

Uther felt the blush crawl up his cheeks. "I'm serious. I've looked all over the property, and I can't find her. She's not in the garden or on the stream bank. I even looked in her room to be sure she wasn't napping. I'm worried. She didn't say anything to me about running an errand."

"Well, you know she's been alone for a long time. I don't think she would tell you if she was running an errand." The nymph cocked her head from side to side looking at her layout for the May Day festival. "Do you think I could put the gnomes next to the meadow fae?"

Uther looked at the seating chart. "Probably not. Why not put the mountain fae next to the gnomes? They get along better. I keep forgetting how independent Linda is. I mean, she doesn't always tell you if she's running an errand, does she?"

Chrissy had been erasing and rewriting when Uther's question struck her.

"Actually, she tells me where she's going every time she leaves." She turned to him, her brows knit together. "Uther? We need to do another search. It's not like her to take off unannounced."

May Day plans set aside, the odd pair decided to split the property in half and mounted a search. Uther took the building and front of the property; Chrissy opted to fly around the garden and stream. Her ulterior motive was to talk with Trickle and see if her cousin had any pertinent information.

Chrissy buzzed to the stream. *Trickle, you here?* Three tries yielded no results. Chrissy gave up trying to contact her cousin. It was obvious Trickle wasn't home. She checked with the birds and talked to the rabbits and no one had seen Trickle for a couple days. Chrissy hovered above the water and murmured. "Where are you, cousin?"

The garden proved as elusive as the stream; no sign of Trickle or the Librarian. Chrissy was feeling ineffectual and frustrated as she returned to the Library.

By the look on his face, Uther had met the same fate.

"Any luck, Uther?" "No. I checked everywhere I could think of and no Linda. You?"

"Nothing. What are we to do? Call in the local police?"

"No. Other's police are very uncaring and will suggest she left of her own accord. I don't believe it. Do you?"

Chrissy shook her head. "No. She loves this place too much to just walk away. There's something going on."

Uther nodded his agreement. "Yes, and I can guess who's behind it. I'm afraid we'll have to wait until they make the next move."

Chrissy's wings quavered. "Uther, I'm afraid."

"I am too, my little friend, I am too."

The next morning Uther sat at a table near the kitchen, grasping a cup of Chrissy's Killer Coffee. His bloodshot eyes told the tale of his previous night. As he forced the dark brown liquid down his throat, a mouse wearing the maroon vest of the Mouse Network approached him.

"I'm looking for an Uther."

The night elf narrowed his eyes to focus on the messenger.

"You have found him."

"Please sir, a message for you is in the pocket upon my back. I'm to wait for a reply."

The mouse turned his body so Uther could retrieve the paper tucked within the vest.

Chrissy winged in from the kitchen and hovered over Uther's left shoulder. She watched him withdraw a bag with a note taped to the front.

Uther pulled the paper from the bag and sucked in a deep breath when he spotted crimson blotches upon a white item inside. He unfolded the paper and read the cryptic message. Opening the baggie, he withdrew the contents; a washcloth covered in blood. Uther uttered an ancient curse.

Chrissy dropped to the table and reached out a tiny hand to touch the washcloth. "Please tell me this isn't the librarian, Uther."

"I can't, my little friend. The beings we're dealing with have no soul or conscious when it comes to the lives of others." The nymph yanked her hand back and broke into sobs, winging her way to the kitchen.

Uther got up to locate pen and paper. When he found what he needed, he sat at the table and put together a carefully worded reply.

If you value your life, you'll not harm a hair on the Librarian's head. What do you want?

He tucked the reply in the vest of the mouse. "What is the cost?"

"None, sir. It has been prepaid."

He watched the gray creature scamper from the room and out the front door.

It took all his power not to follow the creature. He toyed with the idea of placing a magic tracker on the mouse but knew his adversaries while unable to *use* magic, would be able to spot the magic tracker.

"There has to be a way." Pacing the center aisle of the library, he examined his memory for other times when magic couldn't be used to track a foe. "Why can't I think of...hawks! If I can only remember the spell to call them." Uther stopped his motion and furrowed his brow. His hand rested on a book on the shelves. Eyes shut tightly to recall the proper incantation, he would get close to remembering then feel the thought slip away. He opened his eyes and turned to gaze at the spine of the book where he'd placed his hand. *The Forgotten Spells of Merlin. Can it really be that easy?*

Retrieving the tome from its neighbors, Uther flipped to the page for aviary spells, sliding his finger down the page to the words used for summoning messenger birds. The moment he saw the ancient words, his sudden amnesia evaporated. *Of course.*

He replaced the work on the shelf, which he noted was filled with volumes on magical creatures and spells. Rolling the words around his head, he moved as quickly as his feet would allow to the lane in front of the Lending Library. The sky was dotted with rain clouds in various hues of gray, the sun peeking from behind them. He whispered the words to the chant twice, as recommended, and waited for results.

The air shirred with the languid flapping of powerful wings. Uther looked to the sky. His gaze was captured by the white and tan chest of an American Kestral floating on the thermals toward him. Once the creature leveled out, Uther watched as it flew at him back winging to rest comfortably on his shoulder.

Did you call for me, night elf?

Uther was surprised at the throaty, deep tone of the bird's voice. "I did."

How can I be of assistance? "I need eyes and ears to find something I've lost."

Why not look yourself?

"Because I'm not quite sure where it is. I received a message from one of the Mouse Network representatives and need to see where the creature finally ends up. Are you familiar with them?"

Yes. We're forbidden to eat them. Waste of good food, if you ask me.

"This one left within the last fifteen minutes and is probably heading East."

Can you be sure?

"No, but I know the author of the original message and how devious her thinking is. If you don't find the messenger within the day, don't concern yourself with the hunt. Come back here and we'll agree on a price."

Fair enough. I'll return within twenty-five hours either way.

"Fly safely and don't get caught."

I'll watch my back.

Uther watched the kestral take flight on the spiral winds soaring toward the clouds.

I've done all I can—for the moment.

He watched Chrissy buzz around the Lending Library, putting together plans for May Day and envied her distraction. Waiting was the enemy here, and he knew if he didn't find something to occupy his mind and hands, he'd go crazy.

Chrissy whizzed past him.

"I'm going for a walk, if anyone is interested." Uther exited the building to the porch. The walls inside felt as though they were closing in on him. He pulled in a deep breath of the rain-tainted, spring air and made his way to the entry road. Maybe a walkabout would clear his mind and freshen his perspective. The driveway was lined with tulips and daffodils boldly opening their petals to greet the new season. He marveled at the serenity of the landscape. If he could just stand in the lane and inhale all the spring smells for the rest of his life, he'd be a happy man. At this time, his world was about to implode and he felt powerless to find a simple solution.

A reverberation in the distance caught his attention. Uther stopped and concentrated. He realized the noise was moving toward him at a fast pace. *It's coming this way but not to the Lending Library.* He zeroed in to the direction of the sound.

Narrowing his eyes, he trained them to a road situated next to the farmer's field a quarter mile to the east. The tap tapping from afar morphed into thundering hoof beats. Uther beaded in on the figure of a familiar form racing a finely muscled black horse across the valley. The she elf sat ramrod straight on the stallion's back, her white hair billowing behind her as the animal galloped to their destination.

Gitty. Where are you going in such a hurry? He tried to touch her mind but met a blank barrier. *So, you're either blocking me or have lost your ability to telepath.*

The hurried horse and rider continued their journey up the road to the mansion on the hill.

Uther closed his eyes and mentally searched the area for the other night elf. His mind touched many creatures busily preparing for summer but couldn't sense Morgan. *That's odd.* Since the two-night elf siblings had been deprived of their magic, word was if you spotted Gitty, Morgan was close by. *She's in a hurry and he's nowhere to be found. Unfortunately, I believe my fear has been realized. The Saun family is, once again, right in the middle of trouble.*

~ * ~

Linda smelled food. Her stomach grumbled. She couldn't remember the last time she'd eaten. Slowly, she opened her eyes and panicked. Nothing looked familiar. Where was she? She tried to bring her hands up to rub her eyes but couldn't budge them. Her throat constricted as she tried to swallow. Out of the corner of her eye she caught a quick flash of white and involuntarily emitted a low groan.

Where am I? What's happening and why is my head pounding?

"Where…?"

The question hung in the air. Linda realized her voice was nothing more than a whisper. She tried to get her legs to move but met resistance. Frustration hampered her actions. She cleared her throat with difficulty.

"Where am I?" That seemed to catch the attention of the other body in the room.

"Let me tell you where you aren't…at home."

Morgan appeared within her range of vision and she groaned out loud.

"I was hoping this was just a bad dream."

The night elf sneered. "Lady, when you play with the big boys, you suffer big boy consequences. If you're new *friend* values your life at all, you'll be going home."

"I don't know what you're talking about."

"Right. We'll play that game if you insist."

Linda tried to sit upright. "Please. Can you help me to sit up?"

Morgan's brow furrowed. "If I have to…" He moved to the bed and righted the librarian.

"May I sit on the couch?"

Morgan rolled his eyes. "Look, lady, I've got an important function to attend and babysitting you is not what I planned. I'll put you on the couch if you promise not to try to escape. I'm not as heartless as my…partner but I'll have no hesitation to duct tape you to the bed."

"I promise I won't try to escape. I'd put up my hand but…" Linda shrugged. "…at the moment my hands are unavailable."

Morgan slipped his hands beneath her shoulders and knees. He lifted her from the bed and within two steps had her upright on the couch. "There. Now be quiet."

"Thank you." Linda closed her eyes and slowed her breathing. She knew if she were to have her wits about her, she needed to try and eliminate the pain in her head as much as she could.

"Here." Morgan placed a bowl filled with macaroni and cheese next to her. "I'm going to undo your hands, but if you try anything, well, I'll have to take measures."

"I'm too hungry to do anything but eat."

"Good." Morgan stepped behind the couch and untied the ropes binding her hands.

Linda rubbed her wrists to push blood to her fingers. When the tingling and pain started, she knew she wouldn't lose any digits. Grasping the bowl in her fingers, she noted the lack of utensils.

"I need something to eat with."

"Fine."

She could hear him moving around the kitchen and jumped when a spoon was shoved in her face.

"Remember, I have no compunction about knocking you out." "So noted."

Linda dug into the pasta, reveling in the taste of cheese and macaroni. *Never thought mac and cheese would taste so good.* She took in the layout of the cabin over the top of the bowl: *bathroom behind the bed in the right corner of the building, fireplace in front of the couch, kitchen behind and, most importantly, door to freedom on the left.* For the moment, compliance was the best course of action, but there would come a time in the near future where she *would* escape. When she did, this night elf better watch out. Her Donald had taught her a few self-defense moves from his time in the service. He'd always worried about them being so far from town. She hadn't practiced in a while, but the body had memory that would come in handy.

Morgan watched her devour the food. When she finished, he took the bowl and spoon to the sink. "I'll feed her but I'm not about to do woman's work."

Linda tucked her upper lip between her teeth to keep from smiling. This he night elf was in a foul mood, and she wasn't yet ready to push him to the brink.

"How long are you keeping me here?"

Morgan knelt in front of the hearth trying to figure out how to start a fire. He jumped when she spoke.

"As long as it takes to get what we need."

"I see."

"No, you don't. You've never had magic, and wouldn't have a clue how much it adds to being alive. Not having my magic has been...pure hell." He rose from his knees and stomped out to the porch.

I've hit a nerve. This time Linda let a smile touch her lips. *I have ammunition now. Bad move, night elf.*

Chapter Sixteen

Trickle—Katherine—stretched her arms above her head. She smiled as she crawled out of bed. The he night elf, Morgan, really wasn't that bad. To top it off, he was very good looking. It had been quite a while since she'd indulged herself with a mate. The human ones, while easy to enchant, had such frail bodies. They aged so quickly and couldn't hold up their part of the deal. She'd hated to do it, but the last one she had, she wiped his memory and left him at a hospital. Sad. He was an especially nice man who doted on her. Oh, well.

This he night elf could live quite a bit longer. Katherine loved that idea.

"I'm hungry." The one thing she hated about this form was the need to constantly feed it. She couldn't afford to waste the time doing the shopping thing so she'd magic the body into thinking it was full.

"I'm going back tonight to see if he's there. I've made up my mind I want this man for myself. I know Chrissy won't object because he'll do anything I ask—when I enchant him."

She hummed as she tidied up her land home. She'd need to present a picture of domestic perfection to her object of desire before weaving the spell to make him hers forever. Tonight was going to be the most exciting time she'd had in quite a while.

~ * ~

Chrissy hummed around the Library, adding touches here, moving furniture there. She was expecting a large turnout for the May Day celebration and all had to be in order. When she'd sent Bram and Silas out to warn the locals about the night elves, she'd sent invitations to the May Day celebration with the Sky Network. Surprisingly, they'd returned with responses from nearly all the clans in the valley and the forests. If everyone showed, the local Others were sure to notice.

"Tough. We were here first. They'll just need to adjust." She flew through the coffee shop and out the door to the porch. Uther had taken up camp on the wooden appendage and was currently snoozing in one of the chairs. She hated to wake him, but while he slept, a carrier from the Mouse Network had arrived with another message for him.

"Uther?"

She was greeted with a grunt.

"Uther. UTHER!"

"What!" He jumped upright from his reclining position. The wood nymph hovered before his eyes clutching a large white envelope. "Please take this. It's getting heavy."

He reached for the envelope, the white paper container dropping to the deck when the nymph could no longer hold on.

Uther leaned down and picked up the packet. His name was scrawled across the front in a familiar hand. He placed it in his lap and stared at the paper.

"Aren't you going to open it?" Chrissy winged to his leg and landed. She reached out a finger and touched the packet. "Do you think it's poison?"

Uther sighed. "No, little one. I don't think it's poison, but I believe it carries bad news."

She crossed her arms and tapped a tiny foot on his leg. "Uther. I've seen you face a field of opponents and charge in with no regard for your own life. How can one piece of paper cause you such hesitation?"

"Because on the battlefield, I only had to concern myself with the safety of my troops and myself. Most of my men I'd known from childhood and knew of their bravery and selflessness. This, I know, concerns someone I..." He gazed at the tiny creature before him showing more courage than he felt. "...I love for the first time in my life. I never knew how much she would affect my feelings. What if they've killed her, Chrissy? How could I go on?"

Chrissy unfolded her arms and winged to his face. She laid a small hand on his cheek.

"You'll go on because you know Librarian wouldn't have it any other way. She is nothing if not brave. After all, she did stand up to Morgan and Gitty."

"Which is why we're in this bind now."

"Open the envelope, Uther."

Fingers quavering, he tore open the sealed packet. Inside was a fine linen slip of paper, which he retrieved and unfolded.

Chrissy watched his face turn crimson as he read. She winged away from the chair and waited. Uther crumpled the paper and threw it on the wooden deck.

"I knew it! I knew they'd never sit quietly and accept what they'd done to themselves."

He stomped from the porch. Chrissy watched him disappear around the side of the house. She magicked the crumpled paper and read the contents. *We have one demand:*

Call all the clans together and reinstate our magic—in whole.

If you don't comply in the next 48 hours, we'll start sending the librarian back to you: one piece at a time. Send your reply via the Mouse Network to the family warehouse in Springfield.

G & M

Chrissy buzzed to the side of the house to see if she could spot Uther. He sat in the librarian's favorite spot on the stream bank. She raced to his side.

"Uther?" She kept arm's length away in case he was too angry to think.

"Yes?"

"What are we to do?"

"I don't know, Chrissy. I can't afford to have Linda killed because she stood up to those two, yet giving them back their magic would bring nothing but trouble to the valley and the clans. Gitty would make life hell on all who crossed her."

Chrissy moved closer to him and settled on a stump near him. "She acts as though she is the gift to this valley. I've never seen anyone so self-involved. Well, maybe Morgan, but considering he's her brother, it's to be expected."

The two sat morosely for a moment. Chrissy watched pain flash across his face then noted a change of his body. He sat up straight and his eyes lit up.

"That's it!" Uther turned to the nymph. "You, my dear, are a genius."

"Okay, but what did I say that makes me a genius?"

"Vanity."

"Yeah. The two of them have it by the boatloads."

He turned and gazed at her. "Are you willing to help me free Librarian?"

She humphed. "How could you doubt that?"

"I'll need you to lend some of your magic to me."

"Done. What are you going to do?" "Give Gitty something to think about. Morgan seems to have adjusted to life in the Others' world but Gitty fancies herself above all of us. Are you ready?"

Chrissy nodded and moved opposite him.

245

He sat straight up and closed his eyes. Chrissy hovered and closed her eyes.

"Please put all of your concentration on my incantation.

Gitty,

Every minute as a prisoner she spends,

Brings you one moment closer to your end,

The vigor and vitality you so crave will soon disappear

Replaced by the horror of old age and death you fear.

Your life source will find its way

To one whose life you would betray

Be forewarned

The change begins this very day.

As he'd been taught, Uther uttered the spell three times, lying back on the soft grass when the chant was ended.

"There's your answer, Gitty Saun. I hope you enjoy it."

Chrissy fluttered to the ground next to him. "Whew! That should knock her socks off."

"I hope so."

"Is there any way to reverse it?" Chrissy saw him smile.

"Yes. But the cost of reversing the spell is to accept what she wants changed. I seriously doubt she'll understand the simplicity of it. No, I think we're going to see a change in the she-night elf and a change in our own Librarian."

Chrissy seemed revived. She flew in front of Uther and winged loop-de-loops. "Yeah. We get to see what Librarian looked like when she was young." She stopped and looked directly at him. "Will it last?" Uther sat up on his elbows. "As long as she lives which, now with Gitty's life source, will be quite a bit longer than she expected."

"I have things I need to get done for May Day. Do you want me to make you something to eat?"

"No. You've done more than enough for me today. Thank you." Uther watched the wood nymph fly off toward the Lending Library. He plucked a long piece of grass and stuck it between his teeth. The spell would either put an end to this foolishness or backfire to cause a war no one could win.

He desperately hoped the former would happen. Very shortly, time would tell.

Chapter Seventeen

Gitty stood beneath the warm flow of water and allowed the tension to be swept away with the dirt. She'd sent the second letter laying out their demands. By this time next week, she'd be back in control of her life and have the magic that was rightfully hers.

Turning the water off, she stepped to the rug and buffed her body with the towel until she glowed pink.

"I think my first move will be to bulldoze that miserable hovel, the Lending Library. Then I'll ban Uther from ever coming back to these parts and, in a generous display of compassion, allow the renegade fae the ability to go back to the homeland. Let's see how well they manage on the Emerald Isles."

She chuckled and retired to her room to change into her comfortable jeans and a sweatshirt. Warm slippers on her feet completed her outfit and she meandered to the living room. She was restless but didn't want to read, so she pulled out her Tarot cards and decided to give herself a reading. If she were correct, all signs would point to success. Gitty shuffled the deck and placed the first card on the coffee table.

"What? This can't be!"

~ * ~

Morgan combed his hair for the final time. Looking in the mirror, he smiled at the reflection. "Showtime. Tonight, I'll win—without magic." He winked and entered the living area of the cabin.

The librarian was settled on the couch, watching his preparation with interest.

"Date?"

He glared at her. "None of your business. However because I'm going out, you get to stay on the bed." He picked her up and carried her to the cot, securing her ropes to the head rail and foot rail of the bed.

"What if I have to use the bathroom?"

He turned to her. "Hold it or wet your bed. I don't care. I've been here for the last forty- eight hours, and I have something important to do. I told Gitty I was attending to business tonight and I will. I'll leave the light on for you, but otherwise…you are on your own. See you tomorrow."

He headed for the door.

"HEY! You can't just leave me here." The corner of Morgan's left lip raised slightly. "Yes I can and I am. Deal with it." He started out the door and turned back. "You can yell as loud as you like. There's no one around for miles. Goodnight."

The door slammed, leaving Linda alone. *This is not good. What the heck am I supposed to do?* She figured if nothing else, she'd just sleep. Lately, her energy levels seemed to be dropping. *Must be age.* She tried closing her eyes, but they kept popping open. *What is wrong with me?*

In frustration she tugged at her bindings. She felt them give. *What?* She tugged again and felt the rope move. Normally, she would have been short of breath and feeling the need for a nap, but at this moment, Linda felt strength in her arms she'd not experienced in years.

The night elves perception of her as a weak Other was working to her advantage at the moment. Morgan had tied the ropes with a great deal of slack, expecting her neither to fight nor to be able to yank them loose.

Excitement fueled her. She jerked the ropes and popped to a sitting position. The bindings on her wrists had been tied with no thought of them being undone. Linda slipped her hands through the loops and massaged her chaffed, raw appendages. She needed to hurry, however. If either Morgan or Gitty returned and found her out of her bindings, they'd tie her so tight she could lose a limb.

The ropes on her feet proved more of a challenge, but Linda's energy seemed to be endless. She looked at her fingers in awe. The last few years had proved to be a lesson in frustration, with rheumatory arthritis invading her hands and knees and making everyday tasks impossible. She felt no pain whatsoever.

"I'm not sure what's going on but I'll take it." Linda swung her legs over the edge of the bed. Her feet tingled. She was forced to sit and twist her feet around until the circulation returned. Testing a foot on the floor, she was relieved to find her appendages functional and able to propel her away from the cabin.

Linda scavenged the drawers in the small cottage. She found some energy bars and a flashlight. She tucked the bars into her pockets and flicked the switch of the flashlight, blinking when she got light. In a drawer in the kitchen, she located extra batteries she cached in another pocket.

The librarian padded to the entrance and opened the front door slowly. Twilight blanketed the forest, giving the trees and surrounding plants an eerie glow. She slipped her body out and closed the door behind her. In front of the cabin was a single lane, disappearing into the canopy of trees. Linda bolted down the stairs and began to run. She might not have much energy, but she was going to use what she had to expedite her escape. But how to get back to the Lending Library? "Moss grows on the north side of the tree." All those years in Girl Scouts had given her a bit of forest knowledge. When the lane ended in another road, Linda felt desperation creeping in to her mind.

"No. I'll not give up so soon." She stopped and pulled in a deep breath. When she opened her eyes, she noted horse prints headed in one direction. She looked to the sky and mouthed "Thank you" before proceeding to follow the tracks.

Three hours passed before the forest thinned and the Librarian began to recognize landmarks. She was amazed at her stamina and reasoned it must be the fear of being caught again. The meadow opened up, and she could make out a few lights on buildings close to her home. Now was the time she needed to be especially careful. Just another half mile or so and she'd be in her own home. Linda stopped and pulled in a deep breath.

"It's now or never." She bolted across the meadow, keeping her eyes on the lights of the Lending Library. She stumbled on to the driveway and began to cry. Nearing the porch, she saw a figure in the chair and hesitated. Did she continue forward or try to camouflage her arrival by going around back?

"I'm too tired to circumvent coming in the front. To heck with it." Linda pulled herself tall and walked to the porch, taking the steps confidently. She turned to face the figure on her deck.

Uther had kept an eye on the movement he'd noticed in the meadow. Someone was crossing the fields rather late at night. He trained his eye on the lone figure moving intently in his direction. When the figure started up the driveway, Uther tried his best to identify the person but was having a difficult time. The figure hesitated just out of the range of the porch light. It moved up the stairs and turned to face him, shoulders squared.

"LINDA!" Uther jumped from his chair.

Linda thought she would faint from relief. She'd recognized the long, white hair and angular limbs as that of a night elf, but her recent experience had wiped away any recollection of the night elf who cared deeply for her.

"Oh my god, Uther." Linda pushed out an exhausted breath. "I'm so glad it's you." She stood stiffly, checking the face coming toward her. "It is you, isn't it?"

He wrapped his arms around her and pulled her to his body. He buried his face in her hair and pulled in the essence that was Linda. "Yes, my lady, it is I. And I'm relieved, delighted and a million other things to see you." Linda wrapped her arms around him and immersed herself in his strength. For the moment, all was well.

Chapter Eighteen

Morgan arrived at the pub and took his usual seat. He looked around but couldn't locate Katherine. His stomach dropped. "She's not here." He nodded at the bartender. "The usual, please."

The man pulled a glass from the cooler and filled it with draft beer. "Three dollars, Mr. Saun." Morgan reached for his wallet.

"I've got this. Please get me a blended Pina Colada. Thank you."

Morgan started and twisted to stare into the blue green eyes of Katherine.

"Did you think I wasn't coming?" She graced him with a shy smile.

"I, uh, I wasn't sure." He gave her a lopsided grin.

Katherine let him hang for a moment. "I couldn't wait to come back so I took a little— longer—to get ready. I hope you don't mind?" She twirled around.

Morgan took in the vision. "Not at all."

"Good. Now, where were we when we parted ways?" She looked directly into his eyes as she spoke.

Morgan saw her mouth move, but all he could hear was the sound of the ocean. *This is the most beautiful woman in the world. I don't ever want to leave her.*

Trickle watched his eyes glaze over. *You're mine now...forever.*

~ * ~

Gitty waited impatiently for her brother to show. "Where is that idiot?"

She moved to rise from the couch and caught her breath as pain shot through her hands and knees. *What the hell is happening?* Sucking in a deep breath, she pushed off the divan.

Must be because I haven't done enough riding lately.

A quick trip to the bathroom to get an aspirin would take care of the pain issue. Gitty made her way down the hall, halting to catch her breath every ten or so steps. *This is ridiculous.*

She flipped on the light and opened the medicine cabinet. The aspirin bottle proved to be a challenge to open. Her fingers didn't seem to want to work the way they should. When she finally got two tablets out, she turned on the cold water and filled the glass. Tossing the pills down her throat, she washed them away with a big gulp of water and closed the door to the medicine cabinet. That's when she realized something was horribly wrong.

The face staring back at her was...showing signs of age. Skin sagged at the neck and chin line. The surface of the face was dry and gray looking. There were tiny lines around the eyes and mouth and in her platinum hair were—gray—hairs.

Gitty stepped back and opened her mouth. A blood-curdling scream rent the air. The last thing she remembered was some old woman looking at her from her bathroom mirror.

~ * ~

Linda stepped inside the door and pulled in a deep breath. The smell of her books always settled her nerves.

"Are you hungry, my lady?" Uther gently swept her hand into his.

She turned to him, marveling at the adoration shining from his eyes. "I'm so hungry I could eat a complete cow tonight. I guess it was all that running."

Uther's eyebrows raised and his eyes popped open. "You ran here?"

Linda nodded. "Yeah, and it's really weird because I'm not tired at all. I know it's going to irritate Chrissy, but I want to fix my own dinner. How about you, Uther? You hungry?"

She thought his smile looked a bit odd.

"No, my lady. Just out of curiosity, have you looked in a mirror lately?"

"Uh, no. I was too busy running for my life. I must look a fright."

He chuckled. "No. I'll let you see what I'm talking about."

Linda barreled to the kitchen and found the room empty. "Good. No interlopers in my kitchen." She pulled pots and pans from various cupboards and rummaged in the refrigerator. Not finding much food with girth, Linda opted for an omelet. When she'd mixed the ingredients and put them on two plates, she carried the food to the dining table inside the Library.

Uther had taken a chair and waited until she quit fussing to try and carry on a conversation. He touched her hand and looked up into the steel blue eyes. "Stop fussing. Sit and enjoy the meal. We need to have a serious discussion but not over this marvelous omelet." She felt the color rise to her cheeks. "As you wish, sir."

Silence filled the room as the two indulged their taste buds in the veggie omelet. When Uther had finished, he dabbed his mouth with a napkin, placing it over the plate.

"I received a ransom note from Morgan and Gitty yesterday threatening to send you back in pieces if I didn't gather the clans and return their magic."

Linda coughed into her napkin. "What? Are you serious?"

"Very."

"I hope you didn't do anything foolish, because I couldn't live with it if you gave up something for me."

Uther's sly smile put Linda on guard.

"No, I didn't do anything foolish; well, not too foolish. I remembered an incantation my mother taught me to use on vain people who needed to be gently reminded to stop their self centered ways."

Linda leaned back in her chair and crossed her arms. "What did you do, Uther?"

He squirmed in his chair. "Put a reverse aging spell on her."

"That doesn't sound too bad. Why are you being so evasive?"

"Linda? Go look in the mirror." He nudged her with his foot. "Go."

Linda was looking for the opportunity to wash up from her dusty day walk. She entered her bathroom and put the washcloth in the sink to dampen. Then she looked in the mirror and passed out.

~ * ~

Uther had suspected the shock might be too much, so he'd quietly followed her and was there to catch her when she dropped.

"Who, how, what?"

He put his finger to her lips. "I put a spell on Gitty; for each minute she held you captive, she would age and you would, well, unage. I'm guessing you're about thirty-five right now." Linda's hand went first to her hair. "It's black again. I'd forgotten how dark it was." She then ran her fingers around her eyes and mouth. "The lines are gone."

She pushed off the floor and grasped the sink, looking at the face of the person she'd been thirty years earlier. "Oh my. I'm not sure what I think. I'd gotten used to the old face."

"Do you want me to change it back?"

"Oh, hell no." Linda lifted her blouse to view the young, taut stomach she'd forgotten she once possessed. "I think I like this." Her eyes twinkled a deep blue.

"We need to talk, my lady." Uther took her hand and led her to the porch where they sat in chairs next to each other.

"What's so important?" Linda stuck her hands in front of her to admire the taut skin and lack of age spots.

"I want you to be my life companion."

Linda dropped her hands and faced Uther. "Are you serious?"

"More serious than I've been about anything in my life."

"When?"

"How about we have the clan chieftains approve it at the May Day celebration?"

She took a moment and examined her nails. "I wasn't sure I wanted to ever spend time with anyone after Donald, but..." she looked at Uther. "...you're not anyone; you're special. Yes. I'd love to spend my forever with you."

Uther leaned over and captured her lips under his. His heart pounded in his chest and he felt a stirring in his loins. *Later.*

Chapter Nineteen

May Day

The yard was a patchwork explosion of flowers celebrating the spring. A pole had been erected in the front yard for the young fae to participate in the ringing of the Maypole. Chrissy winged her way back and forth directing the activities and sporting a new outfit for the occasion.

Linda gazed at the profusion of colors highlighting her library.

"I never thought I'd see the day when all of the clans would, again, come together in my home and celebrate."

Uther snugged her close to his side. "They have a special place in their hearts for you, my lady. You accomplished that which no Other has done. Come to think of it, no fae has been able to get all these ruffians to agree."

Linda smiled as she laid her head against his muscled chest. "Who would believe I could be so lucky twice in my life?"

Uther placed a gentle kiss on the top of her head. "It's I who is the lucky one to find you."

The fae children ran and winged their way through the Lending Library and on to the deck; the pounding of little feet reminding the grownups of a simpler time.

Bram and Silas sat in the chairs designated for them as co-heads of the May Day celebration. They were attended by their children and watched their wives talk about babies and childcare issues. Bram's wife was the local midwife who would be attending Silas' Mrs.

When the sun reached its zenith in the sky, each chieftain solemnly marched to the center of the front yard near the Maypole. They stood, waiting for the din of the crowd to lessen. When their presence didn't sufficiently lower the clatter, Kayne, the current clan chieftain of the meadow fae, put his two front fingers in his mouth and whistled. The shrill explosion stopped all the noise in the meadow.

"Thank you." He dipped his head in appreciation. "We have gathered today to join in the celebration of new life. For many of us…" he winked at Ailidh, heavy with child. "…this year brings bundles of joy. For others, the end of a threat we've all dreaded has been achieved. It's for this reason we are happy to join with our friend and ally, Uther, night elf, and Linda, Librarian and Other. "At this time, they've chosen to join their houses together. A mighty spell has brought Linda into our folds and she now bonds with the fae. Will Uther and Linda please join us up front?"

Linda, her long, dark hair braided down the center of her back wearing a tan floor length dress with flowing lace sleeves and Uther, dressed in his finest tan leather pants and jerkin held hands as they walked to the center of the yard to face the chieftains.

Kayne flashed a grin at the pair and cleared his throat.

"Are all the clans represented?"

A roar of "AYE!" rang through the air.

"Does any here denounce or disagree with this pairing?"

"NAY!"

"Then let it be known that Linda, the librarian and Uther, the night elf, shall be joined together until the breath is gone from one or both of them."

The crowd erupted in raucous cheering and Uther bent to his lady, lifting her from her feet and kissing her.

The musicians struck up a wedding jig and the newly twined couple danced until they were breathless.

Bram leaned over to Silas. "What happened to the other night elves?"

Silas raised his head from his paws. "Rumor has it the male got himself tangled up with a merfae and is residing in the stream out back. As far as the she night elf…seems she hasn't left her hilltop home since the librarian was found. Some say she's withered away to dust. Long as she stays away from me, I don't care."

Bram tapped his pipe against the chair. "I agree."

A comfortable silence descended between the friends.

Joining cake cut and devoured, presents given and the newly attached couple on their way to some time alone, Chrissy finally settled in her lounge chair and fanned herself with a leaf.

"Who would have thought we'd ever see the pairing of a night elf and an Other? Guess our librarian was always about defying the odds."

Other books by C. L. Kraemer
Available at Rogue Phoenix Press

Healthy Homicide

Two murders have occurred at the Barrel Springs Day Spa. Police hurry to find the method and reason before anyone else is murdered.

MANIC READER REVIEWS says: Healthy Homicide by C.L. Kraemer is an intriguing plot driven mystery. The plot is well written and pretty much carries the whole story...

Dragons Among Us

In a world full of anomalies such as the platypus and self reproducing Komodo dragon, is the human race willing to accept that dragons may be real?

Sapien Draconi-human-dragon shape shifters-all over the world face this dilemma every day. The question has become life and death as their species is plagued with unexpected and unwanted shifting in the most unlikely of places.

The Ancient Ones-full-blooded dragons-can offer advice, but few seem to put forward workable solutions to the problem.

The fate of the shape shifters hangs in the balance, and an answer must be found before the Homo Sapiens find, dissect, and hunt Sapien Draconi to extinction.

Dragons Among The Eagles

Aleda Sable faces the toughest decision of her life—to stay in dragon form, live as a two-legged or put one foot in the human world and one talon in the dragon world.

An urgent call from her newspaper editor sends Aleda to report on an accident whose driver appears to be a dragon. Authorities have the scene locked down and aren't allowing access to anyone. Television broadcasts flash pictures of scaly legs hanging from a crashed car. However, the bodies disappear into thin air. When the stations try follow-up reports, all they find are state highway workers busily tearing up the roads.

In determining the truth of the shifter disappearances, Aleda finds the truth of her own dilemma.

Shattered Tomorrows

Lucy Daniels has a secret—a deeply guarded secret.

Her life was going along just fine until she accompanied her best friend, Cassie, to her attorney's suite on top of the Equitable Building in downtown Salem, Oregon.

Once inside the lawyer's office, the world turned upside down and Lucy was forced to face a demon from her past. Thirty years ago, life had been different. Lucy had discovered Prince Charming and was headed to her happily ever after.

That's when the devil intervened and because of her brush with the devil, innocent people died.

Joker's Wild

Four brothers raised in the Northwest.

Two choose to stay and pursue life in Oregon. Two are seduced by the promise of Hollywood.

Life throws the Palmer brothers an ugly curve when two are killed in preventable accidents. Even more upsetting is the lack of justice in the trials of the perpetrators.

The remaining brothers will find justice using a shared passion of all the participants—motorcycle poker runs.

Moon in Mazatlan

Detective Corey Williams is content with his small town Virginia home. Normally, his busiest night is Saturday, but when his best friend's ex-wife attempts to have him killed, Corey gives his promise to ensure justice is served. Meeting a red-haired, Harley riding goddess has thrown a wrench in his quiet staid life. Only one hiccup in this situation; the goddess is a reporter. When the ex-wife of his friend flees the country, the reporter makes sure she is right behind Detective Williams. He is oath bound to bring the fugitive ex-wife back for trial. What he hadn't counted on was falling for the Harley riding reporter.

Old Enough

Justin Anderson is recovering from a nasty divorce. An ex-wife who never has enough support income and precious little time with his daughter fill most of his days. When he spies an attractive, self-sufficient older woman, he is intrigued. But can he convince her not all guys are animals who need to be locked up?

With a gentle push from their bartender friend, the two face more intrigue than either thought possible in such a small town. However, each terror filled moment proves to provide the glue that brings them together.

If Only

Widow Barbara Langley, and best friend, Rachel, journey to Tampa, Florida. Barbara left broken-hearted years earlier and returns with her newly surgicized body to mend her grieving spirit. Can she juggle an old love who reappears and the younger man who desires her or will she choose to return to the Northwest still single?

www.ingramcontent.com/pod-product-compliance
Lightning Source LLC
Chambersburg PA
CBHW051424170626
46809CB00006B/2305